THE

MARKOV

ENCRYPTION

by

DAVID N ROBINSON

CROSETS PUBLISHING

Cover designed by BespokeBookCovers.com

Published by Crosets Publishing

For my family, near and far.

Thank you for your support and encouragement.

Prologue

The scruffy-looking passenger has only a single piece of hand luggage on wheels. Less than ten minutes after touching down at Rostock's airport on Germany's north-eastern coast, he walks confidently out of the restricted area and into the arrival's concourse. Scanning the unfamiliar faces, he spots his assigned driver, a man in uniform holding his name on a signboard. The man raises a finger in recognition, and the driver hurries to greet him. Despite objections, the driver insists on taking the small case by its extendable handle. They march at a brisk pace down a set of escalators towards the underground car park. The driver opens the rear door of a Mercedes saloon, waits for the passenger to be seated, and checks to ensure that his seat belt is fastened. The door is then closed and the case placed in the boot.

They make their way in light traffic towards the motorway intersection about two miles from the terminal. The passenger is preoccupied in the back, scrolling through emails and messages on his smartphone. Without warning, the Mercedes brakes sharply, pulling onto the hard shoulder and coming to an abrupt halt. With the engine still running, the driver gets out of the car, slams the door, and presses the button on his key fob to activate the central locking system. Hitting another button, the boot pops open, and he removes the small case before closing the lid. Then, using his free hand, he removes another device from his jacket pocket and flips a special switch on its side.

Two things happen next bin swift succession. A white Skoda pulls onto the hard shoulder behind the other car. The driver of the Mercedes, still holding the other man's case, climbs into the front passenger seat and the Skoda accelerates away. Meanwhile, the Mercedes – driverless, and with the passenger in the back confused and anxious – begins moving as well. Navigating the roundabout, the Skoda joins the motorway heading one way. The driverless Mercedes takes the slip road heading the other. By the time the Mercedes joins the main carriageway, its speed is more than seventy kilometres an hour and accelerating.

In the back, the passenger is panicking. He tries the door handles, but they are locked, neither mechanism on either side seeming to work. He claws at the windows: they, too, refuse to open. He slams the heel of a hand against the windowpane, but it barely moves. He has a go at using his elbows to shatter the glass, but no such luck either. Not even his seat belt seems to be working: the release button is not responding. In desperation, he tries forcing the strap through the metal clasp, creating slack in the webbing to allow him to wriggle under. It's a struggle, the space so confined, but he somehow manages it, allowing him to clamber over the seatback – headfirst, combined with a twisting manoeuvre – that causes his legs to end up in the footwell and his body behind the wheel. The general hope being that this should allow him, finally, to regain control of the vehicle.

It is a forlorn hope.

The Mercedes, already travelling at one hundred and seventy kilometres an hour, continues accelerating. Up ahead, on a section of elevated carriageway, the road veers sharply around to the left. The man stamps with all his might on the brake pedal, gripping the steering wheel furiously to try and point the car in the right direction, but the car doesn't respond.

Instead, it dramatically and unexpectedly lurches to the right, hitting the crash barrier beyond the hard shoulder at well over one hundred and eighty kilometres an hour. The car's momentum causes it to vault the barrier effortlessly. Airborne, the Mercedes quickly falls in a graceful arc the fifty-metre distance to the ground.

Momentarily, time seems to stand still.

Then, with a sickening crunch, the force of the impact thrusts the heavy engine block rearwards. The scruffy-looking man never stood a chance.

Chapter 1

The red dot of light and the uninvited guest appear almost simultaneously.

Both equally surprising. Both potentially lethal.

Ben Lewis had had neither inkling nor prior warning. No indication of any change in circumstances. That is, apart from the text message he'd received less than five minutes earlier. The one saying that his chess companion would be delayed by several minutes. Lewis hadn't, at the time, seen it as a problem. Behind London's King's Cross and St. Pancras stations, the newly fashionable Granary Square is a pleasant enough place to sit outside in the wintry, early afternoon November sun. Watching life go by. Lewis's assigned table was next to a gas heater. A bottle of beer had been placed on the table in front of him by a pretty Romanian waitress. The chessboard he'd brought along was already set up, white positioned nearest to him. Lewis had recently completed a lucrative assignment working for a Ukrainian oligarch and been well paid. Life had even started to feel good, once again.

Which, he should have realised, was usually a bad omen.

The red dot was certainly surprising. Despite the distance the laser must have travelled, the light was intense, the dot stationary on the chessboard in front of him, vibrating lazily. Hovering somewhere between what chess aficionados would be quick to describe as **d3** and **e3**. Not yet on his body. However, close enough to indicate that the rifle was in the hands of a professional. The weapon would undoubtedly be mounted on a tripod, the sniper most likely somewhere overhead, aiming downwards. There were many vantage points encircling his current position on Granary Square that might work. Apartment blocks, office towers, even an old gasworks. The sniper could be anywhere. Lewis briefly considered what he might be doing if the roles were reversed. Assuming that he wanted the ability to hit a particular target, rather than simply send a message with a fancy laser. On balance, he would favour a military-grade sniper rifle armed with laser-guided computerised targeting – something accurate to within an inch over a one-thousand-yard range. Allowing for windage – which today would be minimal – anyone armed with a weapon like that, even an amateur gunman, would appear to be a marksman.

The uninvited guest is arguably the more surprising development.

A man, literally, back from the dead.

A blast from Lewis's past. A reckless fellow-soldier. Even back in those days, this one had had a reputation for being wild and unpredictable. A former Marine who, during one particularly unpleasant drunken rampage, had picked a knife fight with Lewis. It had been an unwise decision. The man had ended up the worse of the two – and been dishonourably discharged soon after as a direct consequence.

A man thus with a chip on his shoulder, certainly concerning Lewis. Someone who, thankfully, had disappeared into the empty void of Civvy Street, dropping both out of sight and out of mind.

Until a year ago.

Out of the blue, there had come news reports that the man had been killed in action: fatally wounded on active service whilst fighting with the French Foreign Legion. Reportedly, part of their Second Parachute Regiment deployment in Afghanistan. Few had shed any tears when news of his death had hit the wires. Certainly not Lewis.

Evidently, the story had been wrong – another piece of fake news.

'Bored playing dead, Keiran?' It is all that Lewis can think to say as the man he once knew as Keiran Doherty sits down in the vacant chair opposite.

'You don't look overjoyed to see me, Ben.'

'It's a somewhat surprising development.'

'Worried that I might be back to settle old scores?'

'I hardly imagine that you've come armed with a rooftop sniper simply for a game of chess.'

'The thing is, Ben Lewis, one-time bane of my life ... we sort of have unfinished business, you and I.'

'If I remember rightly, Keiran, the last time you and I had the pleasure, the result didn't go in your favour.'

'I wouldn't be so cocky. You forget that at the moment I have the advantage.' He points to the laser dot on the chessboard, smiling thinly.

Lewis leans back in his chair, staring at the man across the table. Resurrection hasn't been kind to the former Marine. Like Lewis, Doherty is in his early thirties, yet already he is virtually bald. There is an ominous-looking scar on his right cheek, almost certainly a knife wound. He obviously hadn't learned his lesson the first time around. His skin is suntanned, weatherworn and wrinkled, the area around the eyes sallow. It makes him look at least ten, perhaps as much as fifteen, years older than Lewis.

They had been close friends once. Doherty had even been an usher when Lewis had wed his young bride, Lisa. Doherty had briefly dated Lisa's sister, Holly. It hadn't lasted long; Holly announced one day out of the blue that it was all over. She never explained precisely why. At the time, Lewis wondered whether she simply might have been too good for him. Lisa's subsequent death on their honeymoon had been the first of many things to go wrong in Lewis's life. His friendship with Doherty had been yet another casualty.

'The thing is, Ben, being dead brings certain advantages.'

'I'll take your word for it. Can we get to the point? I worry that your sniper might be developing a twitch in their trigger-finger out of boredom.'

Doherty smiles at Lewis's gallows humour.

'Forgive the theatrics. I didn't want there to be any ambiguity about the message.'

'What message is that, Keiran?'

'I need your help with something. Something that is going to put your life on the line. To be brutally honest, with the two of us meeting like this, the odds of you surviving the week have become slender. Close to zero. With or without the sniper.'

'I hope you're not expecting me to be grateful?' Lewis gives a fake smile and runs a hand through his thick, black hair. All the while, he keeps his gaze fixed on the man opposite. 'What are we are talking about?'

'I need something collected and taken care of. Something very much in demand. Something extremely dangerous.'

'Do it yourself!'

'I can't, not any longer. I've pissed off so many people recently that there's a price on my head. I am officially a dead man.'

'Once a dead man, always a dead man.'

'Very droll.'

'Bullshit, Keiran. You're more than capable of doing your dirty work, dead or alive. Whether you've pissed people off or not.'

'Right. Except, the thing is, this time it's going to give me enormous pleasure to see you jumping through hoops and not me.'

'What are we talking about? Drugs? Guns?'

'Worse. Much worse.'

'I'm all ears. Or are we going to continue playing these stupid guessing games all afternoon?'

.

Chapter 2

It is at this point that Lewis notices the young Chinese woman at a nearby table. She is by herself, immersed in a book and wrapped up against the cold. In the background behind her, the water fountains that in summer would be attracting young children to splash and play are today switched off. Today, the piazza is mostly deserted.

'Since my reported death in Afghanistan, I've been living a new life. Born again and hidden from view. All very hush-hush, but still Queen and Country. One of the beauties of being dead is that, by definition, you can get away with murder.'

Lewis snatches a glance around the square. No one appears to be paying them any attention. Apart from the sniper with the laser scope, that is. The Chinese woman occasionally looks in their direction but seems uninterested in catching Lewis's eye.

'You know as well as I do that life for us military types has been going from bad to worse. The bureaucrats and lawyers seem determined to tie us all in red tape – themselves included. Permission in triplicate before anyone's allowed to fire a bullet. I was getting well and truly hacked off. Hence my interest in something a bit different, when it was offered. Want to hear more?'

Lewis shrugs.

'It's not as if I have the option to get up and walk, is it?'

Doherty looks to the sky for a moment then back at Lewis.

'Let me begin by telling you about a cyber-crime operation based out of Rostock in Germany, run by a man called Gunter Markov. Neither Gunter nor Markov are real names, but it was his way of pretending to be half-German and half-Russian. Certainly not North Korean, which is what he really was. His Korean name was Park. Markov, aka Park, happened to be one of the most gifted computer hackers on the planet. Based in a nondescript building in a dull part of the city, his little enterprise was home to a small army of cyber techies, extorting money for the sole benefit of the North Korean regime. Set up and funded by Moscow, it was Russia's method of having a long-term relationship with Pyongyang behind the scenes. Gunter's operation has been providing the North Koreans with a substantial stream of desperately-needed foreign exchange income. Meanwhile, Markov's wife and family were living under house arrest back home in Korea. It helped keep the man focused.'

'Life's a bitch,' Lewis says, taking another mouthful of beer. 'How do you know all this, Keiran?'

'I was tasked to infiltrate Gunter's operation, find out all of his dirty secrets and make sure the place was no longer open for business.' He smiles thinly at the memory. 'In case you're interested, Gunter Markov and his associates have, shall we say, indeed been put into liquidation.'

The Romanian waitress reappears but Doherty dismisses her with a wave of his hand. Lewis smiles at her, watching the view of her rear with interest as she approaches the Chinese woman at the next table.

'Tasked by whom, exactly?'

'All in good time, Ben. I'm sure you understand.'

'Not really. I'm confused. Why are we sitting here, with a sniper rifle pointed at me from on high?'

'I stole something. An encryption key to a hack that Markov had posted online. One-time encryption. It's completely unbreakable without the key.' The two men eyeball each other. 'One of Markov's sidekicks flew into Rostock airport recently. The man was careless. The briefcase containing the encryption key was taken from him, moments before he became involved in a fatal car accident. Too bad.'

Lewis keeps silent, willing his uninvited guest to continue.

'Gunter Markov was a brilliant hacker but had a massive ego. He'd begun touting himself to the highest bidder, offering to perform increasingly impossible hacks to prove his abilities. Essentially, he was bored, eager to show off, keen to prove that he could go further and be bolder than anyone else. The Americans ending up having the deepest pockets, and they took Gunter under their wing, commissioning him to produce a dynamite version of the Panama Papers Mark II: the inside scoop on slush funds and hidden assets held by the world's biggest political names. The completed report was always likely to be a ticking time bomb, something that no dodgy politician ever wanted to see the light of day. Especially after Markov went and posted the damned thing online, even if it was in an encrypted form.'

'No wonder people wanted him dead.'

'Quite. With Markov, however, things were never simple. Despite the American project, Markov also had his eye on something even crazier – hacking the computer systems of the world's major intelligence services. He wanted everyone to believe that no stored electronic information, however covert, was safe from hackers, even in the world of espionage. For him, it was the ultimate all-time hack, his crowning glory. No wonder everyone wanted him dead.'

'You stole the encryption key. What's the problem?'

'My own stupid fault. Being a man of enterprise, I realised the value of what I had in my possession. So, I foolishly consulted a few people I thought were friends about what it might be worth. Big mistake. Suddenly, I find the world and his wife are also desperate to kill me. Seems they want to bury this fucking encryption key – and me with it, to boot.'

'You can cope. What's new? You've been there, got the t-shirt. Go into hiding and play dead, like you did last time. You seem to have a knack for it.'

The red light shimmers on the chessboard in front of him. A few moments earlier, the tiny dot had disappeared. Now it was back once more.

'Assuming I make it through the day without being killed, that's my plan. As it happens, I did manage to lay my hands on a substantial nest egg, thanks to some end-of-life kindness courtesy of Gunter. He just happened to be in possession of a considerable amount of cash lying around. Iranian money that had been washing through his business, destined for Pyongyang. North Korea's nuclear secrets and missile technologies are, apparently, much in demand in Teheran. Given all the sanctions, Markov was the perfect financial middleman – a safe and proven conduit for yet more foreign exchange. To give Markov credit, he did try to warn me. Stealing the Iranian money and the encryption key, he said, would be my downfall. My 'death sentence' were the words he used.'

'Why not send the encryption key to the Sunday papers?'

'It's not that easy. I haven't told you the whole story, for your own protection. Suffice to say, this thing has become way, way too sensitive. The totality of what Markov uncovered needs to be dealt with by professionals. I've seen it, I know. Already there are a number of desperate, ruthless people who want this damned thing buried – and probably for good reason. My job is to make sure it doesn't fall into the wrong hands. Who can be trusted, that's the killer question? I thought I knew. Instead, because of my naivety, I find myself on the kill list. My plan B, as you surmise, is to take the money and go into hiding. Before that, I need to hand the encryption key to someone who can be relied on to sort the mess out. A ruthless son of a bitch who instinctively knows what needs to be done. Someone professional and dependable. That's you, Ben, in case you haven't yet worked it out.'

'Get fucking real, Keiran! Why the hell should I want to touch such a crazy, stupid thing? This is your mess. Deal with it yourself. Keep your fucking head below the parapet, take the money and scarper.' He scratches his head in disbelief. 'How much did you take from Markov, out of interest?'

'A hundred million.'

'Jesus! Are you out of your mind? I'm not having any part of this. This is lunacy! For the record, my answer is an unequivocal no. Shoot me if you like, my answer will still be no.'

At which point, Doherty takes out his mobile phone and swipes through several screens. He places the device on the table in front of Lewis.

'I thought you might say that. Changing the subject, I went to see Holly yesterday. She and I had a nice little catch-up. She wanted to record her own personal message for you. Shall we have a listen?'

Lewis's stomach turns icy cold. He and Holly have history as a couple. It had taken Lewis a few years to get over his wife's death. With that pain fading, Holly and Lewis had dated for a time. It had been a short but sweet romance. Circumstances and geography had contrived to keep them apart, both agreeing to go their separate ways. Over the last nine months, they had done a commendable job convincing each other that matters had come to a natural conclusion.

'*Ben, you've got to help me.*' Lewis can see Holly's face on the video screen. Her eyes are puffy and she has been crying. '*I don't know what's got into Keiran. He's threatening to kill me unless you do what he asks. Help me, Ben. I think he's serious. I've never seen him like this before. I love you, Ben. Please help. Please!*'

'Touching, isn't it? I think she's genuinely fond of you.'

'You've crossed a line, Keiran. You're a dead man.'

'So, here's the deal,' Doherty says, ignoring the other man's taunt. He reaches into his pocket and takes out a key. He places it on the chessboard, some distance away from the red dot. 'I've hidden the one-time encryption key somewhere safe. The trail begins at a numbered mailbox. You'll need this key to open it. It'll take you on a journey.' He withdraws a slip of paper from his jacket pocket and passes it across to Lewis. 'The journey is as much for your protection as Holly's. This is the address where the mailbox is located. You want box number 236. If you do everything right and keep out of trouble, you'll be directed eventually back to Holly. She'll be safe for the next seventy-two hours. Beyond that, I can't vouch for her. Seventy-two hours. That's how long you've got.'

'I repeat: you're a dead man, Keiran. Where is she? What have you done with her?' He glances at the piece of paper before handing it back to Doherty. The address, like the mailbox number, has been committed to memory. Slowly, he picks up the key. It looks like a million others: flat, several circular indentations on either side, a serial number engraved at one end. He takes a bunch of keys from his trouser pocket and starts winding the mailbox key onto the metal ring. He continues with this circular motion until the key sits flush with the others. Then he places the whole bunch back in his trouser pocket.

'Relax. She's safe. Somewhere you won't find her until you've done what I ask.'

Which is the exact moment the red dot begins to move. Slowly and deliberately it inches across the chessboard towards the black pieces furthest from where Lewis is sitting – what the aficionados would now be calling **d5**. Then **d6**; then **d7**. Curiously, when it reaches **d8**, it still keeps moving.

Lewis, senses heightened, is uncomfortable about what he is seeing. He looks across at Doherty, who hasn't yet noticed. The man is smiling at Lewis, goading him.

'Checkmate, I think the word is, Ben.'

'You'd better believe it, Keiran.'

The red dot has disappeared from view altogether. According to Lewis's calculations, it is now likely to be pointing directly at the top of Doherty's head.

In a split-second's decision, he reaches across and grabs Doherty's phone.

Which is the moment that all hell breaks loose.

Chapter 3

The woman inches her way around the building's rooftop, careful with each step not to make a sound. Dressed from head to toe in black and wearing thin gloves that leave no fingerprints, she is inconspicuous. Two air conditioning units afford a degree of cover. She nestles close to one and peers cautiously around its edge. The sniper is about ten metres away, lying on his stomach, his rifle positioned on a front-mounted tripod. Following him to the rooftop had been straightforward, the agent confident she hasn't been detected.

Deeming herself to be in the best position, she gingerly removes a thirty-centimetre-long section of carbon-fibre tubing from an inside zipped pocket. With it, comes a tiny plastic box. Nestling within the outer tube are two identical tubes, each smaller in diameter, all three tapering slightly. Bit by bit, she extends the inner tubes, pulling each as far as they go until they click into a locked position. Finally, by attaching a small circular disc over one end, a simple mouthpiece is formed. The result is a crude but effective blowpipe about a metre in length.

Next, she removes a tiny tranquilliser dart from the plastic box. Custom-made to fit the device, the dart contains a fatal dose of a compound that will cause near-instant paralysis of all body muscles – a drug designed to point the finger elsewhere. More specifically, to natural causes, the body rapidly breaking the compound down to virtually untraceable elements. Her preparations over, the dart is carefully inserted into the end of the tube by the mouthpiece. Then, taking careful aim, the woman inhales slowly and deeply before pursing her lips around the mouthpiece and blowing with as much force as she can muster.

The sniper is hit in the upper forearm, the impact causing the lethal dose to be injected directly into the man's muscle tissue. She counts to ten, allowing time for the drug to begin working, watching as the confused sniper feels behind him, trying to pull the dart out but failing. Within seconds, his body slumps in a state of paralysis. The woman hurries across to kneel beside him, retrieving the dart and placing it back inside the small plastic box. She collapses the blowpipe with practised ease and puts this, along with the box, inside her jacket and zips it shut. The hard part is dragging the man's body away from the rifle. He is heavy, the procedure requiring all her strength. Eerily, his eyes remain open throughout; conscious but unable to move or breathe. For a moment, she smiles. By the time they perform an autopsy, there will be no trace.

Finally, she is ready to lie down beside the rifle, peering through the sophisticated riflescope at the intended target, refocusing the electronic crosshairs on the chessboard positioned between the two men. She takes her time, controlling her breathing, wanting to get the feel of the unfamiliar weapon. Her instructions had been unambiguous. In time, judging the moment to be right, slowly and deliberately, she swivels the rifle on its stand. The crosshairs, currently shaded blue, move towards the man with the almost-bald head. Satisfied that all is as it should be, she toggles the target verification button. A red dot appears on the screen image of Doherty's head inside the riflescope. Seconds later, the colour of the crosshairs changes from blue to red. Target acquisition confirmed.

Which is when she squeezes the trigger. For a few moments, nothing seems to happen. Then, when she is almost ready to give up hope, the loud and deafening report of the rifle rings out across the rooftops.

Chapter 4

The Americans are watching everything in real-time. Two are inside a black van that, temporarily, has become a makeshift mobile office. From the outside, it looks like a standard-issue Ford Transit except for the blacked-out windows and a small array of antennae affixed to its roof. Inside, a stocky man called Schultz is sitting on a plastic flip-down seat, operating a Black Hornet Nano mini-drone. He controls the device through an app on a tablet computer, his colleague, a wiry individual called Jackson, peering over his shoulder. Jackson has an encrypted phone glued to one ear connected to a senior intelligence officer back in Langley, Virginia. The video feed from the drone is streaming directly to both locations. Jackson is attempting a three-way conversation, although noise from passing traffic makes this problematic.

'Who's on the roof with the sniper?' the voice in Jackson's ear barks. The accent hails from the deep-South, anywhere from Georgia to Texas.

'No idea.' Schultz adjusts the controls on the tablet's screen. The camera orientation changes as the drone shifts position and altitude. 'Maybe we should use the drone to warn the sniper?'

'Forget that. What's the other guy up to? Tell Schultz to zoom in.'

The image enlarges, revealing a shadowy figure in black fiddling with a long, thin tube.

'My God, is that a blowpipe?' They stare, mesmerised, as the rooftop drama plays out. First, the sniper being hit in the upper forearm. Next, the sniper struggling before collapsing to the floor.

'Holy shit! This is fucking unreal!' the pair in the van hear coming down the line from Langley.

'There's going to be another takedown,' Schultz says.

'Focus on Doherty,' the man in Langley tells Jackson. 'Who he's meeting with? A name or ID would be super-helpful, folks.'

'We're running his picture as we speak...' Jackson stares at his laptop, balanced precariously on a small pull-out ledge, '...here we go. Ex-Marine, name of Ben Lewis. Known to us. Been working for a Ukrainian oligarch. Before that, freelancing for the British security services.'

'Well, well, the plot thickens. I am not sure if that makes him friend or foe,' the voice from Langley drawls. 'Always assuming this new assassin doesn't kill him first.'

'What's the big deal? Given our supposed Special Relationship, if the Brits get their hands on this thing, so do we by default, surely?'

'Don't bet on it. The Brits want this more than we do. The way I read it, it's their passport to a great and glorious Brexit trade deal. Anyway, it's non-negotiable. We commissioned the damned project, so be under no illusions. Our orders are to get the encryption device first. No one else is allowed to get a look-in. That includes the Brits. That's coming from the very highest levels, in case anyone is in any doubt.'

'Check this out,' Schultz says suddenly. 'Doherty's passing something to Lewis.'

'Can we zoom in?'

Schultz plays with the controls and the image enlarges.

'It could be a key. In fact, I'm certain of it. Now he's taking something else. It looks like a scrap of paper.' A red warning light suddenly flashes at one corner of the screen. 'Oh, shit! We're out of battery. We're going to have to abort.'

'Get the second drone up, quick!'

'We can't. It's not working.'

'Fucking typical! Okay, listen up! Jackson, I need you down there on the street right now,' the voice booms in his ear. 'Grab that key or whatever it is. I don't care how you do it. I want to know what was on that piece of paper. Do whatever it takes, you hear? You can have Schultz and whoever else you need as backup. Just don't screw up! Now, get a fucking move on!'

Chapter 5

Just as Lewis is reaching across to pick up the other man's phone, Doherty's head disintegrates in front of his eyes. The sound is muted, a sickening soft thud as blood, brain and bone fragments are scattered far and wide. Some reach the adjacent tables, including where the young Chinese woman is sitting. She lets out a scream, quickly getting to her feet and grabbing her rucksack. Which is the moment the rifle shot is finally audible, the sound of the supersonic bullet eventually reaching those in the square.

Lewis is quick to get to his feet. Faced with a sniper with a high-powered scope, Lewis's survival instincts tell him that flight is preferable to staying put and taking cover. In his rush to get away, he nearly sends the Chinese woman flying.

'Quick!' he yells, grabbing an arm to stop her from falling as he speeds past. 'Follow me. Come on!' Finding no resistance from the confused woman, he sprints with her across the square. Lewis's mind is focused on two things: what would a sniper do next; and how best to dodge another bullet?

The sniper is the easy bit.

Bullet fired, kill confirmed, old round ejected, new round in the chamber.

Two seconds at most to complete, probably less.

Shit! According to the clock counting in Lewis's head, three seconds have already passed since the initial shot. Lewis needs to keep moving if he's to stand a chance of dodging another bullet.

Reacquire secondary target, toggle laser-guided target acquisition, wait for verification confirmation.

Five seconds, give or take. With a moving target, perhaps longer.

Lewis deliberately runs in a random, zig-zagging fashion, the pair racing across the square to an exit on the far side.

Perhaps risk a hasty shot?

On balance unlikely but Lewis can't afford to rule it out. The pair duck and weave their way towards the corner of a large building at the piazza's edge. By the time they clear it, the clock in his head has counted eight seconds. Eight seconds and still no second shot. Which is a good outcome on many levels.

'Come on, keep going! We're nearly out of danger.' Their pace slows to a fast jog, each breathing heavily as they emerge into the back streets behind King's Cross station. In time, they come to a halt by a motorbike parked on the pavement. It is Lewis's Honda CB750.

'Come on, let me give you a lift,' he says, inserting the key into the ignition and hitting the start button.

'What on earth just happened? Who shot that man?'

Lewis doesn't answer, glancing sideways at her as he manoeuvres the bike off its stand.

'Ever ridden a motorbike?'

'Sure, plenty of times. Shouldn't we wait for the police?'

'Sure, if you fancy spending all night in a police station answering endless questions. I plan to get away from here as quickly as possible.

We can call them later.' He revs the engine impatiently, his signal to her to get a move on. Without any second prompting, she climbs onto the seat behind. Feeling her arms around his waist, he twists the throttle in his right hand, and the bike accelerates away.

Chapter 6

By the time Jackson enters Granary Square, the sniper has fired the single shot and all hell is breaking loose. In the middle distance, already weaving his way erratically out of the piazza, is Lewis. What's interesting and unexpected is that Lewis has a companion. A young Chinese woman, running with him. Jackson sprints across the square in the same direction, slowing momentarily to a brisk walk when he rounds the corner of a building on the far side, then picking up speed again as he struggles to keep pace with Lewis and the woman through the back streets. To his dismay, in the distance he sees Lewis climbing onto a motorbike. Beside him on the pavement, preparing to ride pillion, is the Chinese woman.

Shit!

Jackson tries putting on an extra burst of speed but fails to close the distance. He watches, dejected, as the bike races away. Gasping for breath, he grabs his mobile and punches the speed dial to connect with Schultz.

'Be with you in two,' Schultz calls out.

By the time the black Transit arrives, Lewis and the Chinese girl have been gone almost five minutes. Jackson climbs into the front seat feeling despondent.

'We need more manpower. We can't run surveillance like this on a shoestring.'

'It wasn't such a high priority when we started,' Schultz replied.

'Well, it is now, that's for damned sure. Where's your tablet? I want to run that drone video one more time.'

Schultz points to the glove compartment. Jackson retrieves the device and turns it on.

'Lewis left the square with another person. A Chinese woman. I don't recall seeing her when we were watching earlier.'

'Take another look.'

They find her on the second run-through, in the corner of one of the segments where the drone is focusing on Doherty and Lewis. She is by herself, at a table a short distance away.

'Lewis's look-out, do you reckon?' Jackson asks.

'She doesn't look the type. In any event, I don't get the sense Lewis is the kind of guy who needs a babysitter.'

'Should we run her photo?'

'Let's do it.' Schultz takes screenshots of the woman's enlarged face from three different angles and uploads them to the NSA portal.

'It'll take a while. It did last time.'

'No big deal. Our immediate problem is finding where Lewis has gone.'

'That'll be easy! We should track his cell.'

'What are we waiting for? Let's get the team back home working on finding the number!'

Chapter 7

Lewis knows a café in Regent's Park that he reckons should be a good place to regroup. Somewhere with facilities to clean up. He parks the bike and helps his passenger to dismount. Unsteady on her feet, the moment she sees Lewis's jacket splattered with Doherty's blood and brain tissue, she retches into the gutter. Lewis places a hand on her back to comfort her. A curious couple stop to stare briefly. They hurry away when they see Lewis's hostile glare.

'I'm going to freshen up,' he says, pointing to the toilets tucked to one side of the café. 'You might want to do the same. We should be safe here. If you'd prefer to head off home, that's fine by me. If not, I'd be happy to buy you a drink or something before you go.'

He doesn't wait for her reply. It takes several minutes to rinse his face and hair and wipe most of his leather jacket clean. When he re-emerges, the Chinese woman is already sitting by herself at a table inside the café.

'Can I get you something?'

'A tea, please,' she replies quietly.

He returns with their drinks and sits down opposite, extending a hand across the table.

'I'm Ben, by the way.'

She takes his offered hand in hers.

'Li-Jing,' she answers. She is pretty. Long black hair, sparkling eyes and smooth, unblemished skin. Age anywhere from nineteen to forty, as far as Lewis can guess.

'What happened back there? Why did someone shoot your friend? I can't stop thinking about it.'

'I've no idea,' he answers half-truthfully. 'He wasn't my friend. Not really. Just someone I hadn't seen for a long time. Someone I thought was dead, to be honest. Well, he is now, that's for sure.' He looks across at her. She looks calm despite the recent trauma.

'Shit, I have to make a call,' he remembers, taking out his phone. He has two missed calls and two voicemails from his friend, Saul Zeltinger. Lewis had been waiting to play chess with Zeltinger in Granary Square when Doherty had made his unexpected appearance. Zeltinger was a detective inspector in the Metropolitan Police. Twelve months earlier, Lewis had unwittingly become involved in a murder case where Zeltinger had been lead investigator. They had become friends and, soon after, regular chess companions. He touches Zeltinger's name on his screen and holds the phone to his ear. He mouths the word 'police' to Li-Jing as he waits for the phone to connect.

'Zeltinger,' a voice answers after the third ring. The stridently familiar Germanic tone makes Lewis smile.

'Saul, it's Ben.'

'Ben, finally! Where are you? A man's been shot in Granary Square. I suppose you know that?'

'A man called Keiran Doherty. Someone I knew from way back.'

'I might have guessed you'd be involved. I was late because someone had kindly slashed both of the tyres on my bike.'

'It was probably Keiran, wanting to ensure that he and I had quality time alone together before you turned up.'

'Were you with him when he died?'

'Sadly. He'd just been showing me this video clip of Holly, for God's sake. The bastard had only gone and taken her hostage.'

'Why?'

'It's very complicated.'

'With you, Ben, it usually is.'

'Listen Saul. Holly was pleading with me to do whatever this man wanted. Keiran had just begun to tell me when, kaboom, his head just disintegrates right in front of me. Now, I've got absolutely no idea where on earth she might be. You've got to help, Saul.'

'We'll get to it, I promise. Right this minute, we're focused on the shooting. The area around King's Cross is in lockdown. Any idea who may have shot him?'

'Not a clue. Almost certainly it was the same person who until a few moments before had been pointing a sniper's targeting laser at me, not him. The whole thing was weird, Saul.'

'Did you see who it was?'

'No way. Most likely, it was someone on a rooftop. I couldn't see.'

'Airborne units are hovering over Granary Square as we speak. Ben, I need you to come in and answer some questions.'

'Saul, I know you mean well, but I need to find Holly. That's now my priority.'

'You'll be a suspect until proven innocent, you know that, Ben.'

'That's bullshit. It'll take five seconds – or less – to work out that the murder weapon was a sniper rifle. I'm not a suspect, Saul, and you know it.'

'That's as may be, my friend, but that's not how the police work. Every important witness needs to make a formal statement.'

'Cut me some slack! My priority's now Holly. Assuming she's found safe and sound, I'll be happy to answer all and any questions.'

'What did Keiran want?'

'He said he'd stolen something. Something that would enable the greatest computer hack of all time to be revealed. As a consequence, he was a wanted man. The fact he's now dead proves he was onto something. He told me he's mailed whatever he stole to a private mailbox for safekeeping and wanted me to be his personal courier.'

'Of all the people he might have chosen, Ben, he just had to pick you. As coincidences go, I find that hard to believe.'

'The fact that Keiran made an appearance this afternoon is tough for anyone to believe, trust me. Twelve months ago, he was reported killed in action in Afghanistan. How does a man who's meant to be dead end up meeting with me not thirty minutes ago, looking and behaving very much as if he is alive?'

'You tell me.'

'Also, why does the sniper shoot Doherty, not me? It doesn't make sense.'

'Why is it, Ben, that wherever you go, there are dead bodies?'

'Look, Saul, my immediate focus is going to be finding Holly. Promise me you'll help?'

'Right this minute, we have a murder investigation on our hands. I'll see what I can do, though.'

Chapter 8

'What happens now?' Li-Jing asks as Lewis ends the call. The place is deserted. An air of calm and tranquillity is trying its best to envelop them. It is fighting a losing battle against the surge of adrenalin that is still racing around their bodies.

'I need to go and find someone, urgently.'

'Would that be the woman, Holly, I heard you talking about?'

Lewis nods.

'Maybe I can help? After all, you've helped me. I'd be happy to return the favour?' She looks at Lewis and smiles.

'Thanks, but this is something only I can sort out. Besides, I'm sure you've got stuff you need to be doing.' Lewis's mind is only half-focused on the woman. His eyes keep scanning the area around the restaurant, constantly vigilant.

'Plenty, but it's only coursework.'

Lewis shakes his head.

'A close friend has been kidnapped. I have to find her. Plus, as you heard me say, I'm meant to go and collect something. I appreciate the offer, though.'

'I could go and collect whatever you need collecting while you go and find Holly?'

He looks directly at her. Lewis finds her vulnerability and innocence distracting. Another time, he might have considered asking her for a date. For the moment, he needs to stay focused.

'You saved my life this afternoon,' she continues. 'If you hadn't dragged me away, who knows who else might have ended up dead?' She pats his arm as she says this. 'It would be no trouble. Just tell me where to go, give me the key and I'll go and get it for you. Then we'd have an excuse to meet up again later?'

'It's a kind offer,' Lewis says, fighting to process what she's just told him. His mind keeps jumping back and forth, trying to replay snippets of his conversation with Doherty earlier. 'I need to do this myself. Anyway, we don't need an excuse to meet up. Maybe I can call you sometime? Where are you staying?'

'In a hostel, just off the Gray's Inn Road. I'm a student at SOAS. Studying for a Masters in International Studies and Diplomacy.'

'I'm impressed.'

'It's okay. The accommodation is cramped and very poky. It's a hard place to make friends, to be honest.'

'I'm surprised. Your English is excellent. Where are you from?'

'Thank you. I'm Malaysian, originally from Kuala Lumpur. Who knows, perhaps you and I might be friends, Ben? I think I'd like that.'

'As you say, who knows? How do I get in touch?'

She recites a mobile phone number from memory and Lewis keys it into his phone.

'Are you going to be all right? I need to get going, that's all.'

'I'll be fine. I can find my way back. Call me later, though. I'd like that.' She gives a warm smile.

'Sure.'

With that, he gets up to leave, slowly heading back towards where his bike is parked. Putting on his helmet, he sees Li-Jing watching. She waves at him, and he waves back.

Chapter 9

In police terms, detective inspector Saul Zeltinger had something of a reputation, principally as a man fixated about the details. Arguably more British in appearance than many of his Anglo-Saxon contemporaries, Zeltinger typically dressed in a well-pressed suit, usually with a tie and matching handkerchief in a breast pocket. He attributed his fondness for detail to his half-Germanic parentage, although some claimed his exactitude was more of an obsession than anything else. Here was a man who had read pure mathematics at Bristol and, like his newfound friend, Ben Lewis, was an avid chess player and an ardent fan of the game. Zeltinger was proud of his reputation as being quirky, meticulous and thorough.

It was only because of being thorough that caused Zeltinger to learn about the Chinese woman. Sitting with his well-thumbed black notebook open, its frayed edges stained with ink, Zeltinger achieved this fact-finding success through painstakingly walking the Romanian waitress through the events of that lunchtime yet one more time. As always, he would be taking copious notes in neat handwriting as he listened, periodically underlining a word or two, perhaps scribbling a hastily written addendum in a margin.

As with any repeated walk-through, Zeltinger always went back to the beginning, to the moment when Lewis first arrived.

'I directed the man you call Lewis to an outside table. He didn't seem fussy about which one, so I indicated the one nearest and he seemed content.'

'What else?'

'He had a chess set with him. The first thing he did before sitting down was place it on the table. I asked if he wanted anything and he said he'd like a bottle of beer. I turned on the outside heater for him then left him to it.'

'Did you talk to him again?'

'Not really. I brought him his beer, and he thanked me, nothing else. The chess pieces were already laid out on the Board. He was waiting for someone, that was clear.'

'Describe to me how busy you were this lunchtime.'

'Not very,' she answers. She has long, flowing, curly brown hair that periodically needs tucking behind an ear. It is a nervous habit, Zeltinger reflects, and he makes yet another a margin note in his notebook.

'Was there anyone else outside apart from the two men?'

She shakes her head as if to say no, then stops. This time she remembers.

'No, wait! There was the Asian woman.'

'What Asian woman?' Zeltinger asks, writing rapidly in his notebook. 'Where did she come from? Can you describe her?'

'Long, black hair. Chinese-looking,' the Romanian says and shrugs. Momentarily, she lowers her gaze before looking back at Zeltinger, running both hands through her hair. 'I don't know how old. Quite young, I think. They look so similar, I'm sorry.' Zeltinger writes another margin note beside the one he'd made earlier.

'Was she alone, or with someone?'

'She was alone for the whole time, I'm certain.'

'Did she arrive before or after Lewis had sat down?' He watches keenly as she tries to remember. 'Take your time, there's no hurry. It is important to get the details correct.'

'Definitely after,' the woman says after a few moments' thought. 'I was about to sit her at the adjacent table, but she chose the next one along.'

'She chose? Meaning that she was two tables away then?'

'Yes, that's correct.'

'What did she order?'

'A tea, I think. Yes, green tea. It's a popular choice.' As she speaks, she wraps a curly strand of hair round and round her index finger. It is a nervous habit that Zeltinger finds distracting. His wife, Hattie, has the same mannerism.

'Was she still there when the man was shot?' The waitress's eyes well with tears. 'I'm sorry about all the questions. Just take your time to answer.'

She removes a handkerchief from a pocket and dabs her eyes and nose.

'Did you notice if she left before or after Lewis?'

She begins shaking her head, but then stops, remembers something.

'No, I remember, they left together! I was so shocked after hearing the shot, seeing the man's head disintegrate. I was inside the restaurant, watching through the window, feeling sickened, numb, hardly able to move. After the shooting, the man you call Lewis got up from his chair and ran off, bumping into the Chinese woman, almost knocking her over.

He grabbed her by the arm, and they ran off together. I thought they were brave. I would have been terrified.'

'Did you notice anyone else? Anyone catch your eye, for any reason?'

'There were a couple of others, I think. All running, trying to get away. One man, I remember, ran across the square in the same direction as the other two. I thought at the time he was taking a risk. In case this sniper was a crazy person shooting at random.'

'Can you describe this man?'

'No chance. I really can't remember that much about him at all, I'm sorry.'

'Don't worry,' Zeltinger says, closing his notebook, the cue that the interview is finally over. 'You have been most helpful. That will be all for the moment.'

The waitress hurries away as Zeltinger's mobile phone buzzes angrily in his jacket pocket. It's a call from his office. He steps outside into the open air to take the call in privacy.

'Zeltinger.'

'Sir?' He recognises the voice of his young sergeant, Meilin. 'A body's been found on the roof of a tower block adjacent to Granary Square.' She reads out an address and Zeltinger heads towards the block in question.

'Have SCO19 been informed?'

'They're already in situ, sir.'

Zeltinger ends the call and goes to find an officer from the Met's armed response unit. It takes time to pin someone down, but eventually he locates the officer-in-command. The man is talking into a headset microphone as Zeltinger approaches.

'I gather a body's been found.' Zeltinger flashes his ID card.

'Yes. The office block over there,' the man nods in the general direction. 'We're clearing the roof as we speak. One dead male, Caucasian, mid-thirties. No obvious cause of death. Also, one long-range sniper rifle with a fancy laser riflescope. Do you want to take a look?'

'If I can, yes.'

'I'll have someone take you up there.' He looks around and beckons to a colleague. 'Hey, Joss, can you escort the DI up to the roof of the building?'

'Just to be clear, we're going to need a full post-mortem,' Zeltinger adds.

'No worries, it's all in hand. A team from Forensics are on their way.'

Chapter 10

Several years earlier, with economic sanctions in full flow, the Russian president had promised the North Korean leader of the day his covert support to assist them in getting access to a source of much-needed foreign currency. Help appeared in the form of the Kremlin quietly investing in Gunter Markov's new operation: getting the business started and setting up banking conduits to allow US dollars earned through cyber-criminal operations to funnel their way back to North Korea, without fear of being frozen or seized by Western banks. The Russians were shrewd enough to realise that Markov's loyalties might prove fickle at best. Which explains why SVR agents had installed hidden cameras and microphones in both Markov's business premises and his apartment.

Matters had bumbled along amicably for a few years. It was fair to say that Markov's surveillance had not been a matter of great importance until recently, when the North Korean had uploaded his encrypted post and tried selling the encryption key to the highest bidder. Suddenly, keeping close tabs on Markov moved back to being centre stage. Which explains how the Russians managed to witness, in graphic detail, the moments when Keiran Doherty and one other had tortured and then killed the North Korean. The Russian president had been outraged. It hadn't taken long to identify Doherty, but when they discovered the truth about what Markov had really posted online, an edict was issued ordering Doherty and his accomplice to be eliminated – and to do whatever it took to secure the recovery of the encryption key. Overnight, this became a top priority for Russian agents worldwide.

Unlike the CIA, the *Sluzhba Vneshney Razvedki* – the former first directorate of the KGB more commonly known as the SVR – had a sophisticated field operation on the ground in London. The moment the assassin emerged from the building, a minivan accelerated from a side alley and drew to a halt at the curb, allowing the woman dressed in black to make a hasty but well-planned escape. As part of the same operation, two Russian agents were in Granary Square taking surveillance photos. Back at the control room located in a safe house in Knightsbridge, there had been much excitement. The man Doherty had been meeting was none other than Ben Lewis. Certain SVR agents had scores to settle with Lewis.

'Oleg Panich will be smiling in his grave,' the new head of London station, Alexei Polunin, said on seeing the photos. 'If only our assassin had used another bullet!'

It hadn't been that long since legendary agent Oleg Panich had been killed – and Polunin seriously injured – following a botched attempt by Panich to set off a dirty bomb in London. It had been Lewis who had been largely responsible for thwarting Panich's plan. A lot had changed since then, not least the number and quality of resources now based in London. The days when the head of station was expected to be involved in active fieldwork were consigned to history. Following Panich's death, Pyotr Ivankov had been transferred to London. Two hundred and twenty-five pounds of well-honed muscle, Ivankov had previously been part of the Russian president's close protection unit. When asked personally by the president if he would consider deployment to London, Ivankov had been only too happy to accept.

'*So,*' Polunin muses as he stares at Lewis's picture. '*How do you fit into this puzzle, Ben Lewis? What is your connection to Doherty? Have you acquired the encryption key, by any chance? Because if you have, you'll soon be rubbing shoulders with Pyotr Ivankov.*'

He presses the intercom button on his desk.

'Where is Ivankov?' he asks abruptly. Before his secretary can reply, he adds, 'Tell him to be in my office within the hour.'

Forty minutes later, Pyotr Ivankov is standing in front of Polunin's desk.

'So, Pyotr. How are you enjoying London? Are there enough pretty girls to keep a healthy Muscovite happy?'

Ivankov smiles but doesn't answer. The man's bulky frame fills the space in front of Polunin's desk, barely fitting the suit jacket he is wearing.

'I have interesting news. The man responsible for Comrade Panich's death is back on our radar. Are you familiar with the name, Ben Lewis?'

Ivankov smiles but again says nothing.

'One of our agents was involved in a small operation today, taking care of a saboteur and thief who had stolen secrets from Mother Russia. We believe that before he died, he passed information concerning the whereabouts of these secrets to Lewis. I need Lewis found and apprehended, and the stolen information recovered. After that, what happens to him is your business. Do I make myself clear?'

'It will be an honour and a pleasure. I will need information about Lewis. His address, his movements. How quickly can these be obtained?'

Polunin passes Ivankov a slim folder.

'We are already one step ahead of you. Here is everything we have. Phone numbers, bank details, addresses and known contacts. I hope that should be enough to get you started?'

'Of course. There will be no failure. You have my word.'

Chapter 11

Lewis tries Holly's landline but gets no answer. Her mobile is switched off and routing through to voicemail. He phones the hospital in Canterbury. Holly had been expected to work the early shift but hadn't turned up for duty. Unusually, she hadn't phoned in with an explanation either. Lewis concludes that he needs to head to Canterbury to see if he can find any clues as to her whereabouts.

The trip down to the Kent city is, for Lewis, a familiar journey. During the ride, he tries imagining what Doherty might have done with Holly. As he approaches the outskirts of Canterbury, one conclusion seems inevitable. If this visit proved to be a dead-end, he'll have little option but to follow Doherty's perverted trail if that's the only way to locate Holly. It is not an option he relishes.

The one-way street past Holly's house is a quiet neighbourhood with little passing traffic. Parking his bike on the road, he removes his helmet and walks up the short path to Holly's front door and rings the bell twice. There is no answer. He tries banging on the door. Again, no response. He looks through the letterbox and calls out her name, placing his ear to the aperture to listen for sounds from within. Again, nothing.

About to head around the back of the house to peer through the windows, he stops in his tracks at the sound of a sash window being raised in the property next door. It is an elderly woman, wearing a purple cardigan and blue-framed glasses.

'What's going on?' she shouts at him angrily before seeing who it is and changing her tone. 'Oh, I remember you. You're the boyfriend. Or rather, you were. About a year ago, wasn't it? Very suitable I thought at the time, not that it's any of my business.'

'I'm looking for Holly,' Lewis says, interrupting her. 'You don't happen to know where she is?'

'Do you still see that German detective?' the woman went on as if she hadn't heard him. 'I liked him. I've still got his card. Actually, I was minded to give him a call.'

'I'm more concerned at the moment to find Holly,' Lewis says, struggling to contain his patience.

'And I'm trying to tell you! The last I saw her was yesterday afternoon. She left with another man – suntanned with wrinkly skin. He looked a bit physical with her to me, grabbing her by the arm and all that stuff. It didn't look right. It struck me as odd, so I made some notes. If she wasn't back by tomorrow, I was going to call your German detective. He had ever such nice manners.'

'Notes about what, exactly?'

'Details about his car! I wrote them all down. I can be a nosy old so-and-so at times, but there we are. These days you have to be, don't you? If you want, I'll go and find the piece of paper.'

When she returns, she is holding a small notebook.

'Here we are. It was a black BMW. I've never liked black as a colour for a car. Do you want the registration?' She passes the notebook to Lewis. He takes a photograph of the page with his phone.

'That's very helpful, thank you.'

'My pleasure. Just make sure you find Holly. Don't go letting her slip through your fingers like you did last time, do you hear me?'

Lewis heads back to his bike and calls Saul Zeltinger.

'Saul, it's Ben. I've got a number plate of a car that might have been used to abduct Holly yesterday. Can you run a trace?'

'Ben. How nice of you to make contact. Exactly where and how did you find this?'

'Holly's next-door neighbour in Canterbury. Holly left the house yesterday with another man. The old lady next door thought it didn't look right and wrote down the car's registration details.'

'I remember her. Quite the busybody, as I recall. Give me what you've got and I'll see what I can do. You're not exactly in my good books at the moment.'

'Thanks, Saul. I appreciate it.' He reads out the licence plate details and Zeltinger repeats everything to make sure.

'By the way, we found the rifle. Plus, another dead body. A man, in his mid-thirties, British. Died from natural causes, or so it would appear, but we're still checking. We ran his prints. His name was Nigel Fisher. Ex-army, held the rank of major – a former marksman who had been a freelance security contractor since leaving the military. Here's the thing. It's like your friend Doherty. Records show that Fisher died twelve months ago. Killed during a failed hostage negotiation in northern Iraq. Fisher was buried in Wells, Somerset last November.'

'Are you positive about the ID?'

'Completely.'

'What the hell's going on? Two men with similar backgrounds, both thought to be dead, are suddenly discovered to be alive. First, what's going on? Second, why does one of them, Fisher, suddenly decide to kill the other, Doherty? Third, and this is the bizarre thing: are we really meant to believe that Fisher, having killed Doherty, drops down dead from natural causes? That is what you're suggesting, isn't it?'

'Current evidence certainly points in that direction, yes. I'm not convinced, either. The body was some distance from the weapon.'

'Why all these dead people suddenly coming back to life?'

'You tell me, Ben. Let me check the licence plate, and I'll call you back.'

Ten minutes pass before Lewis's phone vibrates in his pocket with Zeltinger's return call.

'What news?'

'What are you mixed up in, Ben?'

'What do you mean?'

'I ran the plate through DVLA's system. I have an address, the place where the car's registered. That's the good news. The bad news is that I am not supposed to give it to you.'

'Why not?'

'Because the address is blacklisted. All enquiries to be referred to one Jake Sullivan at Thames House. Ring any bells, by any chance, Ben?'

Chapter 12

Jake Sullivan. It hadn't been that long since Sullivan and one of his MI5 section heads – a frosty and difficult-to-read woman called Laura – had tried to recruit Lewis. He'd declined at the time. Instead, through a connection of Sullivan's, he'd ended up playing minder to a Ukrainian oligarch and his family. Which, in a roundabout way, had directed Lewis full circle back to an operation that Sullivan and his team were interested in. Wheels within wheels.

All of a sudden, a lot of things were not making sense. Someone Lewis hadn't seen for over six years, a man he believed had been killed fighting in Afghanistan, turns up unexpectedly, asking Lewis to do something dangerous. The same man uses a former girlfriend – Lewis's sister-in-law – as a hostage to make Lewis do his bidding. Why, amid all this madness, do MI5's footprints start appearing in the mud?

He thumbs through his contacts and hits the number to connect with Sullivan. Several layers of secretarial vetting later, and he finally finds himself connected.

'Ben! What an unexpected pleasure. Is this a social call, or might we be talking business?'

'For the moment, strictly business, Jake. Does the name Keiran Doherty mean anything to you?'

'The man shot in Granary Square this afternoon?'

Why was Lewis not surprised? There were few flies on Sullivan.

'The same. A former Marine acquaintance. Someone we'd all been led to believe had died fighting in Afghanistan a year ago.'

'Never heard of him before today. Why?'

'Doherty was attempting to blackmail me, moments before he died, having kidnapped my sister-in-law, Holly. He was trying to convince me he needed an errand performed in exchange for her freedom – something dangerous, but of great value. So valuable that having hawked it around one or two foreign intelligence agencies, he believed his life in mortal danger. Events seem to have proved him right on that score. Was he playing a part in one of your operations?'

There is laughter at the other end of the call.

'My dear boy! Even if he was, you couldn't possibly expect me to comment? I tell you what. Between friends and off the record, I'll put your mind at rest. I confess, we did run Doherty's name through our database this afternoon. What I can say is that we've had absolutely nothing to do with Doherty, or he with us. Ever.'

'Given that the man was supposed to be dead, I suppose it wouldn't be beyond the bounds of possibility that he might have been using an alias.'

'Nice try, but we covered that angle as well. Why are you asking, Ben?'

'Holly's neighbour witnessed her abduction yesterday. She took down the details of a car Doherty had been driving. I asked Saul Zeltinger to run the registration through DVLA to find out who owned it. It turns out it's a black BMW, registered to an address with your name as the 'do not disclose' custodian. Presumably, it's an MI5 safe house.'

'What did Doherty want you to do?'

'Collect and look after an encryption key that he'd stolen. Ring any bells?'

'What sort of encryption?'

'Some North Korean hack that's been posted online with a unique, one-time encryption.'

'Nothing like that's crossed my desk. I'll make some enquiries. Meanwhile, why don't you give me the plate details?'

Lewis reads out the registration number that Holly's neighbour had given him.

'Leave it with me and I'll call you right back.'

Lewis paces the pavement next to where his bike is parked whilst waiting for Sullivan's call. Holly's elderly neighbour continues to watch him through the net curtains, and he gives a friendly wave. A black Ford Transit drives slowly past. Something about it strikes Lewis as odd. He is about to take a closer look when his phone buzzes.

'Ben, it's Jake.' The Transit has already disappeared around a bend in the road. 'I've been digging. This is not straightforward. A few months ago, MI5's bean counters decided that we needed to dispose of several of our less-frequently-used safe houses. Yet another cost-cutting exercise. The registration you gave belonged to a car that was once ours, registered to a safe house that has since been disposed of. Someone must have decided to transfer the car to the new owner. Only it appears the registration paperwork never got updated.'

'Do you have an address?'

'Sorry, but I can't. It's still classified. It's in Yorkshire, not far from Whitby. It's remote, if I remember correctly.'

'Can you at least say who bought it?'

'Some anonymous offshore company. You think that's where Holly may be being held?'

'Who knows? If you won't tell me the address, at least can you get one of your people to check it out? Holly's life is at stake.'

'I'll see what we can do. I'll speak with the Yorkshire police and ask if someone can take a look today.'

'Thanks, Jake. Call me the moment you hear anything.'

'I'll do my best, Ben, I promise.'

Chapter 13

Already the light is beginning to fade as Lewis puts his phone away. Hearing a vehicle approaching, he turns around. It is the same black Ford Transit, this time looking for a parking space. It must have done a circuit whilst Lewis had been speaking with Sullivan. Lewis now can see what had been bothering him earlier. The van has blacked-out windows and several antennae on the roof. This is no ordinary delivery vehicle. As Lewis steps aside to allow it to park, the driver clips the front of his motorbike with his fender, sending the Honda spilling onto the pavement.

'Hey, you clumsy idiot!' Lewis bangs a side panel with the heel of his hand. The Transit comes to a halt, the passenger quickly out of the van, followed soon after by the driver.

'Sorry about that, buddy.' The driver is American. Stocky, medium height, muscular, the sort likely to be pulling weights in the gym a few times a week. The passenger, in contrast, is wiry but athletic, definitely agile on his feet.

'I hate driving on the wrong side of the road, I apologise.' The stocky guy looks at his colleague and shrugs. 'We'll help you with the bike, sir. If there's any damage, I'll take care of it.'

The two men stand in the road. The stocky guy grabs the handlebars, the wiry guy the bike seat: both preparing to pull, a procedure Lewis knows is going to be futile. Sure enough, having failed a couple of times, Lewis steps forward to help. He leans his backside against the bike seat from the fallen side and uses muscles in his legs to push the machine to the vertical. In no time, the bike is back on its stand. Lewis walks around to check the chrome and the paintwork. There is a small dent in one of the exhaust pipes. All three gather around and stare. Hunched over, they rub fingers over the freshly abraded chrome.

Which is the moment the other two decide to make their moves.

With Lewis's finger extended, the stocky guy grabs Lewis's wrist. Bending it backwards, he executes a snappy clockwise twist, simultaneously stepping behind Lewis to rotate the former Marine's arm in a circular motion. The driver's arm and Lewis's arm now come to rest in the vertical, both locked together, both tucked in close to the driver's body. In this position, Lewis's wrist is bent uncomfortably backwards by the strength of the stocky man's forearm. It is a smart move that aims to keep Lewis immobile, which is the moment when the wiry guy decides to make his own intervention. A double punch, one-two, directly to Lewis's solar plexus. Lewis's knees sag. He is kept upright solely by the pressure exerted on his wrist and forearm courtesy of the stocky guy's arm lock.

'Sorry about that, buddy,' the stocky driver says, his head up close to Lewis's. Lewis can feel the man's warm breath in his ear. 'Just in case you were planning any funny business. We usually find it appropriate to give a little lesson on how to behave upfront.' Lewis's assailants smile at each other. An untold joke hangs in the air.

Lewis gives no reaction and says nothing. Sadly, for these two goons, he is no amateur in unarmed combat. As a Marine, he'd rarely been defeated. Not even by the training instructors. In situations such as this, when seemingly overpowered, he preferred giving opponents the impression they were early winners. Let them believe they had him on the ropes. Then, when they lowered their guard, Lewis would explode like a tiger out of a cage.

When the moment was right.

Which Lewis judges to be not quite yet.

The wiry guy reaches across to search Lewis's leather jacket. With his colleague still keeping Lewis in check, he pats down all the pockets. Lewis lets his muscles relax and feels a corresponding weakening of the grip on his wrist. A subconscious message delivered and received. *Things are going to plan. This one's a pushover. He's not even resisting. Maybe we can relax things a little too.*

'I can't find the key. He must have it on him somewhere else.' It is the first time the wiry guy has spoken. He, too, is American.

'Why don't we ask?'

Which is when the wiry guy makes a major error of judgement. Moving to a position directly in front of Lewis, he looks the former Marine directly in the eye.

'Where's the key, punk?'

Lewis doesn't answer.

'Do you want me to hit you a second time?' the man continues, now enjoying the show. 'I asked you a question. Where's the key?'

Again, Lewis doesn't answer. The wiry guy is fast becoming irritated. He moves his face closer, now only inches from Lewis's.

'You want to do this the rough way, eh punk?' he growls, full of menace, spittle flying.

Which is the moment the tiger explodes from the cage.

Lewis executes a powerful head-butt directly into the man's face. There is a sickening sound of bones being broken, blood quickly pouring down the wiry guy's face. With Lewis's head still lowered from the head-butt, he checks his right foot. In a combination move, he stamps his heel heavily onto the stocky driver's left foot, simultaneously moving his left hand, open-palmed, in a swinging punch across his body. This connects directly with the driver's face to his right, the heel of his hand powering into the man's nose cartilage. It causes the head to whip back and, as Lewis predicted it would, causes the driver to release Lewis's arm as he struggles to deal with the pain in his face. Lewis next swivels his own body to the right and delivers a left knee directly into the man's groin. Turning around to face the wiry guy, he now gives him a dose of his own medicine too. A double one-two punch straight to the midriff. On the receiving end, Lewis had tensed his abs and exhaled sharply each time he had absorbed a punch. Now the tables are reversed, the wiry guy simply doubles up on the deck and howls like a baby.

Lewis eyes his handiwork and straightens his cuffs.

'I agree with you, by the way. About the need to give a little lesson upfront. On setting the right behaviour, that is.'

Both men are writhing about on the pavement.

'Hardly worth the effort, was it? Trying to find that key, I mean. Are you clowns from Langley? It's no bother to me. I'd just like to know. The accent's a bit of a giveaway.'

The stocky driver gives a pained grunt. Lewis takes this to be an affirmative response.

'We . . . want . . . the . . . encryption . . . key . . .' the wiry guy mumbles. A bloodied handkerchief now covers his nose and face. 'We'll . . . pay . . . good . . . money.'

'Unless you steal it from me first, you mean?'

The wiry guy shrugs, getting unsteadily to his feet.

'Tell whoever sent you that there'll be no deal whilst you two goons are on the case. Two people have died today because of this thing. Too bad the pair of you are going to be out of action for a while. Life's a bitch. The price has just doubled. If I see either of you again, I'll raise it tenfold, do we understand each other? Now, before I go, you're going to pay me for the damage to my bike.'

The stocky driver looks at his colleague, then at Lewis, before grudgingly taking a billfold from his jacket pocket. He counts out five twenty-pound notes and flicks the money in Lewis's direction.

'I'll need double that just to cover labour costs.' The driver counts out five more notes and tosses them across. The wiry guy is now back on his feet, trying to take a few steps, evidently in some pain. He rests a hand on Lewis's bike seat to steady himself.

'A further five as a goodwill payment, then we're done.' He looks momentarily at the wiry guy. 'Don't go pushing that machine over again, or there'll be trouble. Mind there's no blood on the paintwork, either.'

With great reluctance, the stocky man peels off five more notes. Lewis takes time to count each one. He folds them neatly and places the tidy bundle in a trouser pocket. What he doesn't take enough note of is the wiry guy hunched over the bike seat, taking a breather. In reality, the American is affixing a GPS tracking device to the underside of the fuel tank. As Lewis turns towards him and picks up his cycle helmet, the wiry guy moves away unsteadily.

'Another time, another life, gentlemen,' he says, climbing once more onto his bike and starting the engine.

With a wave to Holly's elderly neighbour – doubtless, she would have been watching the whole incident – he revs the engine and drives away.

Chapter 14

Decision time. Head aimlessly to Yorkshire in the vague hope that Sullivan might reverse his decision and tell Lewis the address of the property near Whitby? Or go to the mailbox location, before anyone else – such as the Americans – beat him to it? Overruling his heart, his head tells him that the mailbox should, for the moment, be the focus of his attention.

Shortly before five-thirty in the evening, he pulls into a petrol station on the outskirts of Canterbury and fills the Honda's tank. Using his smartphone, he learns that the mailbox business closes at six and won't reopen until eight-thirty the next morning. The address is close to London's King's Cross station. Over ninety minutes away. He won't now be able to check the mailbox until the morning.

He decides instead to call his chess partner.

'Zeltinger,' the familiar voice replies promptly in his ear.

'Saul, it's Ben. Any progress?'

'Not good. Forensics have conducted a preliminary autopsy on the dead sniper. They're struggling to find a reason for his death other than natural causes. All sorts of complex toxicology tests are underway, checking for poisons and such. So far, we've got nowhere.'

'Who do you think pulled the trigger?'

'You tell me. The evidence points to Fisher, but it doesn't feel right. There are no prints, no eyewitnesses and no video camera recordings. It's highly unsatisfactory. Did you speak with Sullivan?'

'One step forward, one backward. The place where the car's registered is in Yorkshire. It used to be an MI5 safe house. Since sold to an unknown buyer, the location still classified. The car transferred across when the property was sold. Sullivan was not in the mood to give me the details. I don't suppose you might feel so inclined, Saul?'

'Sorry, Ben. Rules are rules.'

'I suppose Yorkshire might be where Doherty took Holly. It feels like a long shot, though. Jake said he would ask the local police to investigate. If you can't tell me the address, can you at least follow up with Jake to make sure this has been given enough priority?'

'I can try. I wouldn't hold out great hope, though. I doubt she's there. Sorry to be pessimistic.'

'I'm clutching at straws, Saul. Holly's missing and I'm frustrated as hell not to have hardly any clues as to where she might be.'

'Leave it with me, Ben. I'll speak to Jake right away.'

'Thanks. There's another angle. Moments before Doherty was shot, he'd been showing me this short video clip of Holly. In the mayhem of the shooting, I grabbed the device before fleeing. I've got it with me. It looks like a cheap burner, but I haven't the time or skills to hack into it. You'll have people who can. It might yield something about who Keiran called the day he took Holly hostage or where he might have taken her. I'm on my way back to London. Can I hand it in so that one of your team can take a look?'

'We could have had it two or three hours earlier if you'd come in for questioning.'

'I'll take that as a yes. I should be in London by early evening. Where do you want it delivered?'

'Come directly to Savile Row police station. I'm bound to be working all night. I was about to call Hattie and forewarn her. One other thing. Tell me about the Chinese woman who left Granary Square with you. How does she fit into the picture?'

'You haven't lost your touch, I see. I haven't figured her out, to be honest. I'll maybe be in a better position to give an answer when we next meet.'

He ends the call thinking about Li-Jing. Something she'd said earlier hadn't gelled. Even though she was Malaysian, she reminded Lewis of Sui-Lee, a female Chinese agent he had once come up against. She, too, had been overeagerly disposed towards him, but then she had also been ruthlessly aggressive in trying to kill him. He didn't sense the same aggression in Li-Jing. However, was it purely coincidental that she was in Granary Square earlier? First Keiran Doherty, then Li-Jing, now the American pair.

Which is when he has an idea about how to resolve this, one way or the other. He searches for her number on his phone and hits 'dial'.

'Hello,' says a quiet female voice.

'Li-Jing?'

'Yes, is that you, Ben? It's so good to hear from you.'

'I wondered how you were. Not in too much shock, I hope?'

'I'm okay, but thanks for asking.'

'Do you fancy dinner tonight? Nothing flash, just something quick and simple.'

'That would be terrific. Do you see? Just like friends already!'

'Where and when would be best?'

They agree on a time and place, and Lewis ends the call.

Before setting off, he has just one more thing he needs to do. If his chance encounter with the two Americans demonstrated anything, it was that his mobile phone was a location beacon to anyone wanting to track him. It was therefore time to turn it off and go off the grid.

Chapter 15

Ivankov has been busy. One of his agents is already staking out Lewis's apartment near Victoria. Meanwhile, SVR eavesdropping specialists back in Moscow have been tracking Lewis's phone. Ivankov now knows a great deal about Ben Lewis and what he's been up to. He knows, for example, that Lewis is heading back to London. He also knows that Lewis has Doherty's mobile phone in his possession and is scheduled to hand it over to the policeman sometime soon. Ivankov has another agent waiting for Lewis outside Savile Row police station. Finally, he has just learnt about the time and location of Lewis's dinner date with the woman, Li-Jing. Ivankov has decided that he also wants to be there. He and four other agents.

Now in position near the restaurant, Ivankov checks his watch. Thirty minutes until Lewis's planned dinnertime rendezvous.

The Eastern Dragon is situated in Lisle Street, in the heart of London's Chinatown district. It is early evening, and the area teems with people. Ivankov has commandeered two vans from Polunin's car pool. They are parked on a nearby side street, available for rapid deployment as and when required. Open-channel communication with his team is through neck microphones and hidden earpieces. Back in the Knightsbridge safe house, Alexei Polunin is keeping watch over the entire operation. Now all they have to do is wait.

'Apparently –' Polunin is speaking to Ivankov through his earpiece '– the target's phone has been off the grid for the last hour or so.'

'Why?' Ivankov asks.

'Probably out of battery.'

'Perhaps, but the man's not a fool.'

Less than two miles away, Lewis parks the bike outside Liverpool Street station and walks into the railway terminus in search of a mobile phone vendor. A while later, he is back outside with two bottom-of-the-range burner phones in his possession purchased from a shop on the station concourse. After discarding the packaging, he places a call using one of them.

'Zeltinger,' comes the familiar voice once more after the third ring.

'Saul, it's Ben. I need a favour.'

'I think you are out of those at the moment, Ben.'

'I need to get Doherty's phone to you, but I don't want to risk coming into the police station. Is there someone who could come and collect it?'

'I could send Meilin,' Zeltinger says. 'Where are you?'

'I can be at Tottenham Court Road tube station, north side entrance by the Dominion Theatre, in ten minutes. Would that work?'

'Let me ask.' There is silence for a few seconds then Zeltinger is back on the line.

'She's on her way. Do you know Meilin? Chinese woman, late twenties. She'll be in uniform. She knows what you look like. Are you in trouble?'

'No, just taking precautions. I'm on my way to meet someone in Soho. Given that the Americans followed my phone all the way to Canterbury, I don't want to risk losing Doherty's I've acquired another for the moment.'

'How do I contact you if I need to?'

'You don't. For all I know, they may be monitoring yours too. I've got to go. Tell Meilin I'll be at the Dominion Theatre shortly.'

Chapter 16

Wang Ming-Tao is not happy about Li-Jing's appearance in London. Not happy at all. In his mind, she is an inexperienced amateur – and therefore dangerous. An arrogant youngster, helped along by virtue of family connections. He had made his position clear the first moment the pair had been introduced. Ming-Tao had his reasons. After all, it had been Li-Jing's cousin, Sui-Lee, who had nearly ended his career. Not Sui-Lee, the legendary field agent who could do no wrong. No, this had been the real Sui-Lee; the conniving bitch, the one who had tried to stitch him up to save her skin.

When Sui-Lee arrived in London a few years earlier, she and Ming-Tao worked a lot together. They had briefly been lovers. Then, one day, she ruthlessly turned the tables on him, making him scapegoat for one particularly disastrous operation. During a botched assassination of an African diplomat in his hotel room in Madrid, a Chinese agent was killed. Sui-Lee had been clumsy as well as careless. Several innocent people died when she accidentally detonated a bomb too early in an adjacent room. Sui-Lee lied and pointed the finger at Ming-Tao. Her connections and her undeniable force of character prevailed. Ming-Tao was sent back to Beijing in disgrace and reassigned to administrative duties. Only later, after Sui-Lee's death, did another agent come forward and admit what had happened. Ming-Tao was exonerated. He even received a letter of commendation from the deputy minister praising him for his outstanding service. Sent back to London to resume his old posting, Ming-Tao had never forgiven Sui-Lee. Not only for the anguish she caused but also for the humiliation and loss of face.

Finding a distant relative of Sui-Lee's back in London on a training mission felt more than a little ironic. Worse, Li-Jing's star as an agent-in-training appeared to be rising all too rapidly. Her Chinese minders seem delighted with how she recorded the conversation between Doherty and Lewis in Granary Square. Beijing was especially happy about the information revealed. Now they wanted Li-Jing to continue her attempts to befriend Lewis.

Not if Ming-Tao had anything to do with it. Li-Jing needed bringing down a peg or two. She needed to fail. Or worse.

Earlier that afternoon, he had tried to ridicule Li-Jing's amateurishness. He had argued for a more aggressive approach. He favoured sedating Lewis, forcibly removing his mailbox key, torturing him to reveal what he knew about Markov's secrets and then killing him for the shame and loss of face he had caused the People's Republic for Sui-Lee's death. His arguments were listened to out of respect but hadn't won the day. Instead, Sui-Lee's cousin was given the green light to continue trying to get as close to Ben Lewis as possible.

As a compromise, three junior members of Ming-Tao's team were assigned to watch over Li-Jing over the coming days. They were already in place in the vicinity of the restaurant where she was shortly expected to meet Lewis.

Ming-Tao remained unhappy about Li-Jing. He had been overruled in an early minor skirmish. However, there were other battles in the war yet to be won.

Chapter 17

Ten minutes before the appointed hour, Li-Jing is walking westward along Oxford Street, about to turn down Wardour Street in the heart of Chinatown. As she approaches the junction, her phone begins vibrating.

'Hello,' she says, answering the call in her softly spoken voice.

'Li-Jing, it's Ben.'

'Hi, Ben. I didn't recognise the number.'

'No, sorry. My phone's died. I've had to borrow someone else's. I'll be quick. Look, I've run into a problem. I'm not going to be able to join you for dinner this evening after all. I'm sorry.'

'Oh, that's such a pity. I was so much looking forward to seeing you again.'

'Me too. It can't be helped.'

'Could we, perhaps, meet later?'

Lewis pauses before he answers.

'I guess it might be possible. I won't know until I've finished what I'm doing. Are you sure you want to?'

'Absolutely. I need cheering up after this afternoon's nightmare.'

'Let's see how I get on. Always assuming it's not too late.'

'Call me at any time. I rarely turn in before midnight. Often later – and I always keep my phone on. I've been so frightened after what happened today, Ben.'

'I'm really sorry, Li-Jing.'

As Lewis ends the call, he is actually only a few blocks away, walking through Chinatown's pedestrianised zone. Dressed in his leather jacket, he could easily be mistaken for a motorcycle courier, one of many delivering packages to and from film production companies based in nearby Wardour Street. He is intent on watching the crowds, conducting his own surveillance around the back streets close to the restaurant. The entrance to the Eastern Dragon restaurant is less than fifty metres away.

Two things have piqued his curiosity.

The first is a pair of Chinese men pacing up and down Lisle Street. Both seem tense and anxious. This is Chinatown, but they look out of place. Both are wearing black leather jackets and black jeans. Both have curly black wires passing behind their ears down inside their polo neck shirt tops. Security guys. Or worse. They are waiting for someone. As Lewis watches, the men stop in unison. They each put a hand to their ear. An incoming communication from somewhere. They wait. Then, they briefly look at each other, shrug their shoulders and head off in the same direction together.

Further down the road, they are joined by a third dressed in a similar fashion. Surveillance has been cancelled. It can mean only one thing. The party meant to be arriving at the Eastern Dragon is now a no-show.

Lewis smiles to himself. Thank you, Li-Jing. Now it's clear who you're really working for.

What keeps Lewis rooted to the spot, however, is the second thing. The second thing is similar to the first thing, only more significant. This time the men are not Chinese. They are white, male, yet more leather jackets and black chinos: indeed, yet more curly wires passing behind the ears. Hired muscle. Or worse. These men don't pace; they loiter. They have their chosen positions. They are static watchers. Lewis counts three of them. One is standing in nearby Wardour Street, able to watch people coming and going to the restaurant from an oblique angle. Another is leaning against a wall just beyond the Eastern Dragon's entrance, on the far side. The third is standing in a small cul-de-sac, immediately opposite the restaurant itself. There may well be others Lewis can't yet see also.

Americans? Unlikely. They'd be in damage limitation mode from this afternoon's fiasco. Re-evaluating options and reconsidering resourcing needs. Unlikely to have spare men easily redeployed. These could be Russians, however, which might explain why they were still here when the Chinese delegation was not. They hadn't yet received the cancellation notice. How could they? Lewis hadn't used his regular phone to make the call.

It was time to send a message.

Lewis chooses the one loitering in Wardour Street to be his messenger. The man is on his own, not in the direct line of sight of the other two. By virtue of a small pedestrian cut-through, Lewis can approach this watcher from the rear, his intended target looking the other way, towards the restaurant. The man stands ten feet from where the cut-through emerges onto Wardour Street. Even though it is dark, illuminations from street and shop lights allow Lewis to see the man's curly wire earpiece.

Lewis approaches and taps the man on the shoulder. As he swivels around, Lewis quickly rips out the neck microphone clipped to the man's collar. To complete the surprise, he also powers a knee directly into the man's groin. Usually, this would be enough to cause a grown person to double up and fall to the floor. This one manages to stay upright. His mistake is to get angry. He lunges for Lewis's throat with one hand and squeezes hard. Lewis responds by tucking his chin down hard against his chest in an attempt to save his windpipe. The manoeuvre doesn't stop the choking pain in his throat, but it does give him the breathing space, literally, to execute a countermeasure. Placing his right hand on the wrist at his throat, Lewis pushes downwards sharply, twisting the man's wrist clockwise, at the same time putting his other hand directly under the man's elbow and pushing upwards.

In an instant, the tables are turned, the pressure on wrist and elbow forcing the man to release his grip. Now caught in a straight-arm wristlock, the man can't swing a punch at Lewis with his free arm, Lewis's torso already a whole arm's length away or more. Lewis's endgame is straightforward. He drags his victim towards the privacy of the pedestrian cut through, away from curious passers-by and their smartphones. With the man's hand and wrist bent back and pinned behind him, Lewis applies pressure on the wrist joint. His opponent cries out, the imminent threat of broken bones and tendons suddenly acute.

'Who are you?'

The man says nothing. Lewis increases the pressure, the man's eyes watering with the pain. Genuine terror is starting to show in his face.

'Do you want a broken wrist?'

'Nyet,' the man says, struggling to stay in control.

'Who is in charge of your operation here?'

The man says nothing. Lewis increases the pressure a notch.

'Ivankov. Pyotr Ivankov,' the man splutters in extreme pain.

'And your head of station?'

Again, silence for a brief moment until Lewis forces a rethink.

'Polunin. Alexei Polunin.'

Lewis smiles. He relaxes the pressure a little.

'A man with knife scars on both cheeks?'

'Da.'

'Tell him that Ben Lewis says hello. Also, a message for your man, Ivankov. The next time I find any of his team on my tail, tell him that I promise to do much more permanent and widespread damage. Is that clear?'

'Da.'

'Good.' With that, he lets go of the man's wrist, but not before grabbing hold of his right index finger and, with a sudden downward force, dislocating it. There is a sickly sound of a finger joint popping out of its socket.

'Just in case you were tempted to come after me.'

With that, he disappears, leaving his victim struggling to bend his finger back into position.

Chapter 18

Deciding that it would be unwise to return to his apartment that evening, he finds himself in need of a place to stay for the night. Searching the area close to King's Cross, he locates a hotel on the Farringdon Road with a cheap walk-in rate. It is also less than a mile away from the Remote Mailbox Company. With his bike parked on a side street not far from the hotel, he pays the receptionist in cash for one night's stay. In return, he is given keys to a room that is clean, quiet and has a large bed. He decides to take a shower before heading out to get something to eat. Lewis lets the warm water splay over his body for several minutes before eventually towelling his hair dry and getting dressed.

There is a steakhouse a few streets away. The place is quiet, and he is soon shown to an empty booth and handed a menu by an Argentinian waitress keen to talk.

'Can I get you a beer?' she asks.

'As long as it's cold,' he replies.

When she returns with his beer, he selects a rib-eye with all the trimmings from the menu. The waitress hovers by his table as she enters his order in her electronic device, lingering long enough to encourage conversation.

'Not too busy tonight?'

'It's okay. For midweek, it's okay.' She has a cute smile and pretty eyes. 'What kind of day have you had?'

Lewis takes a long pull of his drink.

'Not great. I was in Granary Square earlier. A man got shot dead.'

'Oh, my God!' She puts her hand on his arm. Lewis can feel the warmth of her fingers through his shirt. 'You were there? I heard it all on the news. It sounded ghastly.'

Lewis takes another mouthful of beer.

'I was there. Right up close.'

'Oh, my God! I would have been terrified.'

'I was more angry than scared,' he says, draining the rest of his beer in two gulps.

'You need another beer,' she says in a hurry, looking at his empty glass. She is suddenly at a loss for words. 'Let me get this one. On the house, I insist.'

The second beer, on the house, and the rib-eye arrive together, the same waitress trying to give Lewis a genuine smile but failing. She hurries away, no longer keen to talk. The warm hand on the arm and the earlier flirtatiousness have become a distant promise. More's the pity. Two beers and one steak with all the trimmings down, he feels in the mood for female companionship, which is when he has the idea to call Li-Jing again. Chinese agent or not, it was time for another conversation.

He leaves enough cash to cover his food, drink and a generous tip. Using the second of his recently purchased burner phones, he dials her number.

'Hello,' says the now familiar voice.

'Li-Jing, it's Ben. Sorry about earlier.'

'Hi, Ben. That's okay. Where are you?'

'Not far from Gray's Inn Road. Fancy a nightcap?'

'I'd love a nightcap. I'd invite you here, but this place is tiny and I've nothing to offer you.'

'That's okay. What's your address?'

She tells him the house number.

'Okay. Be outside on the pavement in five minutes. I'll drive by and pick you up.'

The drive by and pick up that Lewis refers to involves not his Honda but two taxis. He hails the first one shortly after making the call to Li-Jing. He asks the driver to travel the length of Gray's Inn Road slowly. The driver asks no questions, happy to oblige, Lewis wanting to check whether Li-Jing is where she said she'd be – and secondly, whether she really is alone. Soon he spots her, standing on the pavement and with no apparent minders in evidence. Asking the driver to let him out some distance away, he pays the fare plus a suitable tip then waits a full minute before hailing a second cab. In next to no time, Lewis's new driver is pulling to the curb alongside Li-Jing. Lewis opens the door, and she steps inside.

'I thought you'd be on your bike,' she says as the driver pulls away. 'I'm so pleased to see you again, Ben.' She kisses him on the cheek, before looking momentarily embarrassed.

'Me too. You feeling okay?'

'I guess. And you?' She takes hold of his hand, pressing her body next to his. She has put on perfume. The scent is nice.

'I thought we might use a drink.'

Less than a minute later, the driver pulls to the curb outside Lewis's hotel, and they both get out.

'I saw this place earlier,' he says, half-truthfully. 'It seemed to have a quiet bar. Certainly quieter than most pubs.' Which is evident the moment they step inside. They are the only customers.

'What will you have?'

'A white wine please.'

Lewis orders two glasses of the house white from a bored-looking bartender and then returns to where Li-Jing is sitting. They nestle together around a small table, legs touching, waiting for the drinks to arrive. Lewis checks his watch.

'Damn! I said I'd call that detective back. I've still no battery on my phone. Could I borrow yours a moment?'

'Sure,' she says, reaching into her bag. She unlocks her phone and hands it to Lewis just as the drinks arrive. He takes a moment to familiarise himself with the phone's features before dialling a number from memory. After getting no reply, he ends the call and hands the phone back to Li-Jing.

'No answer,' he says with a shrug. 'He can't say I didn't try.'

She places the phone back in her bag.

'Cheers,' he says to her. They raise glasses and both take a sip.

'Where do you live, Ben? Is it far from here?'

'Normally, yes. However, I thought it safer to stay in a hotel tonight, and because this place was so cheap, I've taken a room here.'

'Here? Wow! Have you been planning this sudden get-together of ours, Ben? I do hope so.'

'Do you? Why is that?'

'Well, for one thing, we might not be having this drink otherwise.' She is suddenly giving Lewis the full 'come-on' treatment. 'Tell me, do you have a girlfriend?' she asks, her eyes wide and glistening.

'Not at the moment,' he answers truthfully. 'How about you? Are you single or are you dating anyone?'

'Oh, I'm single,' she says. 'I have been single for a long time.' She puts her glass down and turns to face him. 'For far too long. To tell the truth, Ben, and I have to be very honest: I've always wanted to date an English man. I never seem to find the right person.' Her cheeks blush as she says this.

'You think there's something special about us English, is that the point?'

'No, Ben. The point is that I've been thinking about you all afternoon.' She places her hand in his lap, the message unambiguous. 'Thinking about what happened. How you rescued me from danger.' She drops her gaze for a second, then turns her head to look him directly in the eye. 'Let's not bother with a drink. Take me to bed. Let's forget about all the unpleasant stuff that's happened today.' There is a strange mix of both embarrassment and desperation in her eyes.

'That could be fun. The room does have a double bed.'

'That's good,' she says, moving even closer. 'Because my place is so cramped and suddenly much too far away. Here would be great.' She leans forwards and places her hand behind his head. They kiss for a long time, her tongue weaving in and out of his mouth, curling around his, her intensity full of surprising passion.

It is a surreal experience that rounds off a surreal day. They make love with a vigour that Lewis finds exhilarating. The second time, they take longer, exploring each other's bodies, stoking lust-fuelled fires within until they finally collapse in unison: spent, sated and exhausted.

'Happy?' he asks her, later, side-by-side, she resting her head on his shoulder, he stroking her arm gently.

'Very.'

'Still keen on paying me back?'

'Of course! I've already offered to help you collect that encryption key.'

'Why?' Lewis asks abruptly, his hackles raised.

'I just like to be helpful, Ben.'

'Tell me something.'

'Okay.'

'What are we doing here?'

This gets a reaction. Li-Jing sits up on the bed, her face flushed.

'What do you mean?'

'Twelve hours ago, we had never met. Suddenly, you're all over me like a rash. It's hardly a normal beginning, is it?'

'I wouldn't know,' she says. Uncertainty about where this all might be heading is written clearly on her face.

'Do you work for the Chinese government, Li-Jing?'

This gets a much angrier reaction.

'How can you ask that? I told you, I'm a Malaysian student.' She looks angry, her eyes filling with tears.

'Earlier today, you offered to help me collect whatever I needed collecting. You told me that I only had to tell you where to go and to give you the key. I'd never mentioned a key before, neither when I was on the phone to my policeman friend nor to you. I had mentioned a mailbox, but nothing about a key. It made me suspicious. I wanted to give you the benefit of the doubt. You might have guessed that I would need a key to open a mailbox. Therefore, I ran a little test. Shortly after I rang and told you our dinner date was cancelled, I saw three Chinese thugs leaving the area right next to the restaurant where we were meant to be meeting. I saw it with my own eyes, Li-Jing. They were stood down because they knew I wasn't coming. Only you could have told them.'

'That's not true.' Her face is expressionless.

'The real reason you're here is that you've been ordered to get close to me, isn't that right? You just mentioned an encryption key, but you and I have never discussed such a thing.'

'That's not true,' she says half-heartedly. 'You've completely misunderstood my intentions.'

'Really?' Lewis says, now off the bed. He is starting to get dressed. 'Tell me how, exactly?'

'I only wanted to repay your kindness from earlier today,' she snarls. 'Whatever it is in your wretched mailbox. I said what I said just now because I thought you might want someone to help you retrieve it. I was trying to be kind, or so I thought.'

'You weren't, and you made a careless mistake, Li-Jing,' he says, now pulling on his trousers and adjusting the belt buckle. 'The only way you would have known about an encryption key was if you'd been listening to my conversation with Doherty this afternoon, just before he was shot. You're a Chinese spy, Li-Jing, and not a very good one at that.'

Li-Jing looks thunderously at Lewis. He pretends to ignore her, instead tying his bootlaces.

'You think you're so clever, don't you, Ben Lewis? Well, you're not! You won't get away from here. My colleagues will be arriving at any moment. They're going to forcibly remove that key and then make you tell them everything you know. After that, they'll leave you alone with me and do you know what? I'm going to kill you.' Her eyes are wide with rage. 'Very slowly and very, very painfully. After what happened this evening, trust me, it will give me even more pleasure to see you suffer.'

'Even more pleasure?'

'In addition to the way you killed my cousin, of course. You surely remember Sui-Lee?'

A moment's clarity appears in the midst of otherwise increasing surrealism.

'One matter you may have overlooked. How will your fellow agents know when it's time to burst through the door?'

'Because they track me all the time,' she says with venom. 'They know where I am from my phone. They listen to everything. They'll be listening to this conversation right now.' This latter statement is delivered in a tone of defiance.

Lewis, unperturbed, stands. He picks up the last item of clothing: his jacket.

'Too bad,' he says, wriggling into first one and then the other sleeve. 'When I borrowed your phone earlier, I disconnected it from the network.' He is standing by the door now. 'As far as your Chinese friends are concerned, you'll have been uncontactable these last couple of hours. No one will know where you are. Sorry about that.' He blows an air kiss. 'For the record, it was fun. Until another time.'

He opens the door and disappears into the night.

Chapter 19

Afterwards, Ivankov was seething. He shouted and yelled, casting blame and profanities far and wide. Orders were issued, revoked and then reissued. The unfortunate who suffered the dislocated finger was singled out for the worst: publicly humiliated, he was sent packing to the Knightsbridge safe house in disgrace. If it hadn't been so serious, Alexei Polunin might have been tempted to laugh. Wisely, he kept a low profile throughout and said nothing.

The pressing problem was re-establishing contact with Lewis. With his phone off the grid and no sign of him at home or near Savile Row police station, it was hard to develop a credible plan. Surveillance remained in place at both locations, but it soon became clear to everyone that they were clutching at straws.

To his credit, once he'd calmed down, it was Ivankov who came up with the idea of tapping the policeman's phone. After all, Zeltinger was the one person they were confident that Lewis was likely to make contact with eventually. Polunin was initially sceptical, worrying about the fallout if the British press ever got wind of Russian officialdom secretly recording the telephone conversations of the British police. When Ivankov pointed out that far worse had already been suggested in the media, Polunin cast aside his caution and turned to Yasenovo for help.

It proved to be a lucky strike. At shortly after eleven that evening, the listeners in Yasenevo recorded the following conversation.

'Zeltinger.'

'Saul, it's Ben. Any news on Holly?'

'Nothing. The Yorkshire police say the address was an old, deserted farmhouse. They didn't have a search warrant, but they were certain it hadn't been used for a while.'

'What about Doherty's phone?'

'Nothing on it. The SIM was brand new, the phone pretty been unused. I'm sorry, Ben.'

'I'm running out of ideas, Saul.'

'Have you eaten?'

'Yes, but I could murder a coffee.'

'There's an all-night coffee shop in Soho. On the corner of Frith Street. It's a short walk for me. How about you?'

'I could meet you there in about fifteen minutes.'

It was all that Ivankov needed to know.

Chapter 20

It takes less than ten minutes for Lewis to get to Frith Street by motorbike at this late hour. The slowest part is the one-way system close to the coffee shop. Even this late, Soho is crowded, the trendy, open-all-hours locale bustling with life. Many clubs have only just got going for the night. Lewis is compelled to travel slowly, weaving his bike in and around groups of late-night revellers. Hyper-vigilant after all that has happened, Lewis is not yet ready to lower his guard. Tempting though it might be to arrive ahead of his friend, quietly order a coffee and wait, he had done enough of that at lunchtime. First, he's keen to check out the neighbourhood.

First off, he makes a large clockwise loop around the northern end of Soho Square before turning into Frith Street heading south. Nothing out of the ordinary tweaks his radar.

Up ahead at the junction, just past Ronnie Scott's jazz club, is the café Zeltinger mentioned. It looks empty, and Lewis can't yet see his friend inside. He keeps going, still seeing nothing out of the ordinary.

He continues the clockwise circuit, taking a right into Old Compton Street, meandering in between pedestrians, looking and behaving like a biker searching for a place to park. He wants to see if he can spot Zeltinger arriving, alone and unaccompanied. Then and only then will he believe that they have not been followed. At the next junction, unable to go straight ahead, he's forced to turn right or left into Dean Street. Choosing to turn right, he waits for a group of pedestrians which is when he sees his friend, sauntering along Old Compton Street, heading directly towards him, fifty metres away.

Again, nothing out of the ordinary.

Zeltinger seems to be alone, but Lewis wants to make certain. In a sudden change of plan, he heads the bike left rather than right and makes a short one-block detour, allowing him to approach his friend from the rear. Which all goes to plan until the final leg of the one-block detour, the moment he is about to turn back into Old Compton Street.

Two men. Both of a type that Lewis had secretly been hoping wouldn't be here. Different from the dinnertime crew in Chinatown. However, the same make and model. Leather jackets and dark chinos. Curly black wires tucked behind the ears – both following a few paces behind Zeltinger.

How did that happen?

Lewis makes the turn.

Then, across the street from Zeltinger, keeping pace with him to his right, is a third. Same uniform, same sturdy frame. This one he recognises. It's the man who had been loitering just beyond the Eastern Dragon earlier in the evening.

Russians. Quite a turnout.

Without slowing or missing a beat, he carries straight on, past Zeltinger and his Russian escorts. Past the junction with Frith Street where the café is located. Continuing straight ahead, travelling eastwards. Would there be a fourth?

In seconds, he knows the answer.

The fourth is easy to spot – a man lumbering at speed in his direction, heading for the café. There can be no doubt. A huge brute of a fellow, well over two hundred pounds. Yet another standard Russian-issue curly black wire down his neck. Most likely Ivankov.

Plan B is urgently required.

Lewis pulls to the curb on Greek Street in urgent need of the internet. Removing his regular phone, he risks connecting it to the network briefly to look up the phone number of the café where Zeltinger will be waiting. This takes a few seconds. Once he has the number, he disconnects from the network. Then, using one of his burner phones, he dials the café. For a long time, the phone just rings. Eventually, a bored, Italian-sounding voice answers.

'*Pronto.*'

'This is the police.' Lewis lies with confidence. 'There is a man who just arrived in your café by the name of Saul Zeltinger. He's wearing a suit and tie. Please bring him to the phone. It's urgent.'

'*Whats'a name again?*'

'Zeltinger. Saul Zeltinger.'

The man drops the receiver noisily leaving Lewis to be treated to a cacophony of spurious kitchen. In time, almost giving up hope, he hears someone approaching.

'Zeltinger,' the familiar voice calls out in his ear.

'Saul. It's Ben. You were followed. Don't ask me how or why, but I counted at least four on your tail. They're Russians. Almost certainly carrying. Are you interested in bringing them in?'

'Can you be certain they are Russian?'

'One hundred per cent. I met one of them earlier. It's a long story.'

'Are you sure they'll be armed?'

'Almost certainly. Definitely dangerous.'

'Then, yes, absolutely.'

'Are you able to call in SCO19?'

'Yes.'

'Good. So, here's what I suggest. The café is at the junction of Frith and Old Compton Streets. Call in the cavalry. If they set up four roadblocks, all at the same time, that should do the trick – one on each of the four sides of the crossroads. Say fifty metres distant from the junction. That way, the Russians will be trapped inside the cordon. They're easy to spot. Big guys. All with curly wired earpieces, leather jackets and the like.'

'You're not about to make a fool of me, are you, Ben?'

'No way, Saul. If you're lucky, I might even bring a couple of them in for you.'

Given the high state of alert across London, Lewis predicts he has five minutes at most before the police cordon is in place. Five minutes to take two, if not three, Russians out of the equation. This was not a moment to try anything clever and complicated. Quick and ruthless was going to have to be the order of the day.

He walks three sides of a square to bring him back onto the street leading to the crossroads where the café is located. This circuitous detour allows him to approach the junction from the south. Up ahead are two Russians: one on the left side of the street and one on the right. The one on the right is the one Lewis recognises from earlier. The pair are again loitering, leaning against the brickwork, watching and waiting for Lewis to make his appearance.

He walks down the middle of the road until directly between the two men. Neither has yet seen him – they're facing the café, not looking out for anyone approaching from the rear, after all.

Coin toss time: heads, Lewis goes left; or tails, he goes right. Lewis chooses left and turns towards the first Russian, the sharp movement finally catching the man's eye. No longer loitering, he turns to face Lewis as the former-marine bears down on him. Without fuss or parrying, once the Russian is within range, Lewis attacks, snapping his left boot in a roundhouse kick to the man's groin. The man doubles up, bringing his torso into range for Lewis's follow-through: another, higher kick with the same leg to his opponent's neck and throat. That's all it takes. One-two. Two seconds to bring the man to the deck and out of action. Lewis spins around and the other Russian, seeing his colleague under attack, is already running towards them. A knife has magically dropped into his right palm. Lewis stands his ground, all too aware that knives in street fights are generally a problem. The advancing Russian will believe he has the upper hand, a smile already appearing on his face. Lewis considers a well-executed kick to the man's wrist but rejects the idea. It would knock the knife out of the man's hand and break a few bones along the way, but it wasn't the best tactic in a crowded area. Instead, he tries to draw the Russian forward, willing him to get him close enough to tempt him to make a lunge.

For a few seconds, the two men parry. Police sirens are now audible in the distance, getting closer. The Russian, sensing an opportunity, rushes forward to slash at Lewis's midriff. Lewis sees it coming and swerves out of the way, able quickly and efficiently to grab the now-exposed knife arm, twisting the wrist sharply and causing the knife to fall to the floor. Lewis kicks it out of harm's way. With the Russian in an armlock, Lewis stabs a left elbow into the man's face whilst simultaneously kneeing him in the stomach. The Russian, winded and out of gas, falls to the floor. Bad move. *'Never hit the deck if you want to stay alive,'* Lewis's training instructor would have said. The reason is apparent in an instant. Lewis deliberately and coldly stamps on the man's knee. There is a sickening crunch. Two down.

Reinforcements arrive courtesy of the Russians' open-channel microphones and earpieces. The man he assumed to be Ivankov and another smaller Russian are already bearing down on Lewis, the sound of approaching police sirens drawing ever nearer. A small circle forms comprising all three, Lewis shuffling his position constantly, willing the smaller man momentarily to be positioned between himself and Ivankov. Suddenly sensing an opportunity, Lewis lunges at the man, grabbing him around the neck front-on in a clinching headlock, drawing his elbows down, thus preventing swinging punches of any force from being able to hit Lewis's torso. Leaving Lewis instead to use his knees to pummel the Russian hard in the chest and stomach. More importantly, it puts the man's torso between himself and Ivankov – a form of human shield. The repeated strikes on the man's chest and ribcage gradually weaken him, Lewis constantly manipulating the man's body to shadow Ivankov's movements. In this awkward manner, they circle each other, first one way then the other. Then, with Ivankov's left knee momentarily exposed. Lewis lashes out at the huge Russian with a savage kick, connecting just above the shin with his right boot. It is a move that would send most men reeling. On Ivankov, it does almost nothing. The man barely flinches.

Blue flashing lights from approaching police cars now fill the street. Ivankov has a decision to make. Stay and face arrest – or escape? He chooses to run, charging angrily away moments before the police cordon is in place. Still holding the smaller Russian, Lewis ends the man's misery by delivering a final body punch, causing the weary Russian to sink to the pavement.

The police cordon ends up ensnaring four Russians: the three that Lewis had felled and one other. Of these, three are found in possession of guns and two with knives. At least one, Ivankov, gets away. Zeltinger is content. At the end of a difficult day, he has made some progress – finally. A conversation will shortly be needed with the Russians at ambassadorial level.

'This has got to look good on your performance review, Saul?'

Zeltinger chuckles.

'Perhaps.' The two of them are downing a snatched cup of coffee together. 'Although it was all down to you, Ben, you know that?'

'Don't put that in your report. Take some credit where it's due, Saul. What news on Holly?'

Zeltinger shakes his head.

'Nothing new. As I said, the old safe house was just an empty old farmhouse. Apparently deserted. No signs of a break-in either.'

'That's disappointing. No other leads?'

'To be frank, given everything else that's been going on today, we've had little time to worry about Holly yet.' He looks at the expression on Lewis's face. 'I'm sorry.'

'I understand. What next?'

'Paperwork.' He looks at Lewis who's laughing at him. 'I'm serious! I've so many reports to write by first light. So, another all-nighter is about to begin.' He looks at Lewis, stifling a huge yawn. 'It's been a long day. Do you think they were tapping my phone?'

'They tap everyone's phone.'

'That reminds me.' Zeltinger digs into his pocket and retrieves Doherty's phone. 'As I said, the tech team tell me it's clean. They've made a copy of all the data and reset the password, but there's nothing on it of any interest, apart from the video. That footage was recorded in Holly's house in Canterbury. You can have it back if you like?'

'Sure. If it's no use to you, I can always use another burner. What's the new password?'

'1-2-3-4. They thought that even I would be able to remember that.'

'Nothing on the SIM?'

'It was only activated this morning.'

'That's too bad. I wish I knew where all this was heading. We're still no closer to finding Holly.'

'It's early days yet. We'll find her, trust me.'

'Which reminds me. Can I borrow you before you go back to your paperwork? I'd like to take a look at this mailbox. I'd rather not wait until opening hours if I don't have to. I have an idea that you showing your police badge might open a few closed doors.'

'Where's the place?'

'King's Cross.'

Chapter 21

When the head of Britain's Security Intelligence Service – commonly known as MI6 – invites a senior officer in the domestic security service, MI5, to be his sole guest for the evening at London's Royal Opera House, it is not usually a social call. Overstretched and with a handful of operations at critical stages, Jake Sullivan had been minded to decline the last-minute request from Sir Philip Musson. It had only been the personal intervention of his boss at MI5, Dame Helen Morgan, that had persuaded him to accept.

'Opera not your thing?' Sir Philip says once seated at their private table in the balcony restaurant for the interval. Throughout the first two acts, Sullivan had been only half-watching the performance, preoccupied with emails on his smartphone.

'I might have said that once,' Sullivan says, looking at his host as if for the first time. Sir Philip could easily be mistaken for a quiet, unassuming individual. On the face of it, hardly the man expected to have overall responsibility for such a substantial network of intelligence assets. Sullivan is better informed. He knows that his host is reputed to possess one of the sharpest and brightest analytical minds in the entire civil service. 'These days, I find myself enjoying it more and more.'

Their food arrives and they get started.

'Thank you for coming at short notice, Jake. I'm sure you have a busy workload.'

'How can I help, Sir Philip?'

Musson rests his knife and fork on his plate and, dabbing his mouth with his napkin, looks directly at Sullivan.

'I've been made aware of a certain independent operative who has decided to put his own interests before Queen and country.'

'Hand in the till, do you mean? Or found a new benefactor?'

'Something like that. In that vein, certainly. Taking what wasn't his for personal gain.'

'Does this individual have a name?'

'Keiran Doherty,' says Sir Philip, watching Sullivan keenly.

'The man shot in Granary Square this afternoon?' Sullivan says, downing the remainder of the wine in his glass. 'Why am I not surprised?'

Sir Philip takes another mouthful and again wipes his mouth, the hubbub in the room making conversation difficult.

'Was he one of yours, Sir Philip? I didn't think he was on anybody's books. Most of us thought he was dead.'

Sir Philip leans forward and lowers his voice. Sullivan has to strain hard to listen clearly.

'I need to take you into a confidence, Jake. Despite the inference the press likes to make about our two organisations not getting on, Dame Helen and I spend a lot of time discussing our more sensitive operations. Twelve months ago, she and I met with two influential and extremely wealthy individuals. To spare their blushes, I shall simply refer to them as our benefactors. For slightly different, but aligned, reasons, Dame Helen and I were, at the time, frustrated about our ability to get things done. Too much political interference, aggressive media scrutiny and far, far too much red tape. We came up with the notion of funding a very small group of operatives: outside of our respective organisations and with no proven links to anybody, accountable only to ourselves. It was to be funded not by the taxpayer but through the philanthropic goodwill of our benefactors. Completely off the books. Nothing recorded in any system that could be audited or reviewed. Operational control to rest only with Dame Helen and myself or our successors – not, and this was important, with our benefactors. We didn't want a private army at the whim, beck and call of people with too much money.'

A waiter clears their plates and enquires about dessert choices. Sir Philip dismisses these with a wave of his hand, both settling for a filter coffee. Once they are alone again, he continues.

'We began scouting for our first agents. We were looking for people who had never been employed by the Security Services. Individuals we believed, nonetheless, had the right characteristics. In the end, we shortlisted two. Having persuaded them both to join, we then faked their deaths in what we hoped were plausible circumstances. It allowed them to take on their new roles with no links to their past lives.'

'Totally deniable.'

'Precisely. One of these first hires was Keiran Doherty. Supposedly killed in action in Afghanistan. Quietly resurrected and rebadged, our dead and totally deniable agent was sent out to do our bidding. Until, that is, he woke up one morning and decided to double-cross us. He has stolen from us, Jake, and we find we desperately need whatever he took back.'

'The other operative wasn't Nigel Fisher, by any chance?'

The first bells indicating the end of the interval service start to ring.

'I see you've done your homework. Yes, MI6 discovered Doherty, Dame Helen proposed Fisher. You knew Fisher, didn't you?'

'Sure,' Sullivan replies, a note of fatigue in his voice. 'A good man.

As you suggest, he never formally worked for MI5. He was a contractor. Dame Helen came to me and asked if Fisher could be released from an operation I was running. She had a special project she needed him for. Dependable, tough and with a ruthless streak: I liked him. When I read the report he had died in Iraq negotiating a hostage release, I was sad. I'd rather assumed that he'd been seconded to your lot for some secret operation.'

'As you now learn, your assumption had been half-correct. Having successfully recruited them both, their first project needed to be a joint one. Dame Helen commandeered an old MI5 safe house in Yorkshire to use for training and planning purposes and then they were on their own. This was a trial, both for them and for us. All was going well until Doherty decided to make himself rich at our expense.'

'What about Fisher? According to the police reports, it was Fisher who pulled the trigger on Doherty this afternoon, using a sniper rifle with a laser sight – only to collapse and die at the scene mysteriously. A suspected heart attack, or so we are meant to believe. It seems implausible.'

'We may never know.'

'Where does all this leave us?'

'Good question,' Sir Philip says as the second set of bells starts to ring. 'We desperately need back what Doherty stole. In particular, we want it before the Americans or Russians get to it. It is a one-time encryption key. It will allow us to decode certain information that is both extremely sensitive and highly valuable. Shortly before he died, we understand that Doherty may have told someone where it was hidden. Someone known to you, I believe.'

'Yes. A former Marine colleague of Doherty's. Ben Lewis.'

'Exactly. How trustworthy is Lewis?'

'Totally. I don't know Doherty, but Lewis is in a different league from Fisher. If you were to ask me to name a few candidates as potentials to join an elite, private army of special operatives, Lewis's name would be near the top of the list. Perhaps even at the very top.'

'He's that good?'

'In my humble opinion. For the last few years, he's been out of the Marines. We've used him as a contractor on one or two operations. Tough projects that proved him to be one hundred per cent reliable.'

'I'm relieved. Well, I need to speak with him urgently. It is critical that we get this encryption key before anyone else. Can you contact him?'

To Musson's consternation, Jake chuckles.

'Perhaps. I may be able to contact him, but there's no guarantee that he'll meet with you. In my experience, Lewis will only do something if he thinks it's worth doing. It may not be straightforward. Right now, he's got bigger problems. Doherty took a former girlfriend of his hostage yesterday afternoon. It was Doherty's way of making Lewis do his bidding.'

Sir Philip stands up, smiling.

'Come on, time for Act Three. We don't want to miss *Nessun Dorma*.'

They reach their seats just as the orchestra is warming up before the start of the final act. Sir Philip leans closer to Sullivan.

'Doherty last made contact with us late yesterday afternoon,' he whispers. 'Trying to negotiate a better price than the one we thought we had already agreed.' He leans back in his seat, to give time for his words to sink in. The house lights dim and the massive red curtains sweep open as the orchestra begins playing. Sir Philip quickly leans forward once again. 'I spoke to him myself,' he whispers. 'GCHQ say the call originated here in London. From Silk Street, right by the Barbican, to be precise. If you put your minds to it, I am sure you can find the address. Who knows, it might even be the place where this girl is being held. Find her, Jake. Use her to reel Lewis in. I do so desperately need him brought to me before others beat him to the encryption key.' He looks sideways at Sullivan to make sure that his words have been heard loud and clear. He then leans across once more. 'If not sooner. For reasons that won't yet be apparent, there is so much more riding on this than you could possibly imagine.'

Chapter 22

Ming-Tao settles back in the driver's seat. He closes his eyes, making a conscious effort to breathe deeply to slow his pulse rate.

The deed was done.

Seconds pass before he opens his eyes and studies his hands. They are small hands. Short fingers and stubby little thumbs. Surprisingly strong, though. Powerful instruments of death, bearing no trace of the dark crimes that they have just committed. There again, why should they? No blood has been spilt. True, before the stupid bitch had died, tell-tale marks had become visible all over her naked body: on her face, her arms, her legs even. But there had been no blood.

It was almost the perfect crime scene. Perfect for implicating the wrong person. Lewis had booked and paid for the room. Lewis's DNA would be in evidence in multiple ways. Not least, inside the woman's body. The battering and bruising would be suggestive of violent assault and rape: the cause of death strangulation.

Ming-Tao had been careful and had worn disposable gloves. The sort that surgeons and nurses wear in an operating theatre. After tying up and gagging the woman, he had struck her repeatedly using a favourite weapon of his: a telescopic baton.

In the end, he had placed his hands around her neck and slowly squeezed the life out of her. She had been strong. He had had to repeat it a second time, just to make sure. It was during the final stages of this second procedure that one of the gloves had split. A small tear, just underneath where his right thumb had been squeezing. He hadn't noticed it until he'd removed them on his way out of the hotel. On reflection, a minor problem. One, in the grand scheme of things, unlikely to cause problems.

Still looking at his hands, he remembers something. Yet more evidence to implicate the wrong person: Lewis's prints would be all over Li-Jing's phone.

Too bad, Mister Ben Lewis. The world was about to discover you to be a vicious murderer of pretty young women.

Ming-Tao takes a disposable mobile phone out of the car's glove compartment and begins typing.

'Body of murdered woman can be found in room number . . .'

He finishes the message, checks it and then presses the 'send' button.

Chapter 23

In a quiet back street close to King's Cross railway terminus, the Remote Mailbox Company's offices appear shut from the outside. It is already after midnight, the road quiet, if not deserted. There are few signs of life in the adjacent buildings. The door to the main office is locked, and all the lights inside the building appear to be off. A slatted metal roll-down door to one side is closed. When Zeltinger peers through a small letterbox, he spots a dim light shining from somewhere within.

'Hello!' Zeltinger calls loudly. 'Anybody there? This is the police!'

There is no reply. Lewis tries a different approach. He bangs loudly on the slatted door with the heel of his hand. Sure enough, a while later, they hear someone inside calling out faintly in response.

'All right, all right, I'm coming.'

They wait and eventually the slatted door begins to rise slowly. When it is two feet off the ground, it stops. Lewis, followed by Zeltinger, stoops under the gap and comes face to face with a bearded middle-aged man hurrying towards them. He is wearing his security guard's uniform without either tie or jacket. The man has been sleeping.

'Who do you think you are coming around here at this time of night? This place is closed.'

Zeltinger holds out his police badge.

'Sorry to disturb you. This man,' he says, indicating Lewis, 'urgently needs to access his mailbox. He has his key. He would have waited but it is, literally, a matter of life and death. I'm sorry.'

The three stare at each other in silence, the security guard deciding whether to believe the story or not.

'Show me that badge one more time,' he says eventually.

Zeltinger passes it across. The man inspects it thoroughly before handing it back.

'Very well. The mailboxes are all in there,' he says, pointing away to his left. 'Just the one, mind, and then you'll need to leave.'

Lewis doesn't need a second prompt.

The boxes are stacked vertically, six to each vertical unit, eight vertical units to a cabinet. Box number 236 is in the fifth bank of mailboxes, the second box down at the cabinet's right-hand end. Lewis takes his keys from his trouser pocket, looks at Zeltinger and shrugs. The security guard hovers in the corner, watching from a distance. Lewis inserts the right key into the lock and turns. The door opens without a fuss. Inside is a single envelope, a small A5 letter-sized padded packet in white. It is addressed simply to: **Ben Lewis, c/o Box 236, The Remote Mailbox Company, King's Cross, London**. Doherty had evidently been planning Lewis's involvement for some time.

He breaks open the envelope and finds it almost empty. Almost, but not entirely. There are two keys inside: a key for a cylinder lock and another that fits a mortice deadlock. There is also a piece of paper. Lewis reads the address that's written on it. He shakes his head, half-smiling as if enjoying a private joke. In no particular hurry, he places the piece of paper back in the envelope and the envelope inside his jacket pocket. Then, removing the bunch of keys from the lock, he inches the mailbox key around the key ring's circular metal clasp until it is free and in his hand. He places this back in the mailbox lock before sliding each of the two new keys, one by one, onto the key ring. Round and round the circular clasp they go until, finally, each is sitting flush with the others.

Which is Lewis's cue to place the bunch back in his trouser pocket. Closing the mailbox, he locks it, withdraws the key and then opens the tiny letterbox flap at the top, dropping the key inside. It lands with a metallic 'clunk' that echoes around the room.

One mailbox down. Lewis can only guess how many more there might be to go.

Chapter 24

The only words they speak as they leave the building are to thank the security guard. No sooner have they passed beneath the slatted metal door than it begins its electrically powered descent into the closed position again.

'Well?' Zeltinger asks. 'What was in the envelope?'

Lewis is about to reply when Zeltinger's phone interrupts them. He retrieves the device with practised efficiency and, giving Lewis a silent nod, he answers it.

For several seconds, he listens in stern silence, staring at the ground. Periodically he looks up, his face set in concentration. Lewis, in turn, busies himself by putting his bike helmet on. 'What time was this?' Again, more silence. Then, with an exhausted sigh, he looks at Lewis. 'Yes, he's here with me. Yes, I'll do that. Bye.'

With a weary finality, he ends the call, puts his phone away.

'Trouble?'

'Where were you earlier tonight, Ben?'

Lewis places the keys in the ignition and prepares to rock the machine off its stand.

'In the depths of Chinatown, meeting a few of the Russian thugs we saw a short while ago. Why?'

'What about after that?'

'I went and found a hotel for the night. I thought it safer than heading home. I had dinner. I spent some time with the Chinese woman I had met earlier in the day. Then I called you.'

'Your hotel. Was it a place on the Farringdon Road?'

Lewis looks at Zeltinger, intuition forewarning him where this might be heading. The bike is now off its stand. Lewis wheels it into the road and sits astride the machine to keep it upright.

'It was, yes.'

'A Chinese woman has been found dead in a hotel room on the Farringdon Road. She suffered multiple bruising to her legs, arms and body before she died. She was also raped. The perp was careless. There was DNA evidence in multiple places. Including inside her. The night receptionist has given a description of the man who paid cash for the room earlier tonight. There's also the video camera footage. It was your room, wasn't it, Ben?'

'I didn't kill her, Saul. She was completely alive and well when I left. She works for the Chinese government, even though she told me that she was Malaysian. She was after this damned encryption key. I'm being set up, Saul. I didn't kill her. You'd better believe it. We went to bed, had a little fun, then I found out who she really was and then I left. Run the hotel video surveillance. Work out the time of death. You'll find it happened after I left. About the time when I was traipsing around Soho watching your back, as it happens.'

'That's as may be, Ben. In fact, trust me on this, I more than perhaps anyone hope sincerely that what you say is true. However, as of right now, I'm supposed to place you under arrest on suspicion of assault, rape and murder. The formal charges will be brought once we are back at the station. I'm sorry, Ben. It's out of my hands.'

The two men look at each other in silence.

'It wasn't me, Saul, and you'd better believe it,' Lewis says eventually. 'I've got things to do. I need to find Holly. I haven't got time to follow police procedures.'

'It's the law, Ben. As I say, it's out of my hands. If you don't come with me, you'll be a wanted man. We'll hunt you down. You won't get away. Eventually, we'll find you, we always do. Then we'll throw the book at you. You might get locked away for years. Trust me on this. Come with me, and let's prove your innocence. If you run away, there's nothing I can do to save you.'

'What about Holly?'

'What about her? She's a missing person. We'll do our very best to find her. However, if we have to deploy scarce police resources to locate a dangerous, brutal murderer, I can't guarantee which will take priority. I suspect the murder will grab the headlines.'

'That's bullshit, Saul.'

'It's how the system works, Ben. If you run away, there'll be no turning back.'

They stare at each other once more, both unwilling to cede ground. Finally, his mind made up, Lewis hits the bike's ignition.

'I'm sorry, Saul. I need to go and find Holly. I didn't kill that woman. Find out who did and get your hounds off my back.'

'It doesn't work like that.'

'I know. But we all have to follow our gut instincts. Mine tells me that Holly has to be the priority.'

Lewis twists the throttle briefly in his right hand.

'See you around, my friend.'

At which point Saul reaches across and touches Ben briefly on the arm.

'Just do me one favour? Assuming you are about to run, give me a call from time to time. One friend to another.'

'Sure,' Lewis says, and then, without a second look back, he accelerates away into the night.

Chapter 25

Lewis parks the bike in a small residential street close to Highgate Village's famous cemetery. The time is shortly after one-thirty in the morning. It is a cold, clear night, with hardly a cloud in the sky. Adjacent to a little-used church hall, several London townhouses of varying age and condition are lined up in a row. Few have any lights on inside. In between the parked cars, nestling in the shadows, is another motorbike, a security chain looped around its rear wheel. It looks ideal for what Lewis wants. He's not, after all, about to steal the machine – merely borrowing its number plate.

Swapping plates in the dark takes a little time. Without using a torch, the resultant fumbling around and trial and error in repositioning retaining screws takes longer than he would have liked. Finally satisfied that both plates are securely affixed, he removes his growing mobile phone collection from various jacket pockets. His phone is switched off. He checks both of his new burners: they, too, are off. Lastly, Doherty's burner – it, also, is no longer connected to any network. Putting them back inside his jacket, he is ready for the long journey ahead. Mounting his bike, he rocks the machine off its stand, presses the ignition and pulls away as silently as he is able. In no time, he is back onto the A1 trunk road, heading north out of London.

With the number plates switched, the network of automated number plate recognition cameras used by the police will be unable to trace where Lewis's bike is heading.

For the moment at least, Lewis and his bike should be hard, if not impossible, to trace.

Chapter 26

The Americans spent the evening regrouping. By their own admission, they screwed up, completely underestimating what they were up against. Jackson eventually returned to base with a broken nose, having called for help to assist with Schultz. Schultz was lucky to be alive. The open-palmed punch that Lewis delivered with the heel of his hand had connected directly with nose cartilage. Schultz was fortunate that it hadn't sheered backwards, straight into the brain cavity. Instead, he was on a Medevac plane back Stateside. With Jackson signed off active fieldwork, CIA head of station, Greg Fuscoe, had been shuffling resources all evening. Luckily, there were a couple of aces up his sleeve. Two experienced agents, Oscar Sanders and Mickey Krantz, were both on the late evening Eurostar from Paris. Their imminent arrival in London would add strength and depth to the team hastily being reassembled to find Lewis. Langley was suddenly giving this their full attention, pressure being exerted from the very top to get a positive outcome. Taking an active interest was Kathleen Thomas herself, the newly appointed CIA deputy director of operations.

Sanders and Krantz reach London shortly after midnight. They are briefed by Fuscoe and then meet the rest of the team. The good news is that the GPS tracker Jackson hid under Lewis's bike seat is still operational. In the CIA's London control room, a specially equipped nerve centre buried deep underground and close to London's Grosvenor Square, banks of television monitors have begun following Lewis in real-time across the city. A detailed street map shows the bike's current position. The *pièce de resistance* was high-resolution images being beamed directly into the control room by two spy satellites in geosynchronous orbit over London.

'One heck of an upgrade compared to the hornet drones we had earlier,' Jackson mutters to Krantz as the team assembles in front of the monitors.

'That's because the A-team's now in town, kiddo,' Krantz joshes.

'What I don't get is why Lewis rushed off to Canterbury?' Sanders asks. 'What's Canterbury got to do with this whole fucking business?'

'There's a girl in Canterbury,' Fusco answers. 'The ex-wife's sister. Name of Holly. Lewis's wife died a few years back. Holly and Lewis have had this on-and-off dating thing going in recent times. Lewis went to her house.'

'Sweet. It still doesn't add up, though,' Krantz interjects. 'Doherty and Lewis have this cosy chat while a sniper hovers in the wings. Doherty hands Lewis what we think is a key, Doherty gets his head blown off, yet Lewis runs off to see Holly in Canterbury. Was this Holly's house key that Lewis was given? If not, unless it opens something else in Canterbury, it doesn't make sense. I'm missing something.'

'Did Lewis and this woman meet?' Sanders asks.

'Apparently not,' Fuscoe says. 'The clean-up squad who went to assist Jacko and extract Schultz spoke with a neighbour. She believed Holly might have been abducted way before Lewis even got there.'

'Might have been?'

'A man came visiting the house the previous day. The neighbour thought he might have dragged Holly out of her house against her will.'

'Doherty?'

'Could be.'

'It's got to be connected. Maybe that's the reason Lewis headed down there. He knew Holly was missing. What's Lewis been doing since he got back from Canterbury?' Krantz persists. 'After you and Schultz had your little punch-up with him, I mean,' he says, looking directly at Jackson. The injured field agent has two large strips of white surgical tape affixed across the bridge of his nose.

'We're still piecing some of the bits together,' Fuscoe intervenes before Jackson can reply. 'And I'm not referring to Jacko's nose.' A ripple of laughter at Jackson's expense eases tensions in the room. 'We've only had the satellite link up in the last hour. Lewis has been wandering around various parts of town all evening.'

'Where's he now?'

'North London. Somewhere close to Highgate Village. Before that, he was at King's Cross with a police detective.'

'Are you sure?'

'Positive. He's a friend. Name of Saul Zeltinger. They visited a business called the Remote Mailbox Company.'

'Exactly the kind of place someone might leave something for safekeeping. All that's needed is a key to open one particular locked box. This is good. Was anyone following them?'

Fuscoe shakes his head.

'We've been stretched too thin until you guys showed up.'

'How about satellite images?'

An operator fiddles with the controls for a few seconds. Two monitors previously blank instantly come to life. Sanders and Krantz stare up at the screens.

'Fast-forward the recording up until they come out again,' Krantz orders. 'There! Pause it right there.' Krantz looks at Fuscoe. 'Neither Lewis nor the other guy is carrying anything. Not even a bit of paper: zilch. So what was in the mailbox.'

Sanders considers this for a moment.

'We're in danger of maybe making a meal of this. This encryption key: it would be on a USB stick or similar, wouldn't it?'

'Probably, I guess. Something easy to conceal, certainly.'

'Assume this thing was in the mailbox. Of course, we can't see Lewis carrying anything! It's only a fucking USB stick, for Christ's sake. It'll be nestling in a pocket by now, surely?'

'I'm not sure I buy that,' Krantz say. 'If I'd just collected something precious, even a USB stick, I'd be wanting to take a closer look once I was outside the place. It's human nature.'

'Sorry to interrupt, everybody.' The room goes quiet as a young technician enters the control room. 'I thought you'd want to see this.' She holds up several sheets of paper and quickly distributes them.

'Well, I'll be . . .' Krantz says as he scans the paper and then reads snippets out loud. 'Within the last hour, the police have launched a nationwide manhunt for, wait for it, Ben Lewis! He's wanted for the murder of a Chinese girl in a hotel near King's Cross! Can someone please tell me what the fuck's going on?'

'Continue running the tape, can you?' Sanders asks. They watch the policeman taking a call on his cell phone; the two men having some kind of discussion; Lewis getting on his bike whilst still talking; and then Lewis driving away leaving the detective on his own.

'What's happening here?'

'They're arguing.'

'Why do you say that?'

'Look at the body language. Here's a scenario. Maybe Lewis kills this Chinese girl; maybe he doesn't. Who cares? Suppose Doherty arranged for Holly to disappear. Lewis will have two things weighing on his mind. Finding her and keeping this encryption device from a growing cast who seem hell-bent on getting it. Maybe, even, one of those cast members is trying to frame Lewis for murder to try and stop him. Where are his loyalties likely to lie?'

''Finding the girl.'

'I agree. Whether he's retrieved the encryption device or not, he'll want to know Holly's safe. Meanwhile, his policeman friend takes a call and learns that Lewis is suddenly wanted for murder. What would you do in Lewis's shoes?'

'Cut and run. Whether this policeman was my friend or not. The murder charge is probably a stitch-up. I'd want to get the hell out of there.'

'Precisely! You'd forget about the arrest warrant, and you'd cut and run. Drop off the grid and find the girl.'

'With a fair wind, you'd have no idea there was a hidden GPS tracker under the seat of your Honda. Good work there this afternoon, Jacko, by the way. Despite you and Schultz being such useless assholes and nearly screwing the whole thing up, you might yet have saved the day. Why is Lewis stopping in Highgate, though?'

'Fuck knows.'

'Hold on – look!'

They stare at the screen. The bike is once more back on the move.

'He isn't any longer. He's back on the road. Heading north.'

'Okay, I suggest we stop playing guessing games. Let's grab a car and a couple of fast bikes and head off after him. If we're quick, he'll have an hour's lead on us, at most.'

Chapter 27

The bedroom is like a million others in countless hotels all over the world. Sterile, nondescript yet functional. Saul Zeltinger shares the experience at three in the morning with a female forensics officer from the Met's SCD 4 unit. It is hardly a romantic liaison. He didn't believe that his friend Lewis had killed the Chinese girl. However, with evidence mounting to the contrary, Zeltinger felt the need to see for himself both out of professional curiosity and out of respect for his friend.

He had, over the years, visited many crime scenes. The degree of violence inflicted on the victim's body in this particular case he finds shocking. The victim had died with her underwear stuffed in her mouth and a torn strip of bed linen tied around her head to hold it in place, the body covered in numerous red marks, welts and early-stage bruises. Sandra Kelly, the forensics officer, explains that the marks had been made by a baton or rod hitting the body repeatedly. She points to where fingers and toes have been broken. On one leg alone, the number of welts suggests at least twenty separate strikes. When Zeltinger asks about the cause of death, whether from the beatings or asphyxiation, Kelly states her belief that the woman would have been alive when she was beaten. She points to several markings around the woman's neck, a probable indication the woman had died from strangulation. It would have been a hideous and gruesome death. There had been semen inside the body but no sign of any genital mutilation or forced entry. It suggested that the woman had had consensual intercourse before being savagely beaten, then strangled.

Zeltinger offers a view that the DNA – the semen at least – might prove to belong to a white Anglo-Saxon male, about six feet in height and weighing about one hundred and sixty pounds. He asks Kelly whether there is anything about the crime scene that doesn't tally with a possible perpetrator of that description.

Which proves to be an interesting question, as it turns out.

'In forensics,' she explains, 'I am always on the lookout for anomalies – parts of a jigsaw that don't quite fit. In a case of suspected strangulation, I look for abrasions of the skin or indentation marks around the neck area. More often than not, there are no visible signs at all. It's usually only during an autopsy that you learn the truth: examining neck tissues in microscopic detail, understanding the force vectors that might have come into play. Usually, it's the only way, especially in cases of strangulation. Laboratory analysis is crucial.'

She moves around the body and, with both hands, rolls the dead woman onto her side.

'If I had to make an informed guess,' she goes on, 'the killer had probably needed two attempts at strangling this woman before she died – certainly before her heart stopped beating.'

'Why do you say that?' Zeltinger asks.

'When you look at the corpse for the first time, what you notice straight away is that this woman was prone to bruising easily. Some people, especially females, are. Normally, people don't bruise much, if at all, once they are dead. The heart stops pumping, and that's the end of it. However, if you look closely, you can see markings at the back of her neck.' She steps aside for one moment, her gloved hand holding the dead woman's neck at an angle to allow Zeltinger to see for himself. 'My guess is that the killer thought he had killed her, but went back to check. On discovering a pulse, he panicked and attempted a second strangulation. That time lapse between the two attempts is critical – sufficient time for red skin abrasions and markings from the first attempt to show themselves around the woman's neck, before her heart stopped beating for good.'

She lets the dead woman's body roll back onto the bed before pulling a sheet up to cover her completely.

'What's puzzling is this. I'd like you to have a go at trying to strangle me. Don't be shy and for goodness' sakes, don't apply any pressure. Simply put your hands around my throat as if you were about to squeeze the life out of me.'

With trepidation, Zeltinger steps forward and does what he's been told to do. He brings both of his thumbs together at the front of her throat – what she describes as the first tracheal ring – and then stretches his fingers tightly around her neck.

'Good. Now apply a little pressure. Tell me what you find yourself doing.'

He moves his fingers and thumbs into different positions for a few seconds and then stops.

'I find myself only able to use my thumbs to exert pressure.'

'Precisely! That is exactly the point. Due to the size of your hands, your fingers are forced to overlap behind my neck. The only purchase that they, especially your fingertips, can bring to bear is on my spine, by definition a rigid object that is not about to yield under pressure.'

'Why's that relevant here?'

'Well, that's all part of the puzzle I was referring to. Nearly all male perpetrators typically have hands that are larger than their female victims' throats. What is troubling here is that I'm not convinced that this was the case here. You saw the markings behind the woman's neck, just in front of the spine. They suggest that the killer was unable to overlap their fingers behind the woman's neck. Their fingers weren't long enough. Instead, he or she dug their nails into the neck on either side of the spine to get a better purchase. Hence the bruising.'

She takes a tape measure from her pocket and measures the woman's neck circumference.

'This woman had a neck circumference of just under thirteen and a half inches.' She measures a second time, this time measuring the distance from the marks at the back of the woman's neck to the centre of the first tracheal ring at the front of her throat where there are also red markings.

'My best estimate for the size of the killer's hands would be six and three-quarter inches. Let's call that a maximum of seven inches, allowing for a little thumb overlap. This is what is bothering me. A man or woman whose hands are that size would not be six foot tall. It is basic evolutionary physics. We can guess a person's height to a very high degree of accuracy by dividing their hand size in inches by a pretty universally constant scaling factor to get to a predicted height in inches. A seven-inch hand size indicates an adult of approximately sixty-three inches tall – just over five foot three. A six-foot male would have hands that were at least eight inches or more. If the DNA inside this woman belonged to a six-foot male, then I have to tell you, Saul, that my professional instincts say this six-foot-tall man is unlikely to have been the person who strangled the woman.'

Zeltinger leaves as two men arrive to help with the removal of the body. As he passes the front desk, he asks the night porter for the tapes from the security cameras for that evening. Placing each in an envelope the man also gives him, he seals the flap before exiting the hotel and hailing a taxi.

Although the middle of the night, there are several people still working. One of these is Meilin, the young trainee.

'I thought you'd be home with your family. Not working the graveyard shift with sad people like me.' Zeltinger gets on well with Meilin. She is hard-working and always dependable.

'You have a lot on, sir, and I thought you might need an extra pair of hands. What did you find at the hotel?'

Zeltinger gives an abbreviated version, removing the envelope containing the security tapes from his coat pocket and placing them on the table.

'I'd like your help wading through these. See if there's anything that might exonerate Lewis. I'm not optimistic, but it needs checking.'

'Of course,' Meilin answers. 'Anything else?'

Zeltinger's mobile phone chooses this particular moment to start ringing. He shakes his head, looks at the unknown caller ID and decides to take the call.

'Zeltinger,' he says.

'Saul, it's Jake Sullivan. Sorry to disturb you in the middle of the night. I had a suspicion you might still be at work.'

'Jake. Yes, it's been rather busy of late.'

'Still got the APB out on Lewis?'

'We don't have All Points Bulletins in this country, Jake, as you well know. I have, however, been at a certain crime scene at a hotel near Farringdon for the last ninety minutes.'

'Do you think he killed the woman?'

'There's a lot of evidence suggesting he did. It's not clear-cut, but it looks possible. Killing is not out of character for Ben. God, though, I hope it wasn't him, Jake. This was brutal. One of the worst I've seen for ages. I count Ben as a friend.'

'Me too, Saul.'

'At this moment, he remains our number one suspect, I'm afraid.' He lets out an exhausted sigh. 'How can I help?'

'Irrespective of the manhunt, I have some very senior colleagues desperate to make contact with Ben. All sorts of people you wouldn't believe. Events are in danger of spinning out of control.'

'This isn't linked to what happened in Granary Square by any chance, is it?'

'You know I can't comment on operational matters over the phone. Let's just say that I am not about to deny that in a hurry.'

'How can we help each other, then?'

'There's a school of thought doing the rounds amongst my lot that the best way to lure Lewis back to the mother ship might be to locate Holly. Find her, let Lewis know that we have her – safe and sound – and we suspect he'll be willing to play ball.'

'You may be right. Unless you have any bright ideas, however, we haven't much to go on.'

'Which is where we might be able to help. We've traced Doherty's movements the day before he was shot. A few hours after Holly disappeared, he made a call from Silk Street, near the Barbican, at about six in the evening. He used a SIM card we didn't recognise, but no matter. Assuming it was Doherty who picked up Holly, we think it possible she might be somewhere in the vicinity.'

'That's a densely occupied area, Jake. If we have to search the Barbican and the surrounding neighbourhood, it's going to require a lot of manpower.'

'I never said it was going to be easy. I simply thought two minds, and our combined resources might be better than one.'

'Which is helpful, thank you, Jake. Let me give it some thought. I'd like to talk to a few people first then call you back once we have more of a plan.'

Chapter 28

Shortly before four in the morning, Lewis approaches Blyth service station on the A1 motorway, heading north. At this time of the night, there are a few long-distance lorries on the usually busy road – but not a lot else. Passenger vehicles are few and far between, and motorcycles even rarer. The outside temperature is a chilly five degrees centigrade. In some rural spots, there's a ground frost. Lewis likes the cold because it keeps him awake and stops his mind from wandering. In twin panniers at the back, amongst other items, he keeps a thermal fleece and a pair of black leather gauntlets for such an eventuality. Under his leather jacket, the fleece combined with the gauntlets are both doing a fine job of keeping the cold at bay.

Lewis decides it's time to take a break. He pulls off the motorway and into the forecourt to top up the bike's tank. As he's stepping inside to pay for the fuel, a police Range Rover pulls onto the forecourt. The patrol car slows to a crawl as it passes Lewis's bike. Lewis hands a twenty-pound note to the bored-looking man behind the till, watching through the glass window as the police driver stares at the bike's number plate. Eventually satisfied, the Range Rover slowly moves on, turning back towards the motorway and accelerating away. All the while, Lewis has subconsciously been holding his breath. Now exhaling, he accepts his change and a receipt from the cashier and turns to head towards the washrooms.

From here, Lewis calculates that it will take another hour and a half to get to the address written on the piece of paper Doherty had left for him in the mailbox. The property, located near Whitby in North Yorkshire, had to be Sullivan's old safe house. Bit by bit, the pieces of the jigsaw were starting to fit together. If he stopped at the service station a little longer, he would be able to grab an early breakfast, plenty of coffee and still be in time to arrive just before dawn broke.

Chapter 29

The farmhouse was four miles outside the coastal town of Whitby, located in an isolated position and approached by a single-tracked lane that meandered its way back and forth from the busy main road running from Middlesbrough to Whitby. The road came to a dead-end immediately in front of the farmhouse. There was even a small turning circle in front. It had to be the same property that Jake Sullivan had referred to.

Shortly before seven, the damp, misty night slowly begins to morph into a dull, grey, overcast day. Lewis tucks his Honda around the back of several disused barns, out of sight from the road leading to the house.

The police report relayed to Lewis the previous evening had been accurate. The place indeed felt deserted. Certainly unoccupied. There are no lights visible nor any sign of habitation. A glance through downstairs windows reveals a few furnishings, but not a lot else. The main entrance is around the side of the property. A small porch leads to a door with two locks: a cylinder lock and a mortice deadlock. Lewis reaches into his pocket for his key ring, locating the keys that he'd collected from the mailbox at King's Cross. First, the mortice key: it fits the lock perfectly. He turns it once anticlockwise and feels the deadbolt mechanism moving. He turns it a second time, and again the deadbolt responds. Next, the cylinder lock. His key, flat with notches down one edge, also fits.

As he's turning the key, he hears the distant sound of another engine. Two engines, in fact. Motorbikes. Then a third, this one more muted, more like a car. Almost in unison, the noises die.

Could he have been followed? Without waiting to find out, he finishes turning the key in the lock, pushes open the door and swiftly closes it behind him.

The first thing he notices is the smell. It is a damp, musty smell. The smell of an unused house. A place where the air has not been circulating for some time. And yet, there is a trace of something. He can't quite put his finger on it. He wants to believe it's Holly's fragrance, but it isn't. Another human being? Perhaps a dog? He's wasting time. There is enough natural light to see without the need to turn on any lights. In case he was followed, he can't waste any time hanging around. He quickly needs to check out the property.

Beside the front door, on the floor, lies a small pile of post in a heap. Mostly junk mail: a couple of local papers; a few flyers. Plus, a single envelope. Lewis picks it up and turns it over. It is plain white, the size one would use to post a sheet of A4 paper folded in three. No stamp; the envelope is of the self-adhesive variety.

On the front, written by hand in block capitals, are two words.

Ben Lewis.

Chapter 30

Holly Williams had never considered herself a tough person. She and her elder sister, Lisa, had grown up in a low-income family without great ambition, her father one of the last tin miners working in Cornwall. He died when Holly was in her teens. It was the first real adversity Holly had had to deal with. Holly's mother was convinced that dust in the mines had been the cause of his lung cancer. Lisa was dating a teenager at school by the name of Ben Lewis at the time.

They had grown up in the same neighbourhood and been childhood sweethearts from an early age. Holly had been not a little envious of her sister. Lisa had Ben to comfort her when her father had died; she had to cope with the loss largely on her own. It wasn't helped by the fact that she also had a secret crush on Ben but resigned herself to the fact early on that it was never meant to be. Ben and Lisa were destined to be together. Marriage was a foregone conclusion, certain to happen once Lewis had finished his Marine training and had a few successful tours on active service under his belt.

As it was, things turned out differently.

Yes, Ben did qualify as a Marine and was undoubtedly heading for high places. Yes, he and Lisa did indeed marry. Eventually. However, less than a week after their wedding, tragedy struck. Lisa drowned in a freak accident at Mawgan Porth beach, where the rip tides catch many a swimmer unawares. In the aftermath, Holly coped better than Ben. Whilst she was discovering an inner toughness, Lewis fared less well. Struggling to come to terms with his loss, he left the Marines a confused and angry man. He spent the next few years blaming himself, drifting and searching for answers. That is until his former CO finally caught up with Lewis and gave him a serious talking-to, effectively ordering him to pull himself together and get on with his life. The tough-love message seemed to work.

In time, there had been an opportunity for Holly to accompany Ben on what turned out to be a dangerous mission through France and Switzerland, though she hadn't realised it at first. As events turned out, she would almost certainly have been killed if it hadn't been for Ben. Throughout, she demonstrated remarkable fortitude, surprising even herself at how she coped under pressure. So much so that once the mission was over, she felt strong enough to date Ben for a few weeks and then end it without feeling overwhelmed by remorse. Her relationship might have continued, but for the complications and practicalities of their working lives. They chose in the end to go their separate ways, her life focused around the hospital in Canterbury whilst Lewis had a new job in London. Holly's life returned to her version of normality: nothing overly adventurous and few, if any, demands made on her hidden reserves of inner toughness.

Until two days ago, when Keiran Doherty unexpectedly re-entered her life.

November had proven to be a challenging month at the Kent & Canterbury hospital. Holly was now a ward manager, a job made more complicated by the early arrival of that season's flu virus. On the day that Doherty made his dramatic reappearance, she was working an early shift. It had been scheduled to finish at midday, but it was nearer to two in the afternoon by the time she was done. The rain was pouring down as she left the hospital on foot, chatting to a colleague on the phone. She was tired, hungry, in need of a wash and not a little irritated that her phone was about to die. Holding an umbrella awkwardly under a chin, she turned off the device to conserve what little battery she had remaining, placing it in her raincoat pocket as she juggled with the keys to her front door.

Out of her wet shoes, the priority was to put the kettle on. Then, with a mug of hot tea in hand, she went upstairs to shower and change before heading back down to grab herself something to eat. It was as she was in the process of making a sandwich that the doorbell rang.

'Hello, Holly. It's lovely to see you.'

The two of them stood, staring at each other.

'Well, are you going to invite me in?'

Which of course she did.

'Keiran, I ... I don't know what to say.' She busied herself by closing the front door, following her one-time boyfriend into the kitchen. He quickly began making himself feel at home, pulling out a chair, sitting down and resting his feet on the table.

'To be honest, Keiran, I'm flabbergasted. I thought, I mean we all thought, that you were, you know ... '

'Dead?' he said with an impish grin.

'It's no laughing matter. What the hell's been going on?'

'It's a bit complicated. Probably best if we don't dig too deeply. Suffice to say that I'm still very much alive. If a bit older and hopefully a fair bit wiser.'

'Why are you here? If it's complicated, why are you bothering me again after all this time? I haven't seen you in, what, six years? Perhaps longer. I'm genuinely delighted that you're alive, but I don't need unnecessary complications at this time in my life, trust me.'

They stared at each other, Keiran looking old and weatherworn. In contrast, Holly felt at least ten years younger.

'I need your help, Holly. I need our mutual friend, Ben, to do something for me. I'm guessing he won't want to do it voluntarily. So, I figured that you were the best person to persuade him to change his mind.'

'What's going on, Keiran?'

'If you want to know,' he replied, a harsh edge creeping into his voice, 'I'll explain.' He took his feet off the table and leant forward, taking hold of her chin in his hand roughly. She made a muffled protest, but he ignored her, refusing to let go. 'I need you to come away with me for a while. Somewhere safe. Somewhere secure. Assuming you do as you're told and behave yourself, you'll come to no harm. I need you to disappear. When Ben learns what's happened, he'll be so blinded by rage, he'll readily do whatever I ask. Once that's all done, you'll be free to go. You'll never need to see or hear from me again. Fair?'

'How dare you! If you think I'm going to do that – ' But before she could say any more, the hand that had been holding her chin hit her sharply across her left cheek. She cried out angrily, almost falling off the chair in the process.

'Shut up and listen. I'm only going to tell you once, Holly. You are going to do this for me, that's not up for debate. If I have to hurt you, I will. If you give me any trouble, things will only be worse for you down the line. Do we understand each other?'

Holly felt numb and shell-shocked. She nodded her head simply to keep the peace, not understanding how Doherty's mood could have changed so rapidly: one minute, an old friend; the next a violent monster.

'Now, get up! Once you've composed yourself, you and I are going to make a short video on my phone, something loving and tender that will appeal to Ben's heartstrings. Then, the two of us are going for a ride.'

It took two attempts to make a recording that he was satisfied with. Afterwards, he tied her hands together using cable ties and then covered her wrists with her raincoat. Grabbing hold of one arm in his vice-like grip, he marched her out of the house and across to the curb to where his black BMW was parked.

After securing her wrists to the passenger door handle, he drove in silence back to London. Holly tried talking to him, but he was having none of it. Instead, he turned the volume up on the radio and ignored her. Somewhere near Elephant & Castle, he pulled the car to the side of the road and placed a heavy-duty blindfold over her eyes. She was no longer able to see anything. He also reclined her seat so that her head was beneath the window line. He then drove for what seemed like an eternity, most of it stop-start driving, the kind you get used to when driving in heavy traffic through the centre of London. In time, Holly felt the car turn sharply left and then drop down a ramp. It felt like they were entering an underground car park. Keiran cut the ignition, climbed out of the car, came around to her side and opened the door. He told her to keep still as he cut the cable tie binding her wrists to the door handle. Without removing her blindfold or the tie that bound her hands together, he placed her coat once more over her hands and together, arm in arm, they walked across the concrete floor. She heard lift doors opening and felt Doherty dragging her inside roughly, Holly hoping that another person would try to get into the lift with them but it was not to be. Eventually, the lift came to a halt, the doors sliding open and Doherty was once more leading her roughly by the arm and along a corridor, the floor underfoot carpet, not concrete. An apartment block, she thought. Holly tried counting the number of steps they were taking, but Doherty kept jerking her this way and that, and she quickly lost count. Finally, they stopped. Doherty fumbled for some keys, a door was unlocked, then the next thing she knew, a hand was pushing her roughly from behind and she nearly stumbled and very nearly fell. The door closed behind her and the sound it made felt odd and eerie.

'Where are we?' she asked. 'Please remove this blindfold, Keiran. You don't have to treat me like an animal, you know.'

Which was when Doherty hit her again, another broad open-handed slap across her face that this time sent her spinning to the floor. Despite her resolve not to break down, the events of the last couple of hours suddenly became too much. She quietly began to sob. Doherty walked off at this point, only to return a few moments later.

'Are you right-handed or left?' he asked, once she had composed herself.

'Right,' she whispered truthfully and then immediately regretted it.

Doherty untied the cable ties around her hands and attached a metal handcuff tightly to her right wrist. Roughly, he then dragged her into another room and removed the blindfold. The room was completely dark except for a small, dim table lamp in one corner. Floor-to-ceiling window blinds blocked any view outside. In the centre of the room was a pillar and it was to a solid metal hoop embedded in this pillar that Doherty attached the other end of the handcuff. There was about two feet of chain between the two ends. On the floor was a mattress, and nearby was a chemical toilet. There were also several bottles of water and some basic provisions. Doherty moved to stand close to Holly, once more taking her chin in his hand.

'Now, listen. If you behave yourself, you will come to no harm, I promise. You're going to be left alone for a few days. Assuming that lover boy Ben does what he's meant to, then he'll be coming to rescue you. You can shout as much as you like: no one's going to hear a thing. We're on the top floor and the place is well soundproofed. I've given you lots of water and some food. Compared to a normal hostage situation, trust me, Holly, this is the Ritz. Sorry there's no pillow, but I'm sure you'll make do. Any questions?'

Holly was too shocked to say anything. All she could do was shake her head.

'Good. I'll be off then. Fancy a quick tumble in the sack before I leave?' He saw the terrified look in her eyes and burst out laughing.

'Only kidding. Once upon a time, I'd have been up for it. I had a real crush on you all those years ago, did you know that?' He leaned forward to kiss her on the cheek, but she backed away in disgust. 'Until you dumped me, that is. That was too bad. Still, a lot of water has passed under the bridge since then. See you anon, Holly dearest.'

The last thing she heard was the closing of the door and then keys turning in various locks.

Then she was alone. A prisoner in a tower block. Chained to a wall and with the door locked and bolted.

This was going to test her toughness like nothing else before.

Chapter 31

Lewis opens the envelope. Inside is another key. Not the sort of key one finds on a keychain. The kind of key one is given when checking into a hotel room. Plastic. Similar to a credit card, but completely white. Like the card he'd been given to his hotel room in Farringdon. The kind you leave in the slot by the door to turn on the lights. Designed to fit into a wallet, which is precisely what Lewis now does, carefully placing the key in an empty slot next to his cash card. The same slot he had used for the Farringdon hotel key a few hours earlier. Also in the envelope is a single piece of white card. On it is written a number in black ink. The number seven. Drawn with a circle around it. Beneath, in handwritten script, presumably Doherty's, are the words:

There's only one No-Tell Motel

Lewis gives a tiny exhalation, a form of ironic laugh. He knows exactly where he's going next.

It'd been an old joke between them, at a time when they had both been Marines. It is a clever clue because it is something to which only Lewis and Doherty would ever know the answer. He places the white card back inside the envelope and the envelope inside his jacket pocket. Two envelopes thus far. How many more will there be on this wild goose chase?

Decision time. Lewis wants to check the house out, to make sure that Holly isn't holed up in some hidden basement. It feels unlikely, but he needs to make sure. However, the sound of two motorbikes and a car in the nearby vicinity was worrying. He is about to have visitors. He decides to make a quick search of the house. Downstairs is easy. Several rooms lead off a central living area. Each looks undisturbed and, apart from the main room, have only basic furniture. As Lewis passes through, he checks for hidden panels or a door to a basement. Nothing. The place doesn't feel as if it has been used for a while. Next the stairs. As he starts climbing, his nose once again picks up the distinctive odour. He is nearer the source now. It is more pungent, less pleasant than he'd first sensed. The smell of decay. Then he sees it, at the top of the landing. A dead rat, its body distended, lying on its back. More evidence that the house has been empty for some time.

Upstairs, there are four bedrooms, each with the doors closed, each of them empty. No hidden panels, no sign of Holly, no sign of anything. Until the last bedroom. This also happens to be empty, but it has one added advantage. It affords a view over the drive. With Lewis standing back from the window, he can see a fair distance down the lane leading to the house.

Which is why he observes two men slowly and cautiously approaching the house. Another two are fanning out towards the outbuildings to the side. All four look as if they mean business.

At seven-thirty in the morning, this lot aren't likely to be making a social call.

Chapter 32

While two colleagues circle the outbuildings, checking the property from the rear, Sanders and Krantz approach the front of the house directly. Side by side. Full of confidence. As if they owned the place. When they reach the small porch, they both draw guns from shoulder holsters positioned under jackets. Sig Sauers: the P320 compact with the polymer frame. Nice and light, with a magazine that holds fifteen 9mm rounds.

'Feel like picking the lock?' Sanders whispers to Krantz.

'Not especially,' Krantz replies.

'Cover me,' Sanders says and, with that, swings a roundhouse kick with his heavy boot directly at the door. It flies open with a 'bang' and the pair move quickly inside. Backs against walls, they slowly move through the house. With guns held in a two-handed grip, they edge cautiously into each new room in a well-practised rhythm. Initially, their weapons are held close to their bodies, barrels pointing to the ceiling. Then their arms swing down to the horizontal, the Sig Sauers aiming at multiple imaginary targets. It is a textbook demonstration of everything they learned in spy school. Except that Lewis isn't here. The ground floor clear, they move up the staircase and pass through all the top floor rooms. Past the rat, which Krantz kicks in frustration. Still no sign of Lewis.

'Let's see what the boys have found outside,' Sanders whispers.

Outside, the boys, as Sanders calls them, haven't yet made it to the house. Nor are they likely to any time soon. The first one goes down without a sound about ten metres away from, and five seconds before discovering, Lewis's bike. Farmyards can often be full of builders' rubble and this one is no exception. Lewis picks a well-chosen lump of old brickwork. Throwing objects with accuracy is a Ben Lewis party piece. Lewis is good with a gun, no question. For preference, though, he's more comfortable using old technology. It's stealthier and, for Lewis, just as accurate. The good news is that most opponents never hear or see it coming. The bad news is that for many, it can be lights out. All Lewis needs is to judge the weight correctly, assess the distance and get a good stance.

Thus, whilst Sanders and Krantz are playing FBI officers, Lewis is having fun with the boys. With the first one down, Lewis runs over to assess the damage. The brick fragment has hit the side of the head, and the man is out for the count. It's going to hurt a lot but is unlikely to be fatal. Lewis leaves him alone and sets off to find his companion. As he approaches from the rear, the second man is easy to spot. He, too, has been watching the FBI training film. The one where they hug the wall of an outbuilding with their back, furtively peering around the corner when they feel it safe to do so. Lewis finds another suitable piece of brick. This one a bit smaller than the first. He takes aim and throws. It hits the man on the jaw. The man drops to the floor and Lewis jogs over to check him out. He's just about conscious but in severe pain.

'Don't make a sound, my friend. Otherwise, like your colleague, the lights will be going out. Nod if you understand.'

The man tries to nod but winces.

'Who are the two goons in the house?'

'Sanders and Krantz,' the man mumbles, struggling to get the words out.

'How did you find me?'

The man says nothing. Lewis grabs the man's fractured jawbone with one hand and applies not-too-gentle pressure.

'Tracker . . .' the man yells out in agony. Lewis relaxes his grip. 'On . . . your . . . bike.' His eyes are welling up as he struggles to cope with the pain. The jaw is broken, and blood is flowing from a puncture wound. 'Jacko . . . put . . . it . . . there.' Lewis senses the man is about to lose consciousness. His eyes are starting to roll behind the eyelids.

'What are your orders?' He squeezes the jawbone once more, and the man's eyes open wide temporarily.

'Find . . .you . . .'

'What next?'

'Get . . . encryption . . . key . . .' he says groggily.

'You're CIA, right?'

The man doesn't answer. He's gone under. Lewis searches the body and finds a BlackBerry phone, a communicator and a large billfold of money. He pockets all three. With Sanders and Krantz still in the house, Lewis concludes that it's time to leave. He wheels his bike with difficulty over the rough ground behind the outbuilding, taking care to avoid being seen from the farmhouse. A short while later, he reaches the road. In one direction, around the corner, is the farmhouse. In the opposite direction is the way out of there. Before leaving, he wants to locate the Americans' transport. This proves easy to spot. Tucked in a passing place surrounded by trees, about twenty yards distant, are two bikes and a car.

The bikes are impressive. Both Yamaha XSR 900s. They look brand new. Serious bits of kit. It goes against Lewis's love of bikes to damage such fine pieces of equipment. Instead, he kneels beside the front wheel of one and undoes the dust cap. Using a pocket penknife, he depresses the valve with the tip of a blade and the air comes gushing out. Once it's deflated, he removes the valve and tosses it into the undergrowth. He does the same with the rear wheel, then repeats the procedure with the other bike. Immobilised but not ruined. The car he is less concerned about. He simply stabs each of the tyres with the knife and makes a large gash in the sidewall. Job done. No one will be going anywhere fast. Folding the pocket knife, he takes out the American's BlackBerry, removes the battery and slides the SIM card out of the back. Snapping it in two, he hurls the phone and battery as far as he can into the trees. Finally back on the Honda, he restarts the engine. One last thing before he drives off. He pulls out the American's communicator. It is a multi-channel device, currently turned off. He flicks the switch to on.

'Hey guys,' he says into the device in a fake American accent and then releases the toggle switch. There is a burst of static. Then another voice.

'What's up? Where are you?'

'Listen up, Sanders. Or perhaps it's Krantz? Who cares? You want this encryption key? How much are you offering.'

'Is that you, Lewis? What's happened to my men?'

'They're resting. They both have headaches.'

'If you've hurt either of them, you're going to be in so much shit. I promise, you'll wish you'd never been born.'

'Cut the crap. I thought you lot were supposed to be good? So, make me an offer.'

'We agreed a price with Doherty. Twenty-five million dollars. The deal's unchanged.'

'You think so? The price has just doubled. Because of your fucking ineptitude. The price is fifty million. US. Non-negotiable.'

'That's bullshit, Lewis. Money like that doesn't grow on trees.'

'Your choice. Take it or leave it. Just call me if you want to do a deal.'

'How do we find you, you bastard?'

'Come on, guys! You're the fucking CIA! You can find anybody when you put your mind to it. Always assuming you can organise transport to get you out of this place. So long!'

With that, he tosses the communicator into the woods, takes a final, longing look at the Yamahas, then accelerates away.

Several miles along the main road, there is a dirt track off to one side. Lewis pulls off onto a woodland trail and continues until he comes to a clearing. It's time to locate the tracker. Having rebuilt the Honda a couple of times, he's familiar with almost every inch of the machine. However, after spending minutes scouring the obvious places, he still can't find it. He even looks inside the fuel tank but to no avail. It is only when, in near desperation, he peers under the fuel tank that he finds what he's been searching for. A small circular device, about the size of two one-pound coins stuck together. He is about to toss it away when he has a better idea. Placing the device in his pocket, he turns the bike around and heads back towards the main road.

A few miles further on, there is a petrol station. A tanker is parked on the forecourt, refilling the underground tanks. Lewis gets off his bike and walks alongside the tanker, casually brushing his hand along the underside of the main tank as he passes, the tracking device successfully affixing to one of the supporting struts.

Lewis approaches the driver.

'Got far to go after this?' he asks casually.

'Why aye, man! Back tuh Teesside,' the man says in a thick Geordie accent. 'Then up North the morra.'

Lewis smiles and carries on towards the coffee shop, removing both envelopes he'd been keeping in his jacket pocket and dropping them into a bin as he passes. No point in carrying things he no longer needed. Inside the café, he sits on a stool by the window, sipping yet more coffee and watching the tanker driver finishing up. A while later, with refuelling complete, the driver drops off the paperwork with the forecourt manager, Lewis feeling a certain satisfaction when the lorry finally pulls out of the service station. Teesside, and then North, most likely into Scotland. With luck that might keep the Americans off his back for the next twenty-four hours.

Chapter 33

Shortly after seven-thirty in the morning, Saul Zeltinger is still at his desk at Savile Row police station, this time attempting to write up the report of his interview with the waitress at Granary Square the previous afternoon. He is in the dead zone, as he calls it. The time shortly after sunrise when he's been up all night and his body is craving sleep but knows it can't have any. Everything feels numb, his brain acting as if full of cotton wool. There is a knock on his door and Meilin walks in.

'I've had a look through those surveillance recordings, sir. The ones from the hotel.'

'What did you find? Anything useful?'

'Possibly. When you have a moment, I have the machine set up in the Ops room.'

'No time like the present.'

A small conference room has been converted into a makeshift nerve centre for the various linked murders of the previous twenty-four hours. Meilin pulls up a chair for Zeltinger before inserting a disc into the machine.

'First, we have footage showing Lewis and the girl, Li-Jing, heading up to Lewis's room.'

The picture is grainy but shows Lewis and the girl in an amorous embrace.

'That was timed at 9.47 pm yesterday.' She fast-forwards the recording to another segment and presses play. 'Now we see Lewis leaving the hotel on his own. The time is 10.54 pm. They were alone together in Lewis's room for just over an hour.'

Zeltinger studies his friend on the screen to see if he can discern signs of guilt or anything incriminating. Anything that might hint that Lewis had just viciously beaten a woman to death. The images reveal nothing. Only a man in an elevator heading out for the night. Meilin switches discs and inserts a different one, this time from the camera in the hotel lobby. It shows Lewis purposefully walking out of the hotel. The video picture quality is much higher, Lewis easily identifiable.

'I have a horrible feeling about all of this, Meilin. Unless we can pull some kind of rabbit out of the hat, I think Lewis is going to go down for this woman's murder.'

'I know what you mean, sir. That's why I wanted you to see this next clip.'

Meilin fast-forwards the recording another eleven minutes and presses play. A Chinese man can be seen entering the hotel, making his way to the lift. His face is partially hidden from view. The time is 11.05 pm.

'Damn, I couldn't see the face at all. Can we switch to the camera in the elevator?'

Meilin swaps over discs and fast-forwards to the correct place.

'There!' Zeltinger says. They watch, transfixed, as the man looks around the elevator car as it makes its ascent. 'Go back and freeze the frame, can you? I want to see his face when he's looking directly at the camera.'

Meilin plays with the controls and then pauses the playback.

'Got you!' says Zeltinger. 'So, my friend, who exactly are you? Which floor did he get out on, Meilin?'

'The same floor as Lewis's room.'

'Is that it or did he leave again later?'

Meilin doesn't answer, fast-forwarding the recording another twenty-three minutes before pressing 'play' once more. The image on the screen shows the same man back inside the elevator. The man is smiling. He is fidgeting with something in his hand. The time is recorded as 11.28 pm.

'Freeze it again, Meilin, can you? What's he got in his hand?' Meilin plays with the controls and the image advances frame by frame until a reasonably clear shot appears on the screen.

'Could that be a wooden or metal baton, do you think?'

'It's hard to say, sir. It's why I wanted you to see it. It certainly looks something like that.'

'It's all too circumstantial at the moment.' He rubs an unshaven chin in his hand, thinking through the implications. 'However, it's a positive development. I'd like to find this man. Can you run his picture through the system and see if he is known to any of us, including MI5? It won't be sufficient to exonerate Lewis. However, it might allow us to consider the possibility of an alternative suspect. Even if we don't yet know who he is or what his motive, if any, might be. Good work, Meilin. Very well done.'

Chapter 34

Wheels had spun within wheels all night. The Chinese ambassador in Pyongyang had shared with the North Koreans snippets of the information that Li-Jing had recorded between Doherty and Lewis. When hearing about the destruction of Gunter Markov's cyber-crime operation for the first time, the treasury minister firstly appalled, then latterly terrified for his life. A critical source of North Korea's foreign exchange income had just been wiped out. Worse, the thief who had stolen the Iranians' one hundred million dollars, destined for Pyongyang, was dead and the money missing.

The Supreme Leader, predictably, was incensed. A curt ultimatum was issued to the treasury minister. A new cyber-crime operation had to be built and launched without delay and the missing money recovered, or else lives would be lost. At which point, the North Korean treasury minister knew that he would be doomed to failure without further assistance from Moscow. It had been Russia, after all, who had been so obliging in supporting Markov's operation in the first place. Within the hour, the Russian ambassador was summoned and was learning for himself some of the gory details about what happened to Keiran Doherty and the missing Iranian millions.

Two hours later, the information about the stolen money is thoroughly analysed and debated by a team at SVR headquarters, a large, nondescript building directly to Moscow's south in the district of Yasenevo. Dialling in by secure satellite link is head of London Station, Alexei Polunin. Sitting next to Polunin, still fuming from the disastrous events in Soho only a few hours earlier, is Pyotr Ivankov.

'So, now we know the whole picture,' Polunin says, once he has listened to Doherty and Lewis's conversation in Granary Square the previous afternoon.

'Alexei, none of us ever knows the whole picture.' It is Mikhail Volkov speaking, the SVR's head of field operations. 'Trust me. I've learned that the hard way.' Volkov had been a career field operative and, latterly, agent handler before receiving his latest promotion. As agent handler, he had gained notoriety for having run the legendary agent, Oleg Panich.

'The question is, where do we focus our efforts now?' Polunin looks purposefully at Ivankov. 'Do we go after Lewis and the encryption key? Or do we help the North Koreans get their money back?'

'We find Lewis.' The chill evident in Ivankov's slowly spoken, deep-throated drawl is felt down the line in Yasenevo. Whatever Volkov declares to be the priority, Ivankov is not yet ready to bury the hatchet. Not so far as concerns Lewis. There are now scores to be settled.

'We do both,' Volkov says to settle the matter. 'We have a team here in Moscow more than capable of tracing whatever Doherty might have done with the one hundred million dollars. I have already warned the foreign minister. We'll do our best, but there can be no promises. It wasn't our money in the first place. We are, after all, only trying to be helpful. Now that Markov's operation is no more, the North Koreans urgently need to build a replacement, but it's going to take time. In the short term, that and the missing Iranian money will give them a catastrophic foreign exchange headache. Beijing will doubtless have to bail them out as usual. On a related subject, how have we been getting on with finding Lewis, Alexei?'

'Actually, Mikhail, not as well as we'd like,' Polunin says hesitantly. 'A few hours ago, an attempt to ambush Lewis went badly wrong here in London. We were trying, in hindsight, to be too hasty.' He glances at Ivankov, but the Russian has his head down, glowering angrily to himself. 'Four of our team were arrested. To make it worse, they were armed.'

'Arrested!' Volkov explodes. Polunin and Ivankov listen in silence as streams of profanities and insults are hurled at them. In the Yasenevo conference room, the female clerk taking minutes judiciously omits these from her record of the conversation. 'Are we about to have a mass expulsion of diplomats from London, Alexei? I sincerely hope not for your sake. The president will be apoplectic! How can four have been arrested?'

Ivankov, who has had his fill of reprimands for the night, chooses this moment to re-enter the conversation.

'Mikhail, even the great Oleg Panich suffered under this man Lewis. He is a highly problematic person. Good men went down tonight. Of course, we could have done better. It is regrettable. However, Lewis is a cunning bastard. We need fresh thinking. I have an idea.'

Ivankov looks at Polunin, who nods for him to continue. Ivankov pauses. He wants to hear Volkov's reaction first.

'Well, go on, Pyotr. Tell us,' the voice from Moscow says over the secure line.

'We use the woman – a spider to trap the fly. We don't know where she is. In my plan, we don't care. All we need is for Lewis to think *he* knows where she is.'

'How do we do that?'

'We spoof this woman's email. Then we send a bogus message to Lewis. He thinks it's from her. *'Help me, darling. I need you to rescue me! Come to this address. Hurry! Save me!*''

Ivankov's rendition of a Russian man trying to speak like an English woman causes amusement back in Yasenovo.

'I like the plan, Pyotr. We might revisit your acting career another time. Alexei, would that work?'

'I think it might. Lewis has been off the grid these last few hours. He'll be using Wi-FI hotspots to check emails, I'm certain. All we need is a suitable location to direct him to. One where he will walk confidently right into our trap unawares.'

'Yes, somewhere he can suffer unfortunate accidents,' Ivankov says with a lopsided grin. It is the first time Polunin has seen him smile all evening.

'Very good. I'll get people here to start hacking this woman's email account. Just tell me the location we are going to pretend she's being held at and I'll have someone draft a suitable message.'

Chapter 35

Shortly after nine-thirty in the morning, Lewis again approaches Blyth Services on the A1 motorway, this time heading south. He needs to risk a phone call. Where better than a busy service station? Somewhere with less risk of his location being pinpointed by the telecommunications wizards. The person he wants to call has, after all, access to some of the smartest telephone interception resources on the planet.

Using one of his burners to dial Jake's office number, he places the phone to his ear as it starts to ring at the other end. Almost immediately, the call is answered.

'This is Ben Lewis. I need to speak to Jake Sullivan urgently. I'm going to hang up and call back in exactly four minutes. Please be ready to connect me.' With that, he ends the call and checks the time. Precisely four minutes later, he dials again.

The second time around, without anything being said, there are several clicks and beeps on the line before, moments later, he hears Jake's voice in his ear.

'Ben! I can't tell you how pleased I am to hear from you. You still on the run? I spoke to Saul earlier. Some godforsaken time it was. He was working hard, trying to prove your innocence. Where are you?'

'You tell me, Jake.'

'Blyth Services it says here on my screen.' Why is Lewis not surprised?

'That was fast. I thought you needed at least a couple of minutes to trace calls?'

'Not these days. Everything happens in real-time. I can have someone come and collect you in less than thirty minutes. We need to speak. You've got something. Doherty gave it to you. Or rather, you might know where or how to get it. Whatever it is, it's red hot. Almost radioactive, it's so damned hot. Can we please work together on this? We desperately need your help.'

Lewis exhales heavily. He is standing in the car park beside the service station, stamping his feet to get the circulation going.

'I didn't ask for any of this, Jake. In the last twenty-four hours, I've had a sniper nearly kill me and been attacked by Russians, Chinese and now twice by Americans. I know what you want, Jake. Trust me on this. I'm prepared to give it to you, too. However, that bastard Doherty took Holly. Until I know she's safe, that's my priority.'

'Cut me some slack, Ben. I understand where you're coming from. We're all busting a gut trying to find her. However, we also need that encryption key. Tell me where it is, and we can sort everything, I promise.'

'I'm a wanted man, Jake. On the run for something I didn't do. I've been stitched up by people I've never met. Until the police are off my back, I have to stay in the shadows. It's not that I don't trust you. I do. I am just not prepared to give up my aces when the poker game's a long way from being finished. I'll promise you this much. I won't let anyone else have it. That's as far as it goes for now. Get me off the hook from the police, find Holly and tell me she's safe. Then I'll come in.'

'You drive a hard bargain, Ben. When this is over, you and I need to have a serious talk. You're too good to be wandering around as a freelance.'

'A quick question, Jake. The car that Doherty borrowed. The one from your old safe house. When it was MI5's car and when it was your safe house: it would have had a tracker fitted, wouldn't it?'

'Sure. Standard MO. Why?'

'Well, if they forgot to transfer the registration, do you think they remembered to disable the tracker?'

There is a long pause on the line.

'I don't know, Ben, that's a good thought. I guess we should check. How do I get in touch with you?'

'You don't. I'll call you.'

'Let me investigate. Meantime, keep out of trouble. Call me in four hours. Let's both hope that we have some information on Holly by then.'

The line goes dead.

Chapter 36

At about the same time that Lewis is talking to Sullivan, Holly Williams is calculating that she's already been in captivity for almost thirty-six hours. If she hadn't been wearing a wristwatch, she'd have completely lost all track of time.

The first few hours had been the worst. She had screamed, shouted, and yelled herself almost hoarse. Her cries went unanswered. The two-foot length of chain that kept her tied to the pillar had been well-calculated. It allowed her, just, to lie down, sleep, eat, use the chemical toilet – she just couldn't go anywhere. At full stretch, with arms extended, she was about four feet away from touching the blackout curtains. About ten feet from the door. Six feet from the main light switch. She had already drunk nearly a whole bottle of water. There were just three remaining. For food, she had eaten biscuits, peanuts and some raisins. The biscuits were tasteless, the raisins dry. The peanuts were actually okay. Somehow, she had slept. There was little else to do. She kept waking intermittently, thinking she could hear someone outside the door. It had all been in her mind, but it hadn't stopped her from being hopeful. She had cried a lot, too.

Her eyes are, by now, totally used to the dark. Down the side of one of the three blackout curtains, there is a small sliver of daylight. Not enough for her to discern what might be outside. Enough for her to know the difference between night and day. Over breakfast of nuts and raisins, she resolves to try and find a way to break free. She has already studied her handcuff and chain at great length. She has also studied the hook in the central pillar, trying to work out which of the three is the weakest link. Her conclusion, thus far, is that it has to be the handcuff. The lock mechanism has a tiny keyhole to one side of the cuff. She has never picked a lock before, but she has seen the films. She tries to imagine what Ben would do. '*Show me what to do, Ben,*' are what she mutters to herself frequently, convinced that Ben would be able to pick the lock – using what, though? She racks her brains but draws a blank. She looks at the mattress, but there is nothing there that's going to be helpful. Nothing amongst the food items, either. She thinks about the chemical toilet: sure that it must have some kind of metal handles on the side, only to discover that, yes, it did once have handles, but someone had already thought of that: the handles had been detached.

Then an idea strikes her. Why not the buckle on her belt? She slips the strap off her trousers and takes a look. The long metal prong has a slight kink in it, but it might be possible. How would Ben have done this? He would jiggle the metal prong around in the hole of the padlock and it would come undone in seconds, that's what he would do. For Holly, it doesn't work like that. She tries it on the handcuff attached to her right wrist but finds it difficult working the metal prong with her left hand. Then she has a different idea. Standing up and holding the buckle pin in her right hand, she tries picking the lock of the handcuff attached to the metal ring on the central support pillar. This is easier though, after twenty minutes of fruitless effort, she is no further forward. She sits back down on the mattress, overcome by emotion, sobbing with frustration.

She is tough, though, an inner voice telling her to think about the problem logically. The handcuff must have a ratchet mechanism that engages on metal teeth within the cuff. When the handcuffs first went on, they hadn't needed a key. The ratchet had simply engaged on the teeth. As the cuff had been closed tighter, it had remained locked. Similar to a cable tie. Once it was on, it couldn't be pulled off. So how could she force the ratchet to release the teeth on the handcuff? Logic says that if she sticks the belt buckle pin into the hole in the padlock, turning it might help. Anti-clockwise to undo seemed logical. She tries sticking the pin in the hole one more time, sensing a slight movement from within the mechanism as a result of pressure from her finger. She tries twisting anticlockwise. Nothing. She tries putting the buckle pin in at an angle – still nothing. '*Show me how to do it, Ben,*' she mutters and tries again. And again. Still with no joy. She takes the belt buckle out and sees that the end piece of the metal prong has now bent from all the downward pressure. She is about to straighten it when she has the idea to perhaps bend it even more, almost to a ninety-degree angle. Why? Her contorted logic is that if there was more than one ratchet in the cuff, then the greater surface area afforded by the flattened pin might release them all. She tries once more, twisting anticlockwise. Nothing. Again, one more time with slightly more pressure.

Suddenly, there is a small clicking sound. Amazingly, the cuff releases!

Filled with emotion, free at last, her immediate thought is to find out where she is. She rushes to the window to open the blackout curtains, but they resist being raised by hand. Finding a bank of switches by the door, one by one, she tries them all, pressing eventually on a rocker switch which causes the curtains slowly to rise. The bright light is instantly too much, forcing her to look away. When, finally, able to see, she discovers that her prison cell is at the top of a tower block. She spots several familiar landmarks and, whilst geography wasn't usually her strongest subject, she thinks she recognises the Gherkin and the NatWest Tower not far away – meaning that she was in or near London's financial district. Down below was an enclosed garden.

There had to be a way out. Leaving the room, she finds herself in a corridor. The walls and ceiling are heavily padded. On her right is a door, which opens into another room identical to the one she has been living in. Same blackout curtains. Same central pillar. Same dirty mattress on the floor. Only the space is empty. What is this apartment? She shudders, turns around and heads back into the corridor. At the end is a heavily padded door. She tries to open it, but it is locked. There are no keyholes and no handles: it has been locked from the outside. She tries banging on the door but the padding instantly mutes the sounds. It is made of thick material and scraping at it is useless – even making a small tear appears nigh on impossible.

After the initial euphoria of releasing her handcuff, her heart now sinks again like a stone. There seems no way out.

If Ben doesn't come and rescue her soon, she might never get out of here alive.

Chapter 37

Lewis has been worrying about Holly, in particular, whether he might have done anything differently. Thus far, he has concluded that he probably wouldn't. Or couldn't. That doesn't stop it gnawing away at him. The last twenty-four hours have been a wake-up call. He'd been persuading himself up until recently that his relationship with Holly was over. Just good friends, or so he thought. He realises, now, that he might have been deluding himself. With the time already approaching mid-morning, he feels a sudden need to call Saul Zeltinger, to get the latest update. Passing a sign indicating a lay-by shortly to his left, he slows the bike and pulls off the carriageway. It is a large rest area, and Lewis comes to a halt about halfway down. Apart from himself, the lay-by is deserted.

He has any one of four phones to choose from. For a change, he uses Doherty's. It still has a near-full charge. He keys in the passcode, 1-2-3-4. The signal reception is good. Seconds later, he is dialling his friend.

'Zeltinger,' a tired voice answers.

'No sleep either, Saul?'

'Only because of you. Are you about to turn yourself in? It would make all our lives so much easier.'

'You need to find out who killed the Chinese girl.'

'All the evidence still says that you did, Ben.'

'That's bullshit and you know it. It wasn't me, Saul.'

'Ben, to be clear: there's a warrant out for your arrest. I am not even supposed to be talking to you.'

'You asked me to call, remember?'

'Touché. Where are you?'

'Driving back from visiting that safe house. I ran into yet more Americans on the way.'

'Did you find anything?'

'Thus far, no sign of Holly. I found a tracking device on my bike. Put there by the team from Langley. They've now been pretty much immobilised. Those not requiring medical assistance will find themselves on something of a wild goose chase. What news from your side about Holly?'

'We might have a lead. We think she's may be somewhere either in, or close to, the Barbican.'

'How did you find out?'

'Jake's team traced a call from Doherty sometime shortly after he'd picked Holly up from Canterbury. The call originated from Silk Street. That's right by the Barbican.'

'I spoke with Jake earlier. I asked whether the BMW still had its tracker activated. Did he mention that?'

'No, but it doesn't matter. He and I have been talking. Mostly about you, as it happens. We found the car. In the Barbican underground car park. I sent a team looking for it as soon as we knew roughly the area where she might be located.'

'We're getting closer, Saul.'

'I hope. Only two thousand, one hundred residential properties to investigate. Plus various offices, storerooms, cellars and the like. Are you coming to lend a hand, Ben?'

'If it would help. However, I suspect I might get myself arrested in the process. There has to be a smarter way. Who's allowed to park down there? Anybody?'

'As long as they pay. The car had an annual parking permit in the windscreen.'

'Annual? That means Doherty must own or rent a property. Can we get an address from the parking records?'

'No such luck. The mailing address on both the application and the debit card used for payment is a faceless mailbox number in a distant, offshore paradise.'

'He was really living off the grid, wasn't he? He certainly liked his mailboxes.'

'We are looking into the ownership records of all the properties in the Barbican right now, trying to find out who has bought and sold in the last twelve months, which properties are being rented and so on. As best we can guess, at any rate. It's a mammoth job, Ben.'

'I understand that.'

'You need to come in. It's not just the police who are after you. Jake's team are desperate to meet as well.'

'I know. Nothing about this business adds up, Saul. I've become the reluctant star in a game where the rules keep changing. It's like I'm being made to dance to someone else's tune. Sure, a lot of money has gone missing. I sort of get that this one-time encryption might be of value to all the wrong sort of people. However, any number of things simply don't make sense. For instance, why did Doherty send me on this wild goose chase in the first place? He told me that he was working for some private enterprise outfit. Queen and Country but off the books. Do you believe that units of that sort exist, Saul?'

'I have no idea.'

'Me neither. I like Jake but do I trust him, that's the question? If I hand myself in before you've scrubbed my name off the most wanted list, I have no chips left to bargain with.'

'The case against you for murder looks strong, Ben. You're going to need a good lawyer.'

'I can't worry about that right now. I need to find Holly. I'll call you soon.'

He hangs up, watching in his rear mirror as a black saloon car pulls off the busy road into the lay-by behind him.

Lewis puts away the phone and restarts the Honda's engine.

Curiously, the car behind isn't stopping – it's accelerating. Silent warning bells are sounding as Lewis revs the engine. Quickly he rechecks the mirror. The driver of the other car is Chinese. So is the man in the passenger seat. Despite the overcast day, both are wearing sunglasses.

Definitely trouble.

Lewis releases the clutch and the bike roars away. The Honda's acceleration from a standing start is impressive. Even so, the black car only just fails to connect with the bike by a small margin. Lewis is not out of the woods yet. At the exit back onto the motorway, another black saloon firstly stops and then begins reversing into the lay-by to block Lewis's exit. Both front doors have been flung open, blocking Lewis's path. Lewis continues accelerating. If he undertakes on the left, he's screwed. If he overtakes on the right, he's screwed. There is only one thing he can do. As he gets close to the car in front, he brakes rapidly, pointing his machine directly at the car's bumper, the vehicle behind perilously close to crashing into him. Just as Lewis is about to become the meat in the sandwich, he pulls in the clutch then releases it fast, at the same time applying a twist of acceleration. The front of the bike lifts into a wheelie allowing his tyre to make contact with the boot of the stationary car in front. Instantaneously, Lewis's bike is up and onto the car's roof. Revving the throttle mid-operation, the bike becomes airborne, just clearing the vehicle's front before falling gracefully into a controlled landing. As Lewis races away, the car at the rear isn't so lucky – it crashes with force into the vehicle blocking its exit.

Chapter 38

Ten-forty-five in the morning in London is five-forty-five in the morning in Langley, Virginia. Jake Sullivan has been summoned to join Sir Philip Musson in the latter's office in Vauxhall Cross. Sullivan and the head of MI6 sit side by side as they stare at a television monitor positioned on the desk in front of them. On the other end of the secure video link is Kathleen Thomas. Thomas has, by the look of things, been enduring yet another all-nighter, just like Sullivan. Sir Philip, in contrast, looks as relaxed and unruffled as ever. Coffee, the all-nighters' fuel of choice, is in active service at both locations.

'Kathleen, you called this little get-together,' Sir Philip begins. 'How can we help?'

'Thank you, Sir Philip. Can we start by being totally candid? It's not been a great night for US-UK relations.' She takes a large mouthful of coffee from a Styrofoam beaker. Then, replacing the plastic lid, she positions the cup beside her on the desk.

In London, the two men exchange glances, their faces showing confusion and bewilderment.

'I hope, as you get to know us better, Kathleen, you'll appreciate that in London we always try to be candid with our friends in Langley. What appears to be the problem?'

'Let's cut to the chase. It's been a long night. For some while now, we've had an operation underway in Germany that involved someone I suspect you're familiar with. Gunter Markov. Markov, real North Korean name Park, was recently brutally murdered. Markov had been doing a little work for us on the side. Something highly-sensitive. Shortly before he was murdered, he encoded a file containing the finished product with a one-time encryption key. For reasons only a hacker would understand, he decided to post it on the internet. The encryption key has been stolen. By one of your people, a man called Keiran Doherty. Who then got himself shot dead for going rogue and touting the key around to the highest bidder. I don't need to tell you this. His death has been widely reported in the British media.'

Sir Philip raises his right hand. It is more a flick of the wrist than a full arm raise.

'May I?' he asks, as she pauses for breath.

'Sure,' Kathleen says curtly.

'I just want to be clear on certain facts. We have, as you suggest, been aware of Park's operation for some time. Just to put the record straight, though: Keiran Doherty, the man you refer to as having been shot and killed in London yesterday, was not, and never has been, part of either MI6 or MI5. Correct me if I'm wrong, Jake?'

'That's my understanding, Sir Philip.'

'Then, I stand corrected, gentlemen. He was a former soldier of yours, though, wasn't he?'

It is Sullivan's turn to answer.

'He trained as a Royal Marine, yes. However, he left active service under a cloud, and eventually ended up fighting, we believe, for the French Foreign Legion. Being candid, as we are all trying to be this morning, Kathleen, we, that is both Sir Philip and ourselves at MI5, thought he'd been killed. In Afghanistan, over a year ago. We were as surprised to see him pop up in Granary Square yesterday as you were.'

'Our sources in London tell us that before Doherty was killed, he coerced a former Marine colleague to be the custodian of our stolen secrets. A man called Ben Lewis. Lewis has since gone into hiding. We happened to have an inside track on Lewis's location and sent some people to try to negotiate with him. In good faith, I may add. Only, when they got there, your man, Lewis, overreacted. He destroyed our team, nearly killing two of my best people.'

Again, Sir Philip has his right hand raised.

'Once more, if I may?'

Kathleen, visibly angry, says nothing, taking a pull of coffee from her Styrofoam beaker. Sir Philip looks directly at Sullivan.

'Have you been made aware, Jake, of any American operation currently underway on British soil?'

'No, Sir Philip. Sad to say, such incursions are not without precedent. I had hoped we'd seen the last of those, but clearly not.'

'So be it. Another question. Kathleen's assertion that Lewis works for us. Is that correct?'

'Categorically not. We have used him as an occasional contractor from time to time. But not recently. Certainly not on any operation to do with Doherty or the missing encryption device Kathleen is referring to. The truth is, I suspect Lewis is on edge, at the moment. Doherty ran off with Lewis's former girlfriend before he died. She was taken hostage – but no one knows where. Lewis seems a bit preoccupied trying to find her..'

'One more thing,' Sir Philip continues. 'Isn't Lewis the man currently being hunted by the police? Wanted for the murder of a Chinese woman. I haven't got my wires crossed, have I?'

'No, Sir Philip. That's about the sum of it. It looks like Lewis will be in custody any time soon. So, Kathleen, what is it exactly that you'd like us to do?'

'We need that one-time encryption key, gentlemen. We'd also like you to rein in this rogue agent, Lewis.'

'I understand your frustration, Kathleen, but we seem to be speaking at cross purposes. If you'd like formally to request our help in trying to locate this thing, I suggest one of your people give Jake here a proper briefing. I'm sure we'll be only too happy to help. As to reining in Lewis, it really is out of our control. As Jake has just said, he'll likely be in police custody soon anyway.' Sir Philip shrugs his shoulders and looks at Jake, who nods.

'Kathleen. Why don't you send one of your team over to Thames House to brief us on whatever is missing?'

Kathleen Thomas exhales loudly at the other end of the call.

'Very good, gentlemen. I'm not sure we've all been totally frank with each other during this conversation, but at least we've made our positions clear. Jake, I'll send someone over within the hour. Any help in recovering what has gone astray will be appreciated. Good day to you both.' She punches the 'end call' button with some force and the screen in London clears.

'What did you make of that?' Sir Philip asks, his fingers steepled together under his chin as he looks at Sullivan.

'It sounds like Lewis really pissed them off.'

'Doesn't it? I like the sound of this man, Lewis. Any luck in finding the girl he seems infatuated with?'

'We're still searching.'

'Keep looking. I urgently need to talk with Lewis. We need that encryption key more than ever. We can't let it fall into American hands,

Jake.'

'If we find the girl, the rest will start falling into place. Now, if you'll excuse me, I'm due at the Foreign Office in fifteen minutes. The foreign secretary has summoned the Russian ambassador.'

'Ah, yes. I'd heard about that. I've sent my apologies. I have another rather delicate matter to attend to. In any event, I knew you were going. I hope it goes well. Ambassadorial bollockings can sometimes be quite entertaining.'

Chapter 39

The appearance of Chinese agents catches Lewis off guard. Having thoroughly searched his bike earlier, he had been convinced that there weren't any more tracking devices. So, how had they found him?

As he approaches the turn-off to Peterborough, Lewis has an impulsive idea. If the Chinese have tracked his bike, then a change of tactics was needed. He would ditch the bike and continue his journey to London by train. So, turning off the motorway he follows the signs to Peterborough city centre. On the way towards the main railway station, he passes two police vehicles heading rapidly in the opposite direction. Neither seems interested in Lewis.

With the morning rush hour over, there are just a few people milling around at the station. Even though the car park is full, there are still a few spaces remaining for motorbikes. Lewis weaves his machine into the specially designated area and pulls his bike onto its stand. He locks his helmet in the pannier and searches for a machine to pay for parking. There is one a short distance away, on the other side of the lot, the sort that requires both a licence plate and a credit card. Both are problematic. If the stolen plate has been flagged, keying in the details simply broadcasts where Lewis and his bike are located. Likewise, with a credit card. Deciding not to bother with a ticket, he turns to head back towards where his bike is parked, which is when his luck runs out.

Two black saloon cars have arrived whilst Lewis has been busy with the payment machine. The first has drawn silently to a halt a short distance away. The second, sporting a badly dented front bonnet and bumper, is parked behind the other. The windows of both have been buzzed down. As Lewis turns, guns are being aimed directly at him.

Four guns, to be precise. Four men and four guns.

This time Lewis has no room for manoeuvre.

Chapter 40

They shove him roughly into the back seat of one car, making him shuffle across to the far side, behind the driver. Following quickly behind is a minder who sidles up close, thrusting a gun aggressively into his ribs. Lewis recognises both this agent and the driver from the aborted surveillance of the Soho restaurant the previous evening. A third man, smaller than the others but seemingly in charge, climbs into the front passenger seat – a man he hasn't seen before. As the passenger door closes, it is the cue for the driver to follow the other car, already making its way out of the car park. The man in the passenger seat swivels around to face Lewis. He, too, has a gun in his hand, the same make and model as his colleague's. A CF-98, a 9mm Chinese-made pistol. With eyes fixed firmly on Lewis, they exchange words in a coarse dialect that Lewis has no hope of understanding. This turns out to be an instruction for the man in the back to tie Lewis's wrists together using nylon handcuffs. The sort that are almost impossible to break out of.

They drive in silence, Lewis quickly losing his sense of direction. The landscape changes as they head into open countryside. This is the start of the Fens, a coastal plain stretching from the Norfolk coast inland. Once marshland, now it is mostly flat arable countryside stretching for miles in all directions. There are few landmarks, only occasional banks of trees or hedgerow. In time, the car in front slows to a halt before turning sharply to the right, down a dirt track obscured from the main road by trees. Lewis's car follows in its wake. Reading the signage by the roadside, Lewis understands where they are headed. A landfill. More than likely, a disused brickworks or an old quarry. It turns out to be both.

They come to a halt in a large open space that had long since been excavated from out of the earth. Discarded white goods lie in disorderly stacks along the entire length of the pit. There is evidence of industrial-scale landfill activity, although none of it looks recent. The site has been abandoned. Several pieces of plant and equipment stand idle to one side: a large mobile crane; two industrial-scale compactors; and a heavy-duty earth mover. To the other side, a small office cabin, with a glass window and a wooden door. The place looks – and feels – deserted. The driver of the first car, gun in hand, is already out of the vehicle. He opens Lewis's door and stands back, beckoning Lewis to get out. The other three Chinese join them. Each has guns in their hands. All CF-98s.

'So, the tables are finally turned on the legendary Mister Ben Lewis!' It is the smaller man speaking. The one evidently in charge. He is enjoying his moment of superiority over Lewis. He is also showing off to his colleagues.

'Do we know each other?' Lewis asks.

'We do now!' the man says, again laughing. 'My name is Ming-Tao. You, however, Mister Ben Lewis,' he says, spitting the words out one by one, 'are the infamous killer of Sui-Lee. Everyone in China knows Ben Lewis. Many Chinese people want to see Ben Lewis dead, I hope you realise?'

'But not Li-Jing?'

This gets the reaction that Lewis is expecting. Ming-Tao steps closer, their faces separated only by the height difference between the two men.

'Your little Chinese girlfriend! Your *dead* little Chinese girlfriend,' he says, emphasising the words deliberately. 'Very careless, Mister Ben Lewis. Now you have two Chinese deaths to atone for. Trust me. It will be a very great honour and privilege to kill you personally.'

'Anything to become a national celebrity, is that it?'

'Why, of course!' The man laughs out loud. 'Ming-Tao slays the mighty Ben Lewis. Ming-Tao recovers the missing encryption key. Perhaps Ming-Tao locates the missing one hundred million dollars?'

'How about Ming-Tao kills poor, defenceless Li-Jing to further his own career?' Without warning, Ming-Tao unleashes a well-aimed roundhouse kick to Lewis's midriff. Lewis only catches the movement at the very last moment, managing to tense his stomach muscles a split second before contact. The force of the blow nonetheless causes Lewis to sink to the floor.

'Be very, very careful, Mister Ben Lewis. No more impudence. It is time to stop playing games and to hand over the encryption key.' Ming-Tao issues more commands in rapid dialect. Moments later Lewis, hands still cuffed at the wrist in front of him, has each arm roughly pinned by two Chinese whilst a third systematically conducts a search. The contents of every pocket are emptied onto the floor in front of him: keys, a wallet, and several mobiles. At one point, a small piece of plastic the size of a thick credit card is removed from an outer jacket pocket. Ming-Tao steps forward admiringly.

'Aha! See, Mister Ben Lewis! This is what Li-Jing placed in your pocket last night. Before her unfortunate death. No wonder we find you so easily!' His eyes gleam with satisfaction as he looks at the thin plastic before throwing it on the floor with the other items. He picks up Lewis's wallet and begins to search through it.

'Quite a lot of money here, Mister Ben Lewis. And what is this?' He holds up the white plastic key card that Lewis had retrieved from the house near Whitby and waves it under Lewis's nose. 'What is this for?' he asks, his eyes again staring up into Lewis's.

'It's for the hotel room on Farringdon Road. You should know. You came visiting just after me.' Lewis surprises himself how easily he manages to tell the lie. Ming-Tao shows no sign of disbelieving Lewis. Nonetheless, he places the key card in his own jacket pocket before discarding the wallet on the ground once again. He picks up Lewis's key chain.

'What are these keys for, Mister Ben Lewis?' He slowly thumbs his way through each of the keys. There are five on the chain in total.

'Two are for my flat in Brixton. One for my Honda bike. The other two,' he says as casually as he is able, 'were given to me by Doherty. One was for a property in Whitby. I went there last night, as I am sure your tracking device will have told you. The other is for the next place. The place that should lead to the one-time encryption key.'

'Which key, Mister Ben Lewis?' Lewis watches as Ming-Tao touches each of the five keys in turn.

'That one,' Lewis says when the Chinese man places his fingers on the mortice key that had opened the lock in Whitby the night before.

'I hope you are telling the truth,' Ming-Tao says.

'There's only one way to find out,' Lewis says indifferently. 'They're only keys.'

'Where is this next mailbox located?'

'Why should I tell you?'

Which turns out to be a foolish thing to have said since it unleashes a rapid response from Ming-Tao. A quick one-two-three combination punch directly into Lewis's solar plexus. It causes Lewis once more to sag to his knees.

'We can go on like this all day if you like? Perhaps we should stop playing games, Mister Ben Lewis? The address?'

Winded, Lewis takes a moment to regain his breath. Rising deliberately slowly to his feet, he gives an address in north London. In Highgate Village. The street where he'd found the bike the previous evening. The place where he'd changed number plates. Bluff and double bluff. The question is: will Ming-Tao swallow it? If he does, it is only going to buy Lewis some time.

Ming-Tao throws the bunch of keys to one of the other agents. The driver of the car that had brought Lewis to this place. The two men exchange words in Chinese before the driver, and one other, head towards one of the black saloon cars. As they drive off, a trail of dust and smoke fills the air in their wake.

Now there are just the three of them – two agile, quite lethal Chinese agents, both armed; and Lewis, hands cuffed, unable to move and currently defenceless. Not great odds in Lewis's favour, although marginally improved now that two opponents are temporarily out of the picture.

All Lewis now needs is to find a way to shorten the odds even further.

Chapter 41

Back at Savile Row, Saul Zeltinger was running on caffeine and nervous energy. After years of working erratic and unpredictable hours, all-nighters were nothing new. He'd managed a snatched telephone call with his wife and twin sons a little earlier. The family had been eating breakfast. The short snippets of conversation they'd exchanged seemed to be increasingly par for the course these days, each in a hurry to go their separate ways, either back to work or off to school.

The windowless space in the police station serving as the Ops centre for the investigation had become busier since the start of the morning shift. It was quickly becoming the nerve centre for everyone focused on finding Holly Williams. Besides himself and Meilin, two other officers had been assigned to help full-time. Since finding the car in the Barbican's basement garage, the priority had been to see if CCTV footage might tell them anything about when it arrived and who the driver was. This had been their first setback. The cameras nearest to where the BMW was parked had been vandalised. No video footage was available, not even in the lifts leading from the garage. It had not been a promising start.

Two of Zeltinger's team had headed to the Barbican Estate's Office, the department overseeing the administration and management of the residential site. The pair had been outside, on the pavement, since eight that morning, waiting patiently for the first member of staff to arrive at work. Their request was straightforward: a list of the ownership and tenant records for every apartment within the complex. Zeltinger was especially interested in any that had been sold, transferred or newly rented during the last twelve months. They were also after parking permit information for the BMW found in the basement. Whilst the latter proved relatively easy to obtain, accessing up-to-date ownership and tenant records for every apartment was more problematic. It involved accessing several different computer systems and paper records, and lots of photocopying. Therefore, it wasn't until nearly ten-thirty in the morning that the team had been ready to return to Savile Row with all the information they needed. Since then, everyone had been poring over the records, trying to narrow down which of the flats and apartments Holly might possibly be located in.

'What if she's not in the Barbican?' Meilin asks at one stage.

'Then we have to widen our search,' Zeltinger replies curtly, Meilin putting his unexpected abruptness down to lack of sleep. 'My gut tells me she'll be there. Somewhere. The car is the clue. Doherty wouldn't have parked in the basement if it meant him having to drag Holly through an entire neighbourhood against her will.'

'Unless he'd used Fisher to help,' she adds.

'It can't be ruled out,' he sighs. 'However, I think it unlikely. We should check the street cameras in the neighbourhood. About the time the car arrived in the car park. The BMW has to have been recorded somewhere on its journey to the Barbican.'

It is a young graduate, Winston, who gives them their first breakthrough. Using footage taken from a surveillance camera positioned on the corner of an office block on Silk Street, Winston tracks down Doherty's black BMW arriving at the underground car park. The recorded time was shortly after 5.30 pm. It is the same car, no question, the number plate clearly visible, and just two occupants – one behind the wheel, a man, and a female passenger reclining in the passenger seat. Backtracking, Winston traces the path this vehicle had taken to get there. It came across London Bridge, through Bank and along Moorgate before arriving at the Silk Street car park entrance. From this point onwards, Winston begins a much slower process of trawling through all available video footage from every CCTV camera in the surrounding area. When it finally comes, the breakthrough is courtesy of the same Silk Street camera that had recorded the arrival of the BMW at the car park entrance.

'Got him!' an excited Winston shouts to the assembled room.

On the laptop is a frozen screenshot, the image in reasonable focus. It is of a man walking along Silk Street, away from the Barbican, with a mobile phone glued to his ear. Doherty. He is on his own, Holly no longer with him, all evidence suggesting that she might, indeed, be somewhere inside the Barbican complex.

The question now is where?

Zeltinger faces a big dilemma. Whilst desk-based screening was likely to focus search efforts more productively, going by the book suggested that he ought to initiate a full-blown house-to-house police enquiry in parallel. After much deliberation, he concludes that he has to go by the book, a decision likely to be neither easy nor quick – not least because so many Barbican apartments were unoccupied during the daytime. Quite a number, the Estates Office had already told his team, were empty for extended periods. By mid-morning, photographs of Holly Williams are being widely distributed across the City of London police force. Ten constables, operating in five pairs, have been assigned, the task being to knock on each door to see if anyone recognises Holly's picture. Two thousand, one hundred dwellings, to be precise, within and across the whole Barbican Estate. Four hundred and twenty properties per pair. Even assuming that each team can visit sixty properties an hour, Zeltinger knows this is likely to take at least seven hours – and that's just on the first run-through, the number of unoccupied properties only making the task more complicated. Each unanswered door was going to need to be revisited at least once. Perhaps more than once. The chances of anything useful being revealed in a quick timeframe was therefore slender.

Very slender, in all honesty.

Chapter 42

'So, Mister Ben Lewis. Now we wait to see if you are telling the truth!' Ming-Tao tries to smile, but it comes out more of a grimace. He waves a mobile phone in front of Lewis's face. 'If my men don't find what they're looking for in Highgate, they'll quickly let me know!' This time the smile seems more genuine. 'Then, you are going to be in deep shit.' He steps forward so that his body is up close to Lewis's. Without warning and with lightning speed, he delivers another one-two double punch directly into Lewis's midriff. The speed and power of the delivery catch Lewis off guard. He sinks to the floor, winded and in pain.

'Just a little reminder, Mister Ben Lewis, about what happens when you play games. Do we understand each other?'

Lewis gets slowly to his feet and nods. Ming-Tao speaks rapidly in dialect to his colleague, and Lewis is led back to the car. Here, he is shoved once more into the rear, his already handcuffed hands cuffed a second time with yet another nylon cable tie. This time to one of the two metal headrest pillars in the passenger seat in front. The side nearest the door. Satisfied that Lewis can't escape, Ming-Tao retrieves a small chessboard from the glove compartment. Then the pair wander towards the office cabin some distance away to smoke cigarettes, play chess and wait.

Left to his own devices, Lewis spends the time thinking and calculating.

The thinking bit is straightforward. His current predicament is what his Marine colour sergeant would have called a 'lose-lose' situation. Assuming the other pair made it to Highgate, Lewis was about to be worked over, one way or the other. Then either left for dead or killed outright. The logic was simple. Supposing, by some miracle, the Highgate pair found something they believed to be the encryption key. Very quickly, they would be on the phone to Ming-Tao with the news. It wasn't going to happen, but Lewis liked to think through the angles. In this hypothetical situation, Ming-Tao would conclude that there was no reason to keep Lewis alive any more. He imagines Ming-Tao taking enormous personal satisfaction in killing Lewis. It would make him something of a legend – the man who tracked down and slain the killer of both Sui-Lee and Li-Jing. There would even be a witness to attest to Ming-Tao's heroic act. Lewis's body would end up tossed into the landfill, a place where it would never be discovered. It was the principal reason why Lewis wasn't being dragged along with the other two to Highgate. The end-game had always been to kill Lewis. This particular location was perfect.

What was really going to happen, however, was more problematic. In a short while, the two who had been sent to Highgate were going to discover that Lewis had sent them on a wild goose chase. Ming-Tao would then receive a different sort of phone call. The sort that would make Ming-Tao very angry. Threats would be made, bones would get broken, and it would all get extremely unpleasant. They were unlikely to kill Lewis immediately. Not until he had told them everything that he knew. Which again explained why he had been left behind at the landfill with Ming-Tao and the other guy. Just in case Ming-Tao received the different sort of phone call. The Chinese excel at getting their victims to talk before they die. A deserted landfill was an ideal location. Here, a man's screams could never be heard.

Definitely, lose-lose.

Which is why Lewis has been calculating. The time is now just after eleven in the morning. It will take the other car two hours to get to Highgate. About twenty minutes have already passed since the vehicle left. That leaves one hundred minutes at the earliest before Ming-Tao receives the different sort of phone call. Just after twelve-thirty, or thereabouts. Unless Lewis can turn the tables on his Chinese hosts first.

Which he had been dubious about, until a few moments ago. About the time he calculated that, quite possibly, his Chinese captors were perhaps not being quite as smart as they thought.

Both driver and passenger headrests have metal support pillars, a pair on each side, each with indentations cut along one edge. These are not close enough together or sharp enough to allow the post to act as a makeshift serrated knife to cut through the nylon cable ties. However, they do form part of a mechanism that enables the headrest to be raised and lowered. To do this, there is a button which needs to be depressed, set to one side, closest to the bottom edge facing the middle of the car. What Lewis won't know until he tries is whether there will be sufficient headroom, with the seat at its current angle of recline, to allow the headrest to be removed completely. He needs the headrest out of its slots in order to release his hands.

With both wrists tied to the left-hand pillar, he shifts his body awkwardly to the right, towards the centre of the car, neck and arms stretching almost to bursting as he struggles to get into a position that allows him to get purchase on the button with his nose. By exhaling as much air as possible from his lungs, he gains precious extra millimetres of wriggle room. After several attempts and using his wrists as a lever, the pillars slowly rise from their retaining slots until the top of the headrest hits the ceiling. The pillars, however, are still not yet out. He gives one final push with his shoulder, in effect compressing the headrest against the roof. Finally, his efforts are rewarded. Now free but with both hands still joined at the wrist, he lifts the headrest back into its original position, aligning the two pillars with their respective slots. It requires yet more pushing and shoving to force them back into position, but this time it's a little easier. He finishes just in time since this is the precise moment that Ming-Tao and his colleague decide to come and pay another visit.

Lewis sits impassively, trying to control his breathing, once more holding his wrists close to the headrest, pretending that they are still handcuffed to the pillar. The two Chinese men, therefore, arrive with false confidence. Their guns are no longer on display. Why should they be? Their prisoner is still restrained. They approach the door next to where Lewis is sitting and open it without caution.

'Mister Ben Lewis!' Ming-Tao begins, leaning into the car. His breath smells of stale cigarette smoke. 'We thought you might need some exercise.' He looks at his colleague and they grin. It is another private joke. 'Perhaps a little walk? Something to get the heart rate going?' They are evidently bored, itching to play some rough stuff.

Lewis doesn't answer, feigning disinterest and staring impassively straight ahead. Inside his head, he's calculating: every permutation, every angle, every countermove. There is one major problem. The two Chinese are both armed. He's not. The handcuffs are an impediment. The CF-98s are altogether another level of seriousness.

'Let's go for a walk, Mister Ben Lewis.' At which Ming-Tao steps away from the car. His colleague reaches inside with a pair of pliers to cut the cable tie. Lewis stares straight in front as a head appears inside the car, the Chinese man needing to stoop and then peer upwards to see what he's doing. Which places him in an awkward position, his head immediately below Lewis's wrists, his eyes searching for the correct piece of nylon to cut.

Without warning, Lewis brings both hands down hard on the man's neck from above, simultaneously driving his knee with extreme force directly into the bridge of the man's nose, the speed and surprise of both actions causing a dramatic change in fortunes. The Chinese agent drops the pliers, struggling to get away as blood pours from his nose. His head, however, is trapped, unable to escape the hold that Lewis now has around his neck. Lewis uses momentum from the attack to propel them both out of the car and onto their feet, the hold he uses on the Chinaman similar to the one he'd used only hours earlier on the Russian in Covent Garden. Except this time, he keeps raining body blows from either knee repeatedly into the man's chest and face to weaken him, relying on speed and energy from the surprise manoeuvre to drive the man backwards.

With the head-locked man as a shield, Lewis charges directly at Ming-Tao just as the Chinese agent is pulling out a gun in readiness to fire. At the very last moment, Lewis swivels his human shield through ninety degrees and delivers a snap-kick with his boot directly into Ming-Tao's gun hand. Bones snap, and the CF-98 falls to the floor. Lewis manages to kick it away before raining two more follow-up kicks, one to Ming-Tao's head and the next to his collarbone. The once-proud veteran agent falls to the floor, unconscious.

Meanwhile, released from his headlock, Ming-Tao's colleague stumbles around dazed, confused and winded. Lewis puts him out of his misery with a roundhouse kick to the head, causing his knees to buckle and the man to collapse. Just to make sure, Lewis directs two well-aimed, kicks at each man's kneecaps. Neither men will be walking anywhere for some considerable time.

Lewis hurries to the car and retrieves the pliers, snipping through the nylon restraints and freeing both wrists. Returning to the pair on the ground, he searches each thoroughly. He recovers his phones and wallet, taking care to remove the white key card that Ming-Tao had secreted earlier. In addition to the two CF-98s, he finds a strange telescopic metal baton inside Ming-Tao's jacket pocket. Also, a set of car keys for one of the black saloon cars. Picking up one of his burner phones, he turns it on. It has a nearly full battery and two bars of signal strength. He dials a number from memory and waits for it to ring at the other end.

'Zeltinger,' a familiar voice answers almost immediately.

'Still short on sleep, Saul?'

'Where are you, Ben?'

'A disused quarry. Or perhaps an old brick kiln. Who knows? It's currently an abandoned landfill site, not far from Peterborough. I have a present for you. Or perhaps it's for you and Jake. Two Chinese men. Both foreign agents. Both with guns. One has a strange telescopic metal baton on him. Ring any bells?'

'Sounds like someone who could have visited your Malaysian friend at the Farringdon hotel yesterday.'

'I sincerely hope so.'

'How do we come by and pick them up?'

'You send a police car from Peterborough. Track the mobile phone I'm using, and it will lead your colleagues to two men currently enjoying some forced rest.'

'Do they need a doctor?'

'Probably. I did give them both a helping hand to send them to sleep. One certainly has a few extra kinks in his nose. Perhaps it might be best to have a medical crew check them over, just to be safe.'

'What about you, Ben?'

'I'm coming to join the hunt for Holly.'

'Good. I could use a helping hand.'

'You're not going to arrest me?'

'That might be tricky. Police machinery still has to follow due process. I did warn you, Ben.'

'Then I'm going to remain in the shadows. I'm sorry, Saul. Tell your Peterborough crew to be quick. Two more Chinese agents will be back in another couple of hours or so, looking for their colleagues – and me, I hasten to add.'

'What's the story?'

'Everyone's desperate to get whatever it was that Doherty stole. I sent the other two on a wild goose chase – to Highgate and back. It bought me a little time. They also stole my house keys. I'd be grateful if one of your lot could try and recover them for me.'

'One step at a time, Ben. We're not out of the woods yet.'

'Not until we find Holly, right.'

'Don't forget to leave that phone behind when you go, Ben.'

'Just tell your Peterborough crew to get a move on.'

Chapter 43

Less than an hour after his conference call with Langley, Jake Sullivan finds himself attending a different meeting in yet another government building. This time it is an austere room at the Foreign Office. The building, full of faded grandeur from times gone by, is designed to intimidate. Judging by the well-practised confidence with which the visitor greets the conveners, there is little to suggest from the Russian ambassador's demeanour that he is the least bit intimidated. Sitting directly opposite him is the foreign secretary. To her right, her permanent secretary. On her left, in the absence of Dame Helen Morgan, is Sullivan. All three are positioned along one side of the long, rectangular table facing the Russian. There is no hospitality tray. It is part of a coded message. A rebuke is being sent and received. This is a formal summons, the matter serious. Teas and coffees are not on the agenda.

'Foreign Secretary,' the ambassador begins, speaking in fluent English. 'You called this meeting. How may the Russian Federation be of assistance?'

'Ambassador,' the foreign secretary replies, shuffling the papers on the desk in front of her into a neat pile before continuing. 'Four Russian nationals were arrested here in London during the early hours of the morning. There was an incident in the heart of Soho. All four were armed, either with guns or knives. We have reason to believe they are agents of the SVR, isn't that right, Jake?' she asks, looking directly at Sullivan.

'We believe so, yes.' Sullivan stares directly at the ambassador whilst reeling off the names of each of the four men from memory. The Russian sits silently with a poker face.

'That is indeed unfortunate, Mister Sullivan. Perhaps you can send me their details together with a brief description of what they are supposed to have done? I can then investigate and report back.'

Sullivan selects a single piece of paper from within a file and slides it across the table. Without looking at it, the Russian folds it in three and places it in a jacket pocket.

'Needless to say, but just for the record,' the foreign secretary continues, removing a pair of thick-framed glasses from her nose before looking directly at the ambassador. 'We do not tolerate agents of any foreign government operating within our national borders without both our prior knowledge and the direct approval of the Security Services. Do I make myself clear, Ambassador?'

'Perfectly, Foreign Secretary.'

'Jake, am I correct that neither you nor your colleagues had any prior notification that these four individuals were operating within the UK at this time?'

'That is correct, Foreign Secretary.'

'So, it seems we may have something of a problem. If these four are found to have been part of an unauthorised operation run by the Russian government on British soil, there will be consequences. Not least, the men will be deported. Not least, also, we will be seeking financial compensation. For the significant policing costs involved, both in their arrest and in bringing these four to justice. Do we understand each other, Sergei?'

'Perfectly, Foreign Secretary.'

'We also have our doubts that this was an isolated incident. Jake, would you care to elaborate?'

'There was a shooting in London yesterday lunchtime. In Granary

Square, just behind King's Cross station. One man was shot with a sniper rifle. Another also died, although we are not yet exactly sure how.'

'I had heard. It sounded most regrettable. Have you caught the person responsible?'

'No. We think it was some foreign intelligence agency.'

'I hope you are not about to implicate the Russian Federation in any way are you, Mister Sullivan? Those would be most serious allegations.'

'I am not implying anything, Ambassador. We know for a fact that four Russians, men we believe to be agents working for your country's foreign intelligence service, were arrested last night. They were involved in an active operation of some kind, the substance of which we are still investigating. By coincidence, this occurred only a few hours after the Granary Square killings, in which unauthorised foreign agents are also implicated. There are many parallels between the two incidents.'

The two men eyeball each other for a few seconds in silence.

'Coincidences do happen, Mister Sullivan. Unless you have proof of Russian involvement in this other matter, then I respectfully suggest that you keep your suppositions to yourselves. I will, of course, investigate the details of these four men. If your suspicions about them working for the *Sluzhba Vneshney Razvedki* is correct, then you will, of course, receive our full apologies.' He turns to the foreign secretary. 'Including, naturally, appropriate financial compensation.'

'We cannot tolerate incidents like this, Ambassador,' the foreign secretary continues. 'Otherwise, it is going to impair the good relationship we have historically enjoyed between our two countries.'

'That would be most regrettable. Let me investigate the matter for you. Now, since Mister Sullivan is here, there is another matter I'd like to raise if you both have the time? Who knows, it may even be related.'

'Of course. How can we help each other?'

'The man who was shot yesterday that you referred to. His name, I believe, was Keiran Doherty. By all accounts, he was something of a thief. And a saboteur. He had caused our country great harm before he died. He destroyed something of ours in Germany and stole something precious. We have reason to believe that Doherty might have been working for the British security services.' He looks directly at Sullivan. 'If that assumption is correct, we would like the British government's help in retrieving whatever has been stolen.'

The foreign secretary swivels her head to look directly at Sullivan and nods, her cue to the MI5 man to answer the ambassador directly.

'We'd like to be helpful, Ambassador. However, to set the record straight, Keiran Doherty was not, and never has been, working for the British security services. Neither MI5 nor MI6. Most of us, myself included, thought Doherty had died over a year ago, fighting for the French Foreign Legion. We have to conclude, therefore, that he must have been operating independently. Or working for other parties undisclosed. I'm sorry not to be more helpful. What is it that you believe he might have stolen?'

The Russian ambassador dismissively waves a hand.

'Secrets. And money, of course. A great deal of money.'

'Sadly, money won't be of much use to him now, will it?'

'True. However, the money belonged to someone else and has gone missing. It needs to be recovered. We, the Russian Federation, are trying to be helpful. The real owner has become – how can I put it? Desperately unhappy about the fact that it has gone missing.'

'Are you able to give more details?'

'At the moment, no. The situation is delicate. However, if, as you say, Doherty was indeed a lone operator and not working directly for you, any information you glean about where and how he might have hidden the money before he was killed would be helpful. As you continue your enquiries into his death, that is.'

'We'll do what we can. The *quid pro quo* is easy. We can't have foreign agents conducting unauthorised operations on British soil. Assuming that you're happy to fulfil your part in that bargain, we'll do our best to be co-operative with you in return.'

Once the Russian ambassador has left, the foreign secretary asks Sullivan and her permanent secretary to stay behind for a few moments.

'These last twenty-four hours, it feels as if the world's gone mad, Jake. We can't have all these foreign agents charging around as if it's the Wild West. What's been going on?'

Sullivan briefly summarises the events surrounding Doherty's death, including the kidnap of Holly Williams.

'This is crazy. We can't continue like this, allowing foreign agents to run riot left, right and centre. You say the Americans have been in on the act as well?'

'Most definitely, foreign secretary.'

'Then we need to put a stop to this at once. It's getting ridiculous. Please tell Dame Helen that I am expecting her and you to get this sorted without delay. I shall discuss this with the home secretary later this afternoon at Cabinet. Thank you, Jake.'

Chapter 44

The Unit 61398 office building is twelve storeys high. Like most of the Pudong district of Shanghai, the neighbourhood is relatively new, the office building undistinguished. Inside, it is more like a factory than an office – certainly more like a factory than a military installation belonging to the People's Liberation Army. At any time of the day or night, well over one thousand young men and women are at work inside the building, sitting and staring at computer screens. Each is performing one of several, often very routine and, at times, highly monotonous tasks. Tasks that they hope will allow a computer system at some other location on the far side of the globe to become compromised.

These highly intelligent young men and women are allowed to operate without constraint. They are given a target to focus on and left to their own devices. Enough peer group pressure exists across each of the twelve open-plan floors to allow energy to flow and competitive juices to feed imaginations. Competition is actively encouraged by section leaders, themselves promoted largely based on their hacking prowess. Section 23 is led by a woman in her late twenties. Her most recent claim to fame was that she hacked into the Pentagon's secure database and downloaded a list of all current clandestine operations running at that time.

Earlier that afternoon, she had been assigned the task of securing sufficient resources within her team to focus on Keiran Doherty and the missing North Korean one hundred million dollars. She immediately reassigned ten of her best hackers off existing project work and took them to a small meeting room for a briefing.

There are no chairs in the meeting rooms in Unit 61398. It is a deliberate policy, designed to encourage managers to keep meetings short and to the point. For fifteen minutes, she briefed the hackers on what she knew. Her briefing covered not only Keiran Doherty but also Nigel Fisher, before widening to include Ben Lewis and the missing woman, Holly Williams. The entire room then brainstormed the approach they might take.

Five hackers were, in time, assigned to Doherty and Fisher. Even though the pair were meant to have died over a year ago, three of the five would focus on trying to discover recent digital-footprints of either man from mobile phone, email or social media sources. Also from known record databases such as the Driver and Vehicle Licensing Authority, HM Revenue and Customs or even the Ministry of Defence personnel records. Meanwhile, the remaining two would be attempting to trace the Iranian money that Doherty had stolen from the bank in the United Arab Emirates, in particular exploring options for its recovery.

The remaining five hackers were assigned to Lewis and Holly. It was the same drill as with Doherty and Fisher but with a slightly different objective. This time the sole purpose was to pinpoint the exact current location of either party. They too would start with known mobile phone numbers, email addresses, friendship groups and obvious social media connections. After that, they would need to rely on their imagination and ingenuity to get the results that were expected.

Chapter 45

At about the time the Russian ambassador is receiving his public dressing-down at the Foreign Office, Holly Williams' initial euphoria at being free from her handcuffs is turning to despair. She has returned to the room where Doherty left her chained to the central pillar, having searched the entire apartment for a possible means of escape and finding nothing to give her hope. In addition to the room next door, identical to her own, there are only two other rooms: a pantry-style kitchen and a small toilet. The kitchen has a kettle, two mugs and basic tea and coffee-making facilities. Otherwise, the cupboards and drawers are empty. No biscuits or food of any kind. No knives or sharp implements. A quick tour of the rest of the property also yields nothing that she considers might allow her to escape. No windows that open, no emergency fire escapes, no telephone landlines.

She gives an involuntary shiver, thinking about others who might have been incarcerated here previously. Staring at the view from the windows to distract herself, she tries spotting landmarks she knows. In the distance, the London Eye and the Houses of Parliament stand tall. Nearer, beside the Gherkin and the NatWest Tower, are the Shard and a building shaped like an old walkie-talkie radio. Two high-rise towers close by look to be part of the same development as hers. Her initial assumption that she might be in or near the Barbican still feels plausible.

Only as she is shifting her gaze back inside the room does she notice her raincoat, lying tossed on the floor, in one corner. Doherty had grabbed it to cover her wrists when he'd led her from her front door in Canterbury to his car. The same raincoat he'd used when escorting her from the car to this apartment later that same afternoon. The very same raincoat she'd used when returning from work the previous day. Which causes a sudden rush of optimism. How could she have forgotten?!

Leaping to her feet, she snatches the coat from the floor, frantically checking the pockets and triumphantly finding her phone. Her jubilation, however, is short-lived. When she powers the device on, the battery indicator shows just eight per cent of available power. She waits precious seconds while it searches for a signal, eventually finding a connection with only a meagre one bar of signal strength. She tries calling Ben's mobile. The line crackles as it rings, the signal weak and intermittent. There is no answer. She decides against leaving a voicemail, worried about the battery. Thinking quickly, she walks to the glass window and takes a photo of the view with her phone. This she emails Ben along with a quick message.

'*HELP!! Keiran has kidnapped me. High floor somewhere, lots of soundproofing, in or near the Barbican I think. I now have NO battery on phone. PLEASE find me QUICKLY!!! H xxx.*'

She presses 'send' and waits agonising seconds before a whooshing noise tells her that the mail has been sent. The battery is already down to just six per cent. She keys in the numbers 999 and hits 'dial' before bringing the phone to her ear.

'Emergency,' a calm male voice answers instantly. 'Which service?'

Which is the exact moment Holly's phone dies, the operating system automatically switching off to conserve the barest minimum level of battery charge.

Chapter 46

Saul Zeltinger is enjoying a five-minute catnap at his desk when his phone rings and he wakes with a jolt.

'Zeltinger,' he says, trying hard to suppress a yawn.

'Saul, it's Rachel Paxman at the forensics lab. Is now a good time to talk?'

Zeltinger shakes his head, taking a sip of cold coffee from a mug on the desk beside him. He winces at the taste.

'Absolutely, Rachel.' He tries to sound convincing but is dubious about whether he succeeds. 'What news?' Paxman is the forensic scientist assigned to explore probable cause in the case of Nigel Fisher's death.

'Long story short, Saul, nearly all of the tests we've run have come back negative. On the face of it, all the evidence points to a man that died of natural causes, in particular heart failure.'

'Any known history of heart disease?'

'None that we can find. The heart muscles show no sign of any scarring from previous cardiac incidents.'

'So why did you say 'nearly all of the tests'? What have you found but haven't yet got answers to?'

'On the face of it, not a lot. Though I was put on enquiry by something unusual on the corpse.'

'Which was?'

'The dead man had a puncture mark on his upper right forearm. As if he had been injected shortly before he died.'

'Can you be certain?'

'Oh, yes. Whatever had punctured his arm had penetrated with sufficient force to connect directly through to the bone. There was also some blood near the exit wound, which was how it first came to our attention. Looking at the X-rays, there is a tiny indentation where what looks like a sharp needle had hit the bone. There were also microscopic fibres around the entry point on the surface of the skin. It suggests that whatever it was that punctured his skin passed through the clothes he was wearing.'

'The clothing fibres match?'

'They do.'

'Yet the toxicology results came back negative.' Zeltinger scratches his chin and momentarily tries to stifle another yawn. 'Do you have any theories that you'd like to share?'

'Only one slightly wacky idea.'

'I'm listening.'

'There is a drug used in anaesthetics. It's a muscle relaxant called succinylcholine. More commonly known as Sux. Sux can be given either intravenously or into the muscle tissue and very rapidly causes diffuse muscle fasciculation. That's technical jargon for going into spasm. Sux is used when medics need to stick a tube down a patient's throat to assist them with breathing. Every muscle stops working almost immediately – and I mean every muscle. Because of the spasms, the patient always gets put to sleep before they ever receive Sux. Within twenty seconds of a Sux injection, the drug is effective. Without assistance, the patient would be unable to breathe. They might, if they hadn't received an anaesthetic, be conscious of what was happening even if they couldn't do anything about it. They would also be in a fair amount of pain and distress. The good news is that Sux is quickly and readily metabolised. The effects are short-lived. The bad news for the forensic scientist is that it leaves virtually no trace in the body. In seconds, the body starts breaking down Sux into succinate, a naturally occurring substance. It is arguably the perfect murder weapon. It renders a victim incapacitated almost immediately. Without assistance with breathing, they asphyxiate, their organs stop working and they die. Under autopsy, however, there is virtually no trace.'

'Virtually?'

'Well, in this case, there is the puncture wound on the skin. That's all we have to go on.'

'Off the record, but putting your professional judgement on the line for one moment: do you think Fisher killed Doherty before somehow keeling over and dying from natural causes? Or did someone kill Fisher in cold blood? Perhaps using Sux as the murder weapon. Allowing this same assassin then to use Fisher's sniper rifle to kill Doherty?'

'That's a toughie. My problem is that I can see no reason why Fisher should pull the trigger and then suddenly drop dead himself. What swings it for me is the puncture wound on Fisher's upper arm. I can't prove it, but I'd wager that someone killed Fisher. It would have been a gruesome yet silent death. I think the same person then killed Doherty. That's my gut feeling.'

Chapter 47

In a CIA safe house just off Russell Square, Sanders and Krantz are back from their less than satisfactory trip to the North of England.

Sanders is spoiling for a fight. Raised by a Liberian mother and American father in Alabama, he had worked his way up the CIA's rank and file, earning his stripes on a first overseas posting to Lagos. He had then moved to Kinshasa in the Democratic Republic of the Congo where, in time, he became station chief. Now back in Europe and still on track for higher office, Sanders is well-versed in the practical ways of getting things done. The fact that Lewis got one over them in the first skirmish is grist to the mill as far as he is concerned. Time now for round two. Sanders is confident about being the eventual winner. All that needs to be done to defeat Lewis is to think smarter and act smarter than him, which suits Sanders since he is a confident man. It's a trait he learned the hard way in Africa.

Krantz, by contrast, feels humiliated. Nothing short of Lewis's blood is going to satisfy his yearning to finish the skirmish with him the overall winner. Krantz had been stationed in Beirut for several years. It had been a challenging posting in one of the most challenging regions, running field agents across the Levant from Egypt in the west to Jordan and Iraq in the east. He had served his time, mostly keeping his nose clean. Now, in his late fifties, he was on one final tour of duty before heading back home. He had already bought a retirement condo in Jackson Hole where he planned to ski the winter and fish Wyoming's reservoirs during the summer. The Krantz game plan was to complete his London tour on a high and then head back to the States in a blaze of glory. He didn't need an upstart like Lewis to end his career with a blemish on his record.

Station chief Greg Fuscoe ends a secure call with Kathleen Thomas before his driver drops him off a block away from the safe house.

'We have a lead on Lewis,' he announces to Sanders and Krantz as he enters the living room, heading straight for the coffee machine in the corner. 'Seems you were right, Oscar,' he says, looking directly at Sanders whilst pouring steaming black liquid into a Styrofoam beaker. 'Doherty did take Lewis's girlfriend hostage after all. Smart thinking. Kathleen Thomas has just been speaking to Britain's head of MI6. An underling who was on the call let slip that Holly is somewhere in the Barbican. All we need now is to find her.'

'How big is the Barbican?' Krantz asks. 'How many apartments?'

'Hundreds. Maybe more. In any event, the Brits are crawling over the place trying to find her.'

'Where is it exactly? I've heard the name for some reason.'

'About two miles east of here. A concrete ghetto and theatre complex close to the financial district. Get it up on the screen, and we can take a look.'

Sanders busies himself on the keyboard and, moments later, the search engine throws up street view images of the area.

'Three big high-rises and various other apartment buildings. According to this website,' Sanders says, 'there are over two thousand apartments. Fuck, we are never going to find this woman. It'll be like finding a needle in a haystack. Game over unless we can think of a smarter way.'

'Hang on, hang on,' Krantz says, staring into space. 'Let's brainstorm this. Assume we were Doherty. What if we had someone we wanted to keep hostage, and we needed that person to be kept somewhere in or near Central London. Where would we choose?'

'A vacant rental property somewhere. Maybe a self-storage unit or similar. Thousands of places to choose from. What's your point?'

'My point is that Doherty is ex-Marines, ex-Foreign Legion. He's a man who's meant to be dead but isn't. He's been doing dirty deeds in covert ops mode this last twelve months for some organisation or other. He and this other guy, the one who died on the rooftop.'

'Fisher.'

'Right. Breaking apart Markov's little operation is not something Doherty and Fisher woke up one morning and decided they wanted to do just for the hell of it. This was a professional job from start to finish. I'm one hundred per cent certain.'

'Not working for the Brits, apparently,' Fuscoe interjects. 'Not according to what they told Kathleen, at any rate.'

'I think that's bullshit, but it doesn't actually matter who the fuck they've been working for. The point is that it's been a professional operation and not run by amateurs. If we wanted to keep someone locked up as a hostage somewhere, what would we do?'

'We'd use a safe house or a tailor-made facility,' Sanders says.

'Exactly! However, remember, these guys are in covert ops mode. They won't be going through normal channels. So, why pick the Barbican? Either there's a friendly safe house there that Doherty knows is secure or else a tailor-made facility that he's aware of.'

'If it's a safe house, there'll be babysitters for the hostage and perhaps other hangers-on such as housekeeping and such.'

'Correct. Which is the reason why I like the notion of a tailor-made facility best. Somewhere with good soundproofing. A place he could leave a hostage locked up, out of mischief and where he doesn't need to keep worrying about returning every five minutes to check if they are still alive.'

'You think that such a place might exist in the Barbican?' Fuscoe asks. 'That's weird.'

'Is it? Think about it. Why not? A place at the top of one of the towers might be perfect. No one can see in, the floors are probably made of concrete, so there would be good sound insulation – we could make that work.'

'Always supposing someone might have such a facility. Who would have one of those, for Christ's sake?'

'That's the million-dollar question. Since we're desperately clutching at straws, I suggest it's time you made a few discreet calls, Greg. Pull in some favours. See what rattling the cage produces. We may find nothing, but there's no sense in not asking. I wouldn't know who to speak to, but theoretically, top of my list would be France's DGSE, the Israelis, perhaps even Moscow. Let's go fishing and see what we catch. It's not like Doherty and Fisher just went and bought themselves a place and converted it for the job, right?'

'Unless it is, and always has been, a British facility no one else knew about.'

'Unlikely, in my view. They have so many lock-ups and safe houses they could commandeer, but what do I know?'

'Okay, you've convinced me. I'll go and make some calls,' Fuscoe says, getting to his feet. 'I am not confident it's going to yield anything; however, there're a couple of people on that list who currently owe me.'

Chapter 48

The Chinese have had a breakthrough. One of the hackers in Unit 61398 in Shanghai has managed to clone Doherty's phone. Not the burner he had on him when he was shot, but his regular phone.

Doherty, it would seem, had been a frequent WhatsApp user. Whilst all messages were end-to-end encrypted, one of the Unit 61398 hackers knew that every time an account holder changed their device, a new WhatsApp security key was automatically generated. The hacker had thus managed to set up a brand-new device onto which all Doherty's old accounts were successfully transitioned, thus was able to read Doherty's old messages. In particular, one thread with someone called Elijah. Elijah was the custodian of a particular facility that Doherty seemed eager to borrow. A facility in one of the apartments in a London complex known as the Barbican. An apartment at the top of one of the three tower blocks in the Barbican. The forty-second floor of Cromwell Tower to be precise. Apartment 42-05.

Back in London, with resources much depleted, head of station Cheng convenes a meeting with the three remaining field agents currently unassigned. Despite now being in Ming-Tao's custody, Cheng has been ordered by Beijing to continue to try and find Holly.

'We need the girl as leverage,' he tells his team. 'Lewis has a track record of surprising us. We now know she's being held in a secure facility at the top of a tower block. So, we need a plan.'

'Is this woman injured?' one of them asks.

'I've no idea,' says Cheng dismissively.

'Well, if the woman became ill …,' the same agent persists, '… then she might need hospitalisation. She might even be unconscious. In fact, unconscious would be very helpful. Then she would need an ambulance to take her to hospital.'

'I get it! I like the idea. Okay, but we'd need specialist equipment. Isn't that going to be a problem?'

'No,' another answers. 'The same ploy was used not that long ago, remember? We can find an ambulance easily.'

'What about uniforms?'

'Again, not a problem. You just say the word, we can be ready in next to no time.'

Cheng smiles. Mostly, he has great people working for him in London – many of them only too happy to be preparing a plan B in case Ming-Tao failed to deliver what they needed from Lewis.

Chapter 49

Shortly after midday, Jake Sullivan is in his chauffeur-driven car, being driven back to Thames House after his meeting with the Russian ambassador when his phone rings. He looks at the caller ID and swiftly answers the call.

'What news, Saul?'

Zeltinger tells him the gist of his conversation with the forensic scientist, Rachel Paxman.

'Proving that both Doherty and Fisher were killed by parties unknown. As we suspected all along.'

'Proves might be too strong a word. The evidence certainly points in that direction.'

'It suggests Fisher didn't shoot Doherty. So, who did? We're back to square one, Saul. Clutching at straws.'

'I'm struggling with motive.'

'What do you mean?'

'All crimes happen for a reason. Here we have two men, both of whom were meant to be dead but weren't, for reasons that I don't understand. Maybe you do, but I don't. What appears beyond dispute is that the pair were involved in something kind of espionage operation. More your territory, Jake, than mine. They both get killed in broad daylight yet we still don't know the reason. Sure, they might have recovered something they shouldn't have. Or stolen something that wasn't theirs. But if their crime was so heinous, wouldn't the injured parties want to recover whatever they'd lost before they killed them both?'

'Unless their deaths were intended to shut the operation down.'

'Go on.'

'What if they knew too much about something? Or had seen something. Something that left certain parties with no option but to kill them both? Which, having done, caused them to cover their tracks by dressing up the crime to look like something different.'

'Like being about stolen money or the secret location of an encryption key.'

'I suspect the encryption is real, but maybe the money is a smokescreen. Who knows? Better to prevent an encryption key ever seeing the light of day again than risk exposing something explosive.'

'Which certainly now puts Lewis's life on the line, given that he seems determined to find the wretched thing.'

'Given what happened to Doherty and Fisher, I'd say the chances of him remaining alive for long are fast approaching zero.'

Chapter 50

At about the time Zeltinger and Sullivan are talking, Lewis pulls into a service station. He switches his regular phone on, toggling upwards with his thumb to come out of airplane mode and connect to the network. He lets out a breath as the device finally acquires three bars of signal. About to scan his emails, he notices a missed call – from Holly! At 11.33 am. Less than an hour ago. He dials the number but the phone routes through to voicemail. He doesn't leave a message, instead checking his voicemail to see if she has left him one. His voicemail is empty. Frustrated, he scrolls quickly through his emails, finding one from Holly sent at 11.35 am. He taps to open it, but almost immediately, the message disappears. Equally oddly, another mail from Holly arrives seconds later. Time-stamped 12.17 pm – just a few minutes ago.

Ben darling please get me out of here don't try calling no battery Doherty has me locked in flat 36 in Shire House near the Barbican Help me Ben Love you Holly xx

Quickly Lewis composes a reply.

I'm on my way. Are you hurt or trapped? Alone?

He presses 'send' and waits. Five minutes go by, and there is no reply. Lewis reads the mail once again. Faint alarm bells are sounding. Holly never calls him 'darling' nor has he ever used the same affectation. He forwards the email to Saul Zeltinger, switches off his phone and picks up Doherty's burner to call the detective. This phone, too, shows a missed call. There is also one new voicemail. Saving this for another time, he dials Zeltinger's mobile and waits for the familiar voice to answer.

'Saul, it's Ben. Holly tried to ring me forty-five minutes ago. She's also just sent an email. I've just forwarded it to you. It explains where she's being held.'

'I've just seen it. What do you think?'

'I'm not sure. On the face of it, it seems genuine. Put it this way. Some of the language doesn't sound like Holly. To my knowledge, she's never called me 'darling' before.'

'More's the pity. People do and say funny things stress.'

'Which is why I wondered if this might be a more appropriate matter for the police to sort out.'

'Finally, the leopard is changing its spots.'

'In truth, it's because I'm well over an hour away. You could be there in five minutes.'

'We'll take a look. So that you know, Holly tried dialling the Emergency Services earlier. The line cut out as soon as the call was answered. We've had her number on our watch list. Most mobiles automatically record the location of every call made to 999 and forward this information to the Emergency Services. Holly's call was at 11.36 this morning. The call – and her location – was logged, but no sooner had the call been answered than the line went dead.'

'Hang on, this is weird. She calls me at 11.33 am. I don't pick up, and she doesn't leave me a voicemail. At 11.35 am, she sends an email calling for help and then at 11.36 am she dials the Emergency Services. Then her phone dies.'

'I thought you said she had sent you an email a few minutes ago, not at 11.35 am.'

'That's the weird part. When I first turned on my phone, there was an email from her at 11.35 am. When I went to open it, it simply disappeared – vanished into the ether, replaced by another mail at 12.17 am – the one I forwarded to you. I saw the earlier mail briefly with my own eyes, Saul. Now it no longer exists.'

'You think someone's messing with her email?'

'Hers or mine, yes. Possibly both. Tell me, when she rang the Emergency Services. Where, exactly was she?'

'Right bang in the heart of the Barbican. Very close to the Barbican Theatre. It narrows the search area considerably, but not quite enough.'

'Not near a place called Shire House, then?'

'It doesn't sound like it, no.'

'Shire House feels like a trap. I suspect you're better focusing on finding Holly in the Barbican. Send someone else to Shire House. When they do go knocking on the door of flat 36, perhaps one or more of Jake's people should be on the team?'

Chapter 51

Polunin and Ivankov stare at the computer screen, waiting for Yasenovo to come back online. When the call finally begins, it is Volkov himself at the Moscow end.

'Good news and bad news, gentlemen,' Volkov begins. 'Let's start with the good. We have managed to trace the missing money. The Iranian's one hundred million dollars has been earning frequent flyer points. From the bank in the Emirates, the money routed via Bermuda to Luxembourg, then to Cayman and various tax havens in between. It finally ended up in a bank in London, in an account belonging to the art auctioneers, Tylers. We haven't yet managed to get behind their firewalls, but we're working on it. We might need to put an asset on the inside.'

'We could do that, no problem,' Polunin says without prompting. 'That's good work, Mikhail. Very quick. Please congratulate the team. What's the bad news?'

'The bad news is disappointing. We've been tapping the detective's phone, as you know. Despite a successful email spoof on Lewis and despite him, yes, actually reading our message purporting to be from his Holly, the plan hasn't worked. There were some unfortunate timing issues on this end: we were unable to delete an email that the girl had sent to Lewis quickly enough to prevent Lewis from seeing it and getting suspicious. I want to play two recordings of conversations between Lewis and Zeltinger this last hour. The first is from Lewis, telling his friend how Chinese agents have been playing games, nearly succeeding in kidnapping him. The second concerns the email spoof.'

Polunin fidgets with his pencil as the two recordings play. Ivankov looks at Polunin at one stage and shrugs – *no big deal,* he seems to be saying.

'What do you make of all that?' Volkov asks once the recordings have ended. Ivankov answers first.

'Let me suggest something. Lewis always talks to the same person, this detective – the one with the German name. So, we should visit this detective. Perhaps at home. Maybe he has a nice family. You know, a pretty wife, some vulnerable children? The children could be very helpful – as leverage. That would make Lewis come to us.'

'You're an evil bastard, Pyotr,' Volkov chuckles. 'I like the plan. I like it very much. What do you think, Alexei?'

'I think if anyone can pull it off, it has to be Pyotr Ivankov.'

'Excellent,' says Volkov. 'Then let's not waste time. The sooner this is all over, the sooner we can all get some rest. I am under intense pressure from the very highest levels on this one, Alexei.'

Chapter 52

Lewis is ready to turn off Doherty's phone when he remembers the missed call. He punches the voicemail button and holds the phone to his ear.

'*Keiran, this is Eli. All I keep reading in the papers is that you've been shot. How many times does a man need to die, for goodness' sake? After what happened last time, I figured it might not be beyond the bounds of possibility that, by some sleight of hand, you might yet be alive. If you are, call me. Urgently. I've had the CIA's head of station, Fuscoe, enquiring about our special little facility in the Barbican. Thought I'd give you a chance to explain yourself before I call him back. Ring me, you bastard! You've got two hours. If I don't hear from you, I'm going to have to tell him everything.*'

The message was recorded twenty-five minutes ago.

Weighing his options, he takes out his regular phone, turns it on, checks that there's nothing new from Holly, then hits Jake Sullivan's number.

'Hello, this is Ben Lewis,' he says to MI5's switchboard operator who, without Ben even asking for Jake, immediately routes the call through to Sullivan.

'Ben, finally!' Jake says, seconds later. 'I see you're on your way back into London.'

'Something like that,' Lewis says vaguely. 'Look, I've still got Doherty's phone. Someone called him about thirty minutes ago.

Someone called Eli. I think you ought to listen to the message.' He manipulates Doherty's phone next to his and replays the voicemail message on loudspeaker.

'Did you get all that, Jake?'

'Oh, yes. That was extremely helpful.'

'You know who this Eli person is?'

'Sadly. I've even got the slippery bastard on speed dial.'

'Sounds like he knows where Holly is.'

'It does rather. With Eli, nothing surprises me.'

'He sounded as if he could be Israeli. Certainly Middle Eastern.'

'Just leave it with me, Ben. Keep out of this one. If Eli can lead us to Holly, we'll get her out safe and sound, I promise.'

'Can't I join you?'

'From what I can see on my screen, you're at least an hour away from the Barbican. Leave it to us. We'll sort it. Once we've got Holly, I'll give you a call. I promise. This is really helpful, Ben. Thanks.'

Chapter 53

The Embassy of Israel is tucked out of sight on the western edge of Hyde Park, adjacent to Kensington Palace Green. Knowing that he is unlikely to find Eli Rosin eating in the office canteen at lunchtime, Sullivan sends the Mossad agent a text to find out if he's free for a quick coffee. Within fifteen minutes of Lewis's call, Sullivan is entering Eli's favourite coffee shop off High Street Kensington. The two men greet each other warmly. With a simple hand gesture from Eli to the proprietor, a double macchiato is placed on the table in front of Sullivan. Sullivan forgoes the proffered sugar bowl and receives a snort of derision from Eli as a result.

'Everyone needs sugar in their coffee, my friend. You need to live a little. Have you eaten?'

Jake shakes his head, taking a sip of the hot liquid and looking directly at the Mossad agent. The two have been sparring partners in London for many years. Theirs hasn't always the warmest and friendliest of relationships, but over time they have learned to trust each other.

'To what do I owe the pleasure?'

'Talk to me about Keiran Doherty, Eli. In particular, I'd like to hear about a certain apartment that you appear to own in the Barbican. One which I believe you might have lent to Doherty recently.'

'Is Keiran dead?' He searches Sullivan's face for an answer but gets no clue. 'He used to say, "Once a dead man, always a dead man." Has he disappeared for good this time?'

Sullivan eventually gives the briefest of nods, taking a mouthful of coffee before saying anything.

'The Barbican, Eli. I need to know about the apartment. Where is it and what's it being used for?'

'What if I said that I don't know what you're talking about?'

'Then I would have to refer you to evidence contained in a small but damaging voicemail that you left on Doherty's phone not more than an hour ago.'

Eli looks at the remnants of a small iced pastry on the plate in front of him. He dabs a wet finger on some crumbs and pops the finger in his mouth.

'Too good to waste,' he says, licking his lips. He looks across at Sullivan, who appears unusually restless. 'I think the English expression is 'hoisted by my own petard', or similar. What do you want to know?'

'Where is it?'

'I think you're playing with me, Jake. You already know where it is.'

'I know it's in the Barbican, Eli. I just need the exact address. And I need it right now.'

Eli looks at Jake with a poker face for all of thirty seconds without saying anything. Then he speaks.

'Cromwell Tower. Apartment 42-05.'

'Very good. Thank you.' Jake lifts his mobile from his pocket, flicks through to a particular number and hits 'dial'.

'Dame Helen, please. It's Jake Sullivan. This is a Category One call.' He looks at Eli, who raises his eyebrows.

'Jake?' the voice in his ear says, seconds later.

'I know where the girl is.' He gives the details and listens whilst his superior repeats everything back. 'I am about to head over there. Can you speak with the police commissioner? We need Cromwell Tower and the whole neighbourhood around it in lockdown immediately. That includes all stairwells, lifts and means of entry. We might also need an ambulance or two on standby. I should be there in less than fifteen minutes.' He ends the call and looks back at Eli.

'We have to go, Eli. I have a car waiting.'

'Can't I finish my coffee first?'

'There's a woman's life on the line,' Sullivan says, draining his in one gulp. 'Do you need to collect the keys from anywhere first?'

Eli smiles and pats his pockets.

'I was anticipating something like this. It was either you or Greg Fuscoe, whoever came asking first.' They get up to leave and Sullivan places a ten-pound note on the table.

'Very generous, thank you.'

'You know how it is, Eli. One good turn deserves another,' Sullivan says as they hurry outside to the waiting car. Sullivan opens the rear door and lets Eli get in first before sliding in after him. 'The Barbican,' he says to the driver. Then turning back to Eli, he carries on where the pair of them had left off.

'So, Greg's been asking about the apartment too, has he?'

'In a roundabout way. He left a voicemail a while ago. It was a fishing expedition. Like he knew there might be something in the Barbican but didn't know whose asset it was.'

'What's this place been all about, Eli?'

The Israeli looks at Sullivan, then at the driver and then back at Sullivan.

'Can we speak?' he asks.

Sullivan nods.

'Let's just say that we find it useful, from time to time, to have somewhere we can take people and talk – for those moments when we all need a little peace and privacy. Humanely, of course, nothing unpleasant. Just out of the office and out of the public eye. We haven't broken any laws, you know.'

'Heaven forbid, no. When did Mossad last break any laws? It's probably helpful, for the good of our relationship, if we turn a collective blind eye as to the rights and wrongs of such a facility for the moment. Instead, tell me, how did Doherty get to hear about it?'

'Some time ago, he and I did some business together. Let's also leave it at that. We became friends. We are friends. Or should I now be saying, we were friends? From time to time, we would share a bottle, exchange gossip, compare methods and techniques, you know how it is? One agent to another. No rules were broken, only friendships made. Then, a few days ago, out of the blue, he sends a WhatsApp message. Asking if he could borrow the place in the Barbican. The apartment was empty, I already owed him one for a past favour, so I lent him a spare set of keys. That's all I know, Jake. That's the truth.'

'For which I am grateful, thanks, Eli. Now we need to pray that we haven't left it too late.'

Chapter 54

The area from Goswell Road in the west to Moorgate in the east has been sealed off. Fire alarms are sounding in numerous office buildings, the place teeming with office workers looking bewildered and disoriented. Police and fire wardens are ushering everyone in all directions away from the Barbican complex.

Sullivan's car is equipped with discreet flashing blue lights in the radiator grilles and a loud two-tone klaxon. Using these, the driver navigates past the police roadblocks, eventually dropping the pair off close to the entrance to the Barbican Theatre on Chiswell Street. Several armed police are already patrolling. Two ambulances are parked on the theatre's entrance driveway, their blue lights flashing and one with its rear doors open.

Eli leads the way. They pass around the left-hand side of the theatre towards the entrance to Cromwell Tower itself. Sullivan flashes his card at the armed policemen in the lobby entrance and one of these uses his radio to summon a lift to take them to the top floor. Given the security lockdown, Sullivan and Eli are escorted in the lift by an armed policeman from SCO19. He, in turn, uses the manual override to work the elevator controls and take them to the top floor.

Waiting for them on arrival are two more armed officers. Sullivan presents his MI5 badge. Both officers study this carefully before confirming with colleagues over the radio that Sullivan is expected and can proceed. Sullivan vouches for Eli and the pair stride along the corridor towards the apartment.

'You arrived just in time, sir,' one says as they near the apartment entrance. 'There was already an ambulance crew here when we arrived. They managed to break in and found the woman. She's alive, but they needed to sedate her. She was nearly hysterical. It's weird inside, sir.'

They step through the door. Instantly, Sullivan sees the padded walls and knows that this is no ordinary apartment. He looks at Eli but, momentarily, the Israeli's eyes are elsewhere.

'Where's the hostage?'

'In the next room, sir. With the ambulance crew. They're about to leave.'

Sullivan's professional eye quickly takes in the scene. Blackout curtains. Dirty mattress on the floor. A chemical toilet. Half-finished bottles of drinking water and packets of biscuits, nuts and raisins. He's seen enough. To one side of the room is a stretcher on wheels. On it lies Holly, sedated. Three paramedics in green scrub uniforms stand next to her. One is in the process of putting a drip up, while another adjusts various tubes and monitors to watch over Holly's vital signs. The paramedics are all Asian, of Chinese extraction. Two male and one female.

'Who's in charge?' Sullivan asks the medical crew.

One man steps forward.

'I am.'

'What happened?'

'We were the first on the scene. We heard the call on the radio and were already close by in Moorgate. When we reached the apartment door, all we could hear was this lady screaming for help. We broke the door down to gain entry and took the decision to sedate her before she did herself, or us, any harm. She looks okay otherwise. With your agreement, we'd like to get her to hospital for a thorough examination.'

Sullivan looks at the other two, then at Holly and nods.

'Okay. Where are you going to take her?'

'Barts,' the man replies. 'It's the closest. Just around the corner, in fact.'

'Very well, you'd better get going. Thanks for all your help. Look after her.'

'We'll do our best,' he says and turns towards his colleagues and speaks something to them in a language sounding to Sullivan like Cantonese. He glances at Eli, who has also picked up the language switch.

The ambulance crew wheel the stretcher out of the apartment, heading briskly along the corridor towards the lift bank. Back in the apartment, one of the police officers' radios crackles into life.

'All units, all units, this is a code nine alert! No one, I repeat no one, is to leave the building. I repeat, this is a code nine. Two ambulance crew have been shot dead on the ground floor. Do you copy?'

Sullivan and Eli race towards the lobby landing but fail to get there in time: the elevator doors have closed and the lift has already started its descent.

'Can we disconnect the power?' Sullivan asks the SCO19 officer in charge.

'I wouldn't advise that, sir. If the perps think they're trapped, they'll probably kill themselves and the hostage. For the moment, let them think they've got away with it.' He turns away and barks orders rapidly into his radio.

'I concur with that, by the way,' Eli says to Sullivan. 'No one comes out a winner with a hostage trapped in an elevator.'

'We have teams watching the podium and ground floor levels,' the SCO19 man says. 'We let them exit the lift with the hostage. Then we take them down.'

'What about immobilising both ambulances?'

'I'm sure they're already on to that, Jake,' Eli says.

'How would Mossad do it, Eli?'

'We'd have a bogus police vehicle in the basement. Ditch the trolley and the uniforms, put the girl in the boot of the car, and then drive out pretending to be a police car in hot pursuit.'

'Do you have the basement covered?' Sullivan asks the SCO19 officer, watching the lights above the lift doors flashing on and off to indicate the floor level the lift is currently at.

'On reflection, I think we might need more men down there,' he says, and rapidly barks yet more instructions into his radio.

'What if they get off the elevator before the ground floor?' Eli questions. 'Podium level, for example.'

'We've got all the lower floor lift exits covered,' the SCO19 officer replies.

'Except for the basement,' Sullivan mutters. The lift indicator light briefly shines on the letter P for podium, then off again. Then on the letter L for lobby, and then off again. Finally, it comes to rest illuminated at B for basement level.

Chapter 55

It is almost as if Eli Rosin had written the script. For that reason alone, the Chinese team's planned getaway is doomed to failure. There were just two armed officers in the basement when the officer standing beside Sullivan and Eli had ordered reinforcements. By the time the lift comes to rest at basement level, another four have just run down the stairwell from the lobby and are fanning out in various directions across the car park. Six armed officers against three unsuspecting Chinese. For anyone trying to escape, it isn't great odds.

The three Chinese agents have discarded their paramedics' uniforms during the descent from the forty-second floor. When they emerge, wheeling the trolley bearing Holly Williams' inert form, they look to all intents and purposes like police officers. They walk with the confident air of a team who have just got away with the impossible. Which, in its way, is fitting. They almost have.

Almost but not quite.

The armed units have clear orders. The principal shooter is a top marksman. He is positioned in what turns out to be the ideal location – in the shadow of a small pick-up van, some forty metres to the rear of the Chinese escape vehicle. His tripod is mounted on the van's bonnet. The marksman waits until the Chinese have manoeuvred Holly's inert body into the boot of the getaway vehicle. He then fires off three silenced rounds in rapid succession. One into the calf muscle of each of the three agents. Wounded, but not fatally, they are quickly surrounded by more armed police. Handcuffs are applied and then real ambulances called.

Chapter 56

Lewis needs to be extra-vigilant now that he's back in central London. The security level in the capital remains at an all-time high following the previous day's shooting. He can't afford to forget for one moment that he's a wanted man – for a murder he didn't commit, but still a wanted man. For that reason, he's chosen the same location where he and Li-Jing had regrouped after Doherty had been shot twenty-four hours previously. The same small café in Regent's Park. As before, the place is nearly deserted at two-thirty in the afternoon. It's as good a place as any to make the call he needs to make.

This time, the line goes through to voicemail and Lewis asks Sullivan to call him back urgently on the same number. Sure enough, the phone lights up less than a minute later.

'Jake, what news?'

'We have her, Ben. She's safe. I'm here in the hospital with Saul. She's been through the mill, but she's okay.'

Lewis temporarily puts the phone down and pinches the bridge of his nose. He can feel the release of tension in his body. His mind wanders for a few moments, brought back to reality by the sound of his name being shouted from the phone's speaker.

'Ben? Ben? Are you there?'

'Sorry, Jake. I was having a moment. Can I speak to her?'

'Not yet. Soon, but not yet. You and I need to talk first.'

'I need to speak to her.'

'She's groggy, Ben. We nearly didn't get to her in time. Some Chinese bastards nearly beat us to it. They already had her sedated.'

'Just put the phone to her ear and tell her not to say anything. I'm just going to say a few words. Okay?'

'All right, here goes.'

Lewis waits a few seconds then takes a breath and begins.

When he's finished, the next voice he hears is Sullivan's.

'Whatever it is that you said, it made her smile. Now, you and I need to talk.'

'There's a café in Regent's Park. Just off the Inner Circle. Meet me there in forty-five minutes. Come alone. I'll be watching. If I see a shadow, the meeting's off. Do we have a deal?'

'Yes, Ben. I'll be there. Alone.'

Chapter 57

Forty-five minutes later, Lewis observes from a distance as Sullivan is dropped off by his driver, the car quickly pulling away out of sight. He follows the MI5 man as he enters the eatery and finds an isolated table away from other people. There appear to be no other watchers. He leaves it another five minutes to make sure. Satisfied there are no tails, he approaches Sullivan's table from the rear, pulls up a chair and sits down. The two men shake hands briefly.

'Good to see you, Ben.'

'You too, Jake. How's Holly?'

'She owes you. If it hadn't been for you finding Eli's phone message, who knows what might have happened.' He scrolls down his phone for a few seconds before finding something and passing it across the table to Lewis. It shows a picture, taken in hospital, fifty minutes earlier. Holly is looking at the camera, smiling weakly.

'She told me to say hi. I'll spare you the slushy stuff. Do you want a drink? I bought two bottles of water and some tea for us both. I couldn't remember what you liked.'

'Thanks,' Lewis says, picking up the water and twisting the plastic cap. He takes a swig and looks at Sullivan. 'You say the Chinese had her?'

Sullivan explains what had happened.

'They had some nerve. Right from under our noses, too. How bad would that have been? At least we caught them all.'

'There were another two I had to fend off earlier. Including their main agent. The man I'm convinced killed Li-Jing.' Lewis describes the events at the landfill earlier in the day.

'I'd heard about that from Saul. The Cambridgeshire police picked up the pair of them a while ago. In quite a bad way, apparently.'

'They were lucky to be alive. How's Saul? Does he still think I killed the girl? Or have the lunchtime arrests finally provided him with an alternative suspect?'

Sullivan eyes Lewis carefully.

'Saul's suddenly not in great shape. We've got another situation on our hands, Ben. It's bad. Saul's twin boys, Zach and Nate, have disappeared from school. Taken during the lunch break.'

'Oh, dear God, no!' Lewis slowly puts his head in his hands, the icy feeling returning with a vengeance to the pit of his stomach.

'Saul received a text message a short while ago. Untraceable, of course. Whoever's got the twins wants you in exchange.'

'God help us, Jake! Not the boys! This is over the edge. It's gone way, way too far. Poor Saul. Poor, poor Hattie. This is my fault, I hope you realise that?'

'That's not true, Ben. They're just playing hardball.'

'Bullshit, Jake. I'm going to have this on my conscience all my life. I don't care a shit about those Russian or Chinese bastards. Or the Americans or anyone the fuck else who wants to take me on. But not Saul and Hattie's twins, for God's sake! What have I done, Jake? What have I done?'

The two men look at each other in silence, tears of helpless rage appearing in the corners of Lewis's eyes.

'It'll be the Russians. It can only be them. Ivankov's a bastard. It's precisely the sort of thing he would do. What exactly do they want from me? Where and when is the exchange meant to take place?'

'We're still waiting for them to tell us.'

'Saul must be a mess. Hattie too. What a horrendous, almighty fuck-up.'

'Saul's not taken it well.'

'It can't continue like this, Jake. These last twenty-four hours have been crazy. Totally out of control. Now, Zach and Nate have disappeared and I'm the one responsible. We're not even talking about terrorists here. Just some stupid encryption key and a heck of a lot of stolen money. A rapid change of tempo is needed. Otherwise, this thing will never end without more people being killed. All because of what Doherty told me before he was killed. A man, we shouldn't forget, we all thought was long since dead and buried.'

Lewis reaches into his pocket and retrieves his wallet. From within, he pulls out the white key card that he recovered from the safe house in Whitby.

'This leads to the next stage in Doherty's crazy journey. The more I think about Keiran and his methods, the more I wonder if we might have got him wrong. Perhaps he and Fisher had been a force for good all along? Yes, we had crossed swords in the past. Yes, he had a chip on his shoulder about me in particular. However, deep down, he knew that if he was really up shit creek, I was perhaps one of the very few people he could trust. He knew I might need to be coerced into helping him. Taking Holly was his way of making me jump to his tune. It's the only reason I can think of for him to send me on this wild goose chase. He'd been planning this, Jake. Devising various cryptic clues that led from one mailbox to the next. Clues he knew that only I would ever be able to work out. Anyway, I think you should take over from here. I trust you, Jake. This is the key to a motel room. Room number seven. The clue was this: 'There's only one No-Tell Motel.' When Keiran and I were in basic training, there was this grotty, seedy little motel on the edge of town that just screamed of being a rent-a-room-by-the-hour place. It was on the main road out of Lympstone, on the way to Exmouth. He and I would kid each other that we'd be taking the girls there on our respective nights out. It was our 'No-Tell Motel'. Our little secret. That's where you need to go next. Just you. Please don't tell anybody. Not Saul. Not your assistant. Or even your driver. Not Dame Helen or even Sir Philip. Just go there incognito. Turn off your phone, don't call the office. If these shits have taken Zach and Nate, they will stop at nothing if they find that you are now the man with the key to the portfolio and not me.'

'Thanks, Ben. You've done the right thing. I appreciate it.'

'I suggest a cooling-off period before you pick up Doherty's trail again. Get everyone back on an even keel. Pretend it's all behind us. Perhaps take a well-earned mini-break in a few days? I hear the Devon coastline is stunning at this time of year.'

'I hear you. It's actually a good idea. These last twenty-four hours have been crazy, crazy times.'

'There's only one sensible course of action to end this madness. All roads currently lead to me. The longer I'm alive, the more people will believe I know where Markov's key is. That is going to put people like Holly, Saul and his family – even you, now that I've given you the motel room key – in danger. I can't live with that on my conscience. I'm making a decision, here and now. I want to die, Jake. In a very public manner. With no room for doubt. That way, no one can use my friends and loved ones to make me do things I'm not prepared to do. I need you to promise me that you'll help me with this, Jake. I need to die and I need there to be no ambiguity. All I ask is that you make it quick, painless and very public.'

'You are not serious, Ben?'

'Deadly. If you want Zach and Nate alive and with you still in control of this whole crazy operation, it's the only way. I have an idea how to get them back, by the way.'

'Tell me.'

Lewis explains.

'Does it need to happen this way, Ben?'

'It's the best solution. Otherwise, Saul's boys will end up in body bags. We need a watertight plan. One that, once and for all, will bring an end to this kidnap madness. This plan will work. Don't worry. By the time it's all done and dusted, I should already be enjoying the afterlife.'

Chapter 58

'Good evening, this is the Six O'Clock News from the BBC.

'A man has been shot dead by police this afternoon in London's Regent's Park. The victim, a one-time former Marine on the run and wanted in connection with the murder of a Malaysian student, was named by police this evening as Ben Lewis. Lewis, aged 32, had a history of violent offences. The police had also wanted him for questioning in relation to the shooting of a former Marine colleague in London's Granary Square yesterday afternoon. After a nationwide manhunt, Lewis was spotted and challenged by an armed officer from the Metropolitan Police's Specialist Firearms Command at a café in Regent's Park. Lewis is believed to have drawn a weapon before being shot dead with a single round. No one else was injured in the incident.'

Chapter 59

Saul Zeltinger and his wife, Hattie, huddle around the kitchen table, staring at the television screen. On the table beside them, in addition to half-finished mugs of tea and an unopened packet of biscuits, are several makes and models of phone. Sitting with them is Max, a trained hostage negotiator. Max speaks softly and gently but with an authority that is reassuring and professional. Max exudes knowledge and confidence about every aspect of what the Zeltingers might be facing: how he expects them to be feeling; what the next steps are likely to be; even a realistic assessment of timescales. Also in the room with them is a female police welfare officer, Diane. Zeltinger has never met either of them before but their presence is reassuring. Diane busies herself by making several cups of tea. Even in a half-German household like the Zeltingers', this very British activity proves surprisingly soothing and welcome.

Saul and Hattie are in their version of hell. They have just listened to the bulletin on the six o'clock news, struggling to come to terms with Lewis's death. Saul's lack of sleep these past twenty-four hours only makes acceptance and understanding more complicated. Lewis's death is a hammer blow, felt even more acutely given the close linkages to, and parallels with, the twins' kidnapping. It brings sharply into focus the reality that both boys' lives could also be on a knife-edge. There had been no mention of the abduction in the news bulletin for which Saul, in particular, was grateful.

'What will this mean for the boys, Saul?' Hattie asks her husband, her head in her hands and tears flowing down her cheeks.

Saul doesn't answer immediately. Instead, he purses his lips, finding it hard to keep his emotions in check. His eyes well up as he tries to choose his words with care.

'I expect,' he says with some effort, 'or rather I hope, it will help. We mustn't antagonise the kidnappers. With Lewis dead, they either release the boys, or they make other demands.'

'Won't they simply release them?'

'Who knows? Every hostage situation is different. Max, what do you think?'

When Max speaks, his voice remains calm and even.

'I agree it's less likely that whoever it is will keep the boys for a long period.'

With that, the room falls silent. The Zeltingers sink into their own private, dark thoughts.

'Did you know about Ben?' Hattie asks her husband later. They are gripping each other's hand as they stare at the now-muted television screen.

'I knew he was wanted for questioning. But not this.' Zeltinger looks at his wife and tries to smile through watery eyes. 'He was sitting next to this man, Doherty, in Granary Square. I was meant to be there, playing chess with him. I got held up. Doherty was once a Marine, like Ben. Doherty asked Ben to do something which he knew Ben wouldn't have volunteered to do naturally. So, he kidnapped Holly as a way of ensuring that Ben did what he wanted. Next thing, out of the blue, Doherty gets shot by a sniper and Ben has been on the run ever since.'

'What about this Malaysian woman?'

'She died in Ben's hotel bedroom yesterday evening. On the face of it, evidence points to Ben as being the prime suspect. I was with the forensic team at three o'clock this morning. It was looking conclusive. Then, earlier this afternoon, we got another lead on a different possible killer. We've still more forensic work to do to prove the case against this other man, but I am quietly confident. You know me, I've always wanted to believe that Ben was innocent.'

'In which case, Ben has been killed for no reason! This is madness. What was the firearms officer doing? Ben was your friend! Our friend. Now he's dead. What does that tell us about getting our boys back alive? Oh God, I am so worried about them.'

'We must be patient. I know it's unbearable, but that's the game these people play.' He glances at Max, who reassuringly nods his head. 'The firearms officer was only doing his job. If Ben had pulled a gun, then the other man had no choice but to shoot first.'

Zeltinger's mobile starts simultaneously ringing and vibrating on the table in front of him. He picks it up quickly, looks at the caller ID and presses the button to take the call.

'Saul, it's Jake. Have you been watching the news?'

'We're devastated. In total shock. What happened? Why did they have to kill Ben?'

'I've no idea. I know little more than you. It's the worst possible outcome. How are you coping?'

'Not well. I've been stood down from work until we know the boys are safe. We have a hostage negotiator here with us and a welfare officer.'

'Who've you got?'

'A man called Max and a lady called Diane.'

'If he's the Max I've met before, he's very, very good.'

'I wish I could be confident of a good outcome, Jake. Ben's death has completely spooked us.'

'I'm sure. I just wanted to let you both know that I'm on the case, Saul. Actively on the case. Quietly optimistic. With Ben out of the picture, I suspect perversely that it makes it easier to reach a good outcome.'

'I hope to God something good comes out of Ben's needless death, Jake. Hattie and I are at our wits' end. I'm not sure we can take much more of this.'

Chapter 60

The address – Moscow Road, near London's Bayswater – seems an ironic choice of location for a man in such a position. A specialist from Sullivan's operation had visited earlier in the evening to tamper with the alarm system. Someone extremely skilled. The operative had also found two panic buttons, which she had disabled. Her tradecraft now allows the latest intruder to enter the place undetected at shortly after nine in the evening, the alarm system outwardly giving the appearance that it is still set.

Deep in the intruder's inside left pocket is a Glock 19 handgun. Technically it is a Glock 23, but it had been converted to a 9mm format. Suppressed, of course. Hollow-point ammunition. Fifteen rounds in the magazine. More than enough for the job in hand.

Ten minutes ago, a Tweet had caught the intruder's eye. It was from his new Twitter friend, @MadDog3x. The Tweet was posted at 8.52 pm and simply said: *See you in 20, Honey!*

At 9.13 pm, the intruder hears a key in the front door latch, the sound of deadbolts being unlocked. Then a second key in a different lock, and finally the door is opened. The alarm starts to beep. The intruder hears the sound of the keypad being used to disable the security system, followed by the front door closing. Thankfully, the person is alone. The hall light switches on and the person heads upstairs, presumably to change. Three minutes later, they are back downstairs, heading to the kitchen. The fridge door can be heard opening and a bottle removed. The person then comes down the corridor and into the living room, turning on the lights and drawing the curtains in what is a familiar pattern. It is only then that Alexei Polunin turns around, nearly jumping out of his skin when he sees Ben Lewis sitting in his favourite armchair. The silenced Glock is pointing directly at the Russian.

'Sit down, Alexei. No strange or sudden moves please, or I will kill you.' Lewis gestures with his gun towards the sofa immediately opposite him. Cautiously, Polunin sits.

'We heard that you had died, Lewis. Another fake news story! Too bad. I was about to have a celebratory beer.'

'Don't let me stop you. How's the head?'

A year ago, Lewis had sent a hefty padlock hurtling in Polunin's direction outside an apartment block in Cambridge. It had landed with extreme force.

'Go screw yourself.'

Which causes Lewis to fire off one warning round. It pierces the leather headrest next to Polunin's right ear, missing by centimetres.

'I like the Glock. Such a simple but effective weapon. Even with the gunsight slightly obscured, I find it accurate. Let's cut the abusive talk, Alexei. We have things to discuss, you and I.'

'How did you get in here?'

'You should check your alarm installation company. They're not very good.' Lewis watches as Polunin's left hand, casually sprawled over the arm of the sofa, starts inching its way down the left side panel. Lewis fires off another round, this one almost grazing Polunin's fingertips. 'I wouldn't try, Alexei. Not even the panic buttons seem to be working. Sorry about that.'

'What do you want, Lewis?'

'That, my friend, is simple. What I want is for two children currently held in your custody to be released. We don't have much time, I'm afraid.'

'I don't know what you are talking about,' he says and then screams, as Lewis fires a round that pierces Polunin's left kneecap. The hollow-point round takes no prisoners.

'I think I misheard you, Alexei. Did you say they were in Pyotr Ivankov's care?'

Polunin drops the beer bottle and writhes around on the floor, trying to stem the blood flowing from his knee.

'I didn't hear you, Alexei. Do you need another bullet? Perhaps in the other knee?'

'No . . .' the Russian eventually gasps. 'Please . . . I'll . . . tell . . . you.'

'I'm listening.' Lewis is now standing, his silenced weapon aimed at the Russian.

'One . . . of . . . Ivankov's . . . men . . . have . . . them.'

'Where, exactly?'

'Near . . . Victoria.'

'Very good. So, Alexei, if you want me to spare your life, the drill is this. You're going to phone this person. Tell him to put the children in a taxi and send them directly to Thames House, on Millbank. No tricks. No code words. Tell them that since Ben Lewis is dead, you have new orders. The children go free. Do we understand each other, Alexei?'

'Da,' the Russian says, the pain beginning to throb badly in his knee joint as the initial shock wears off.

'One more thing, Alexei. Someone is waiting outside Thames House right now. If the children are not in his custody in fifteen minutes, you will lose your right knee. Is that fair? One more thing. My Russian's not bad these days. Besides, the electronic spooks will be listening to your every word. So, no tricks. Last and final warning.'

Lewis sits and watches Polunin make the call. He speaks with the other party for just twenty seconds. He puts on a brave act. To Lewis's poor linguistic ear, it sounds as if Polunin plays it straight. Lewis reaches for his new electronic device and sends a Tweet into the ether, timed at 9.22 pm. It comes from his new Twitter persona, @HairyHound4, and reads: *Show-time in fifteen. Coming from Victoria.*

'I hear your ambassador got a mauling, Alexei. Ivankov's been careless, recently. I thought he was meant to be better than Panich?'

'With . . . me . . . Lewis . . . it's . . . professional. With . . . Ivankov . . . it's . . . personal.'

Lewis counts down the minutes. He checks his device at 9.37 pm.

'Sounds like you've been bullshitting me, Alexei. The children haven't arrived. To be fair, I'll give you a choice. Right knee or right ankle?'

'No! Wait . . . Please!'

Lewis aims the gun at Polunin's right knee and pauses.

'You've got a minute's grace, Alexei. Would you like me to count down?'

'You . . . bastard,' is all he says before Lewis hears a ping on his device. He has a new Tweet. It is from @MadDog3x. Sent at 9.38 pm. It simply reads: *All safe, sound and in good spirits.*

'Well done, Alexei.' Lewis beams sarcastically at the frightened man. 'Very well handled. As one professional to another, let me put you out of your misery.'

With that, Lewis raises the handgun and fires a single round at point-blank range, straight between the Russian's eyes.

Chapter 61

Even though he considers himself resourceful, Lewis is still grateful for the one thousand pounds in cash and the pre-loaded disposable credit card that Sullivan has given him along with the Glock. Those items aside, Lewis has brought nothing into his new life from his old. No credit cards, no driving licence, no mobile phones. Nothing. His one guilty pleasure is a small electronic gizmo allowing Lewis periodically to check Twitter feeds on a particular Twitter account. The only method that he's agreed with Sullivan for communication between the two in Lewis's afterlife.

Ordinarily, he might have liked a passport as well. For the moment, he is content to begin this enforced cooling-off period in the UK. His first consideration, therefore, is where to go? The second is transport. Tackling the problems arguably in the wrong order, he realises that solving the transport issue is straightforward. He already has a motorbike, currently at Peterborough station. Although his bike keys are still with the Chinese agents he sent on the wild goose chase to Highgate, that is hardly about to cause him problems he can't solve. Lewis has stripped and reassembled his Honda so many times, he knows the workings backwards. Hot-wiring the starter won't take more than twenty seconds. Perhaps thirty in the dark.

The geographic question is more challenging until he realises that there is a solution staring him in the face. The safe house near Whitby. It's currently empty and thus almost perfect. True, Sullivan knows of its existence. Certainly no one, apart from Sullivan, should be able to link Lewis to the place. If minded to consider it, the Americans would only think of it in terms of a once-used dead letter drop. From Peterborough, it would be a three-hour bike ride.

Trains to Peterborough run late into the night. From Polunin's flat, he takes the Underground to King's Cross station and buys a train ticket on the station concourse using his new credit card. It is made out in the name of Tom Ruff, Lewis's new name. Beggars couldn't always be choosers, but on first impressions, Lewis quite likes the idea of becoming Tom Ruff.

Lewis, or more accurately Ruff, arrives at Peterborough station shortly before midnight. His bike is exactly where he left it, thankfully unclamped and without a parking ticket. With practised ease, he reaches underneath the seat to where the ignition cable connector is located, deftly unclipping the tiny plastic straps that hold the two ends together. Using a paperclip that he has bent double into a U-shape, he pushes the two ends hard into the parallel slots in the connector and is rewarded by the sound of the bike's power switching on. It is as simple as that. All that remains is to press the ignition, and the bike is ready to go – twenty-two seconds from start to finish.

It is a long, cold ride, most of it by the light of a nearly full moon. When he eventually reaches the farmhouse, he parks his bike in the same place he had before, out of sight of anyone approaching the property. For reasons he can't fathom, it feels longer than twenty-four hours since he was last here. All evidence of the Americans, their two Yamahas and the car, has been removed. The front door, however, still has the splintered lock, courtesy of an American boot. Lewis resolves to repair it in the morning. Entering the property and pushing the door as near-shut as it will go, he doesn't turn on any lights, instead letting his eyes become accustomed to the dark. Satisfied that he can see enough, he performs a quick recce, aided by the brightness of the moon outside. The house is spartan but adequately furnished. In addition to a table and chairs in the main living room, there is a large sofa next to the fireplace. A place that, for the time being, is going to serve as his bed for the night. He uses the bathroom, finds a glass in a kitchen cupboard and runs himself a much-needed drink of water from the tap. Then, after testing the sofa for comfort, within seconds he falls wearily into a deep sleep.

Chapter 62

Lewis doesn't stir until after ten the next morning.

His first thought is about Holly. She will be starting her first day out of captivity thinking that Lewis is dead. He wonders how she's coping. He wants to call her. If the roles were reversed and he had woken knowing Holly had died, he would be finding it tough. Though he yearns to speak with her, for the time being it's best for her safety if she remains in the dark about him being alive. Instead, he imagines Saul's and Hattie's faces when the two boys returned home the previous evening, unaware that they had their friend to thank for that.

In daylight, he inspects the upstairs rooms, finding beds that look perfectly serviceable. There is even a linen cupboard with clean sheets and blankets, further evidence that this had been a safe house at one time. Downstairs in the kitchen, all the food has been cleared out, except for basic tea and coffee-making items. Lewis fills a kettle and starts to prepare a mug of strong, black coffee. Whilst the kettle boils, he searches the room leading away from the kitchen at the back of the house. It is a utility room, with a few basic tools – a hammer, saw, some nails and assorted screwdrivers – in one cupboard. He brings these into the kitchen in preparation for mending the splintered door jamb. There are some spare house keys on a dresser in the kitchen, Lewis testing them on both door locks and finding they fit perfectly. Then, taking his newly made mug of coffee, he wanders outside to explore the outbuildings.

In time, he returns carrying bits of wood that he hopes will allow him to repair the door frame. He has also come across a useful length of rounded, wooden fence pole, about three inches in diameter. Cut down to about eighteen inches in length, it will make a useful additional weapon to complement the Glock. Old technology: often the most reliable.

Mending the door takes most of the morning. Nailing the freshly sawn and shaped pieces of timber into the space where the old door jamb had been, he stands back, proud of his handiwork. All that remains is to gouge out the recesses for the locks. In the absence of a chisel, Lewis reverts to using a screwdriver and hammer. It is a slow and not exceptionally tidy piece of carpentry, but the job gets finished and the door can finally be securely locked once more.

Lewis's bereavement doesn't just involve his friends and loved ones. He has arrived in his version of the afterlife with no phone, no tablet computer and strict rules about internet access: only when absolutely necessary and even then, only for checking Twitter feeds. He agreed with Sullivan that he wouldn't connect to any wireless network unless he was well away from somewhere he didn't want to be found, to all intents and purposes making him impossible to track down. It's a slightly scary new world, both unfamiliar and liberating in equal measure. It forces him to revert to old ways to discover more about his new neighbourhood. In practical terms, this means getting on his bike and using two wheels, rather than technology, to go exploring.

Sticking to the back roads but heading generally in the direction of Whitby, he finds a decent looking pub five minutes away called the Lamb and Flag. A signboard outside says that it serves hot food and Lewis quickly realises that he is famished. Inside, the bartender, a pretty woman of about Lewis's age called Sarah, is alone behind the bar and delighted to have company. Lewis orders a beer together with a steak and ale pie and sits at the counter in preference to being consigned to a lonely table in the corner. The pub isn't busy, Sarah finding plenty of time to chat in between serving the occasional customer. She proves fun company, asking few intrusive questions and content to talk to another human being about everything and nothing. It's as if Tom Ruff has stepped into a parallel universe. Living a normal life for once, not worried about who might be following him and whether they might be armed. The food is excellent, the conversation lively and in good humour, and when it's time to go, he finds himself sad to leave. He leaves a generous tip and Sarah, in return, gives him a warm hug. On the way out, she asks whether he will be back sometime soon. To his surprise, Tom Ruff finds himself promising that he will.

Back home, he falls asleep on the unmade bed in the upstairs bedroom. It is a drop-off-the-cliff type of afternoon sleep that Lewis hasn't enjoyed for years. He wakes feeling rested but suddenly missing companionship. If chatting with Sarah had done anything, it had reminded him how much he craved female company. If only he could call Holly. Soon, he reminds himself. This, after all, was meant to be a cooling-off period.

Chapter 63

Three days of enforced rest with not a lot happening, and the man who is now Tom Ruff is bored. He has explored Whitby and the surrounding villages, been back to the Lamb and Flag two days running and concluded that it is only Sarah's gentle flirting that is preventing Tom Ruff from going completely stir crazy. Sarah's end-of-lunch, warm, goodbye hugs have become a highlight. On the morning of the third day he wakes, restless, suddenly feeling a need to check his Twitter feed. He drives along the coast road from Whitby towards Middlesbrough, eventually finding a place to stop near the outskirts of the city. This, he judges, should be a safe enough location to turn on Sullivan's electronic gizmo. He is about to leave the world of Tom Ruff and no commitments and dip back into his old life. There is one Tweet waiting for him that he hasn't read. It is from @MadDog3x. The Tweet, short and sweet, was posted at 8.32 that morning. *Speak soonest.*

Lewis drives into the city centre heading for the main railway station. He parks his bike and hunts for a payphone. Sure enough, near the station entrance, he finds an empty phone booth and dials the number that Sullivan had made him commit to memory.

'Jake, this is Tom Ruff returning your call.'

'Hi Tom, how are you doing?'

'Just fine, thanks. How're things with you?'

'Oh, you know, so-so. I had to go to the funeral of a good friend, yesterday – organised in something of a hurry, but it was a fair turnout. A lot of emotion and a lot of intrigue. How about you?'

'Chilling out and cooling off in equal measure. In fact, rather restless, to tell the truth.'

'Are you staying at that old cottage near the sea, by any chance? The one we were talking about the other day?'

'Yes. It's great. No Americans or anyone. Quite the rest cure. Why? Do you want to drop by sometime?'

'Sadly, I can't. Much too busy at work. Maybe another time. Anyway, Tom, I can't stay and chat. I've work to do. Speak to you anon!'

Lewis hangs up and then feels his electronic device buzz in his pocket. Another Tweet has just arrived. It is from @MadDog3x posted at 9.47 that morning. One minute earlier. *I'll be dropping by this afternoon.*

Chapter 64

Lewis is chopping logs, labouring with a rusty old axe behind one of the brick outbuildings, when he hears the car. He skirts the neat stack of chopped firewood that he's already prepared and peers around the edge of the barn. It is a rental: a white Volvo with the latest registration. Jake Sullivan is the driver and only person in the vehicle. Lewis brushes wood chippings from his body and comes across to greet his friend.

'It's good to see you, Jake. A familiar face, finally.'

'Four days that seem like a lifetime.'

'Tell me about it! Come on in. I've got a pot of tea all ready to go.'

'It's not as outrageous as people think.' He pauses to sip from his mug. 'Heck, that's good tea,' Sullivan says, taking another mouthful. 'Taking a private jet, I mean. The Service has a block deal with one of the charterers. It works out only marginally more expensive in the long run than flying scheduled. Sometimes cheaper.'

'Tell me about the funeral? It must have been weird.'

'You could say that. I don't think anyone found it easy – and I include myself in that statement. It got me thinking. Unless you're planning to remain as Tom Ruff, living out a new life with a new identity in the same way that Doherty and Fraser did, then I think Holly, Saul and his wife ought to be told. It's going to mess them up completely otherwise. Assuming, that is, that you still plan on walking back into their lives?'

Lewis briefly considers the last few days he's spent as Tom Ruff. His new life. There had been a few highs. Undisturbed sleep had been one. Flirting with Sarah at the Lamb and Flag had been another. He can't deny, however, that even after only a short time he's become restless, if not downright bored. His thoughts return to Holly, and immediately he knows what his response to Sullivan's question will be.

'I want you to tell them. Is there any way Holly could come up here?'

'I don't see why not. What about Saul and his wife?'

'Have all murder charges against me been dropped?'

'That question comes with an answer in two parts. The police have charged a Chinese citizen in connection with Li-Jing's murder. When he was arrested, they found a weapon on him that had been used on the girl, exactly as you intimated. There were even traces of the girl's DNA on it. What sealed it was that one of the latex gloves that he'd been wearing when he strangled the Chinese girl had split. Forensics matched a portion of his thumbprint to one or two smudged prints found at the crime scene. They're so damned clever these days. That's one murder that's no longer going to be pinned on Ben Lewis, dead or alive. The record has been struck clean. Expunged. However,' he says, taking another mouthful of tea, 'there is still the murder of Alexei Polunin to be resolved.'

'Do I know the man, Jake?'

'Did you have to kill him, Ben? The Zeltinger kids were free. You could have just left him alive, surely?'

'No, I couldn't. Those bastards would have more than likely murdered the twins out of spite rather than let them go free. Plus, Polunin knew by then that I was still alive. I couldn't take the chance. Anyway, I wore gloves. All the bullets and shell casings were clean. No one will ever know I was there.'

'I am not happy about it, Ben. We've had a hell of a bust-up with the Russians trying to sort everything out.'

'They're the ones who kidnapped the twins, for God's sake. Anyway, it was you who gave me the gun, remember?'

'No need to remind me. We'll let the matter rest for moment, but for the record, I'm not happy.'

'Back to Holly, Saul and Hattie. Please talk to them, now that the funeral's out of the way. Be gentle. Tell them we had to do it this way to spare their lives. If Holly could come up here for a few days, that would be terrific. Tell Saul and Hattie that I'll drop by unannounced one evening soon and say hello. Leave it vague. Tell me, are you planning on taking that holiday to Devon sometime soon?'

'I'm heading down there the day after tomorrow.'

'Good. I'd like to know what the next link in Doherty's puzzle is.'

'That makes two of us. Look, I need to confess something, Ben. It's one of the reasons I came here in person. To tell you. Don't get mad – I gave the matter a huge amount of thought. I decided to tell two people about your current predicament. I know it's not what we agreed, but it's a chain of command thing. The more I considered it, the more I felt duty-bound to let them know. They don't know where you are or what your current alias is. They just know you're alive.'

Lewis looks sternly at Sullivan.

'Jake, that might just have been one of the most stupid decisions you ever made. Who did you tell?'

'Helen Morgan.'

'Bloody hell, Jake.'

'She's my boss, for fuck's sake, Ben. One of the top and most trusted civil servants in the country. Who, having heard the story, insisted she convene a private meeting with Sir Philip Musson at MI6. Same goes for him – one of our most respected senior Whitehall mandarins. I was also invited along. A minion. That was it – no one else. Sir Philip and Dame Helen are the pair who, it now transpires, ran Doherty and Fisher. It was a deeply covert, completely off the books, operation. No one else in either service knows a damned thing. Not even funded out of the public purse. Doherty told you as much when he met you. Both Musson and Morgan are as senior as it gets. Your secret is safe in their hands.'

'Oh, come off it! This is a mistake on so many levels. You knew I wouldn't be happy, and I'm not. We went through this charade to cool things down and protect Holly and the Zeltingers. If this has, in any way, put their lives in danger, then on your head be it.'

Lewis stalks off angrily, leaving Sullivan to stew along with his pot of tea. When he returns, Lewis is carrying the Glock pistol.

'I was going to return this when I saw you next. Now I've changed my mind. I am going to keep it until I know this whole business is over. I just hope to God I don't have to use it.'

'Trust me when I say this, Ben: so do I.'

'What's been everyone's reaction to the fact that I'm dead?' Lewis asks, changing the subject whilst stuffing the Glock down the back of a sofa cushion behind him. 'Let's start with the Americans?'

'We had a big pow-wow yesterday. Kathleen Thomas flew over from Langley. She even came to your funeral. Also at this get-together was Greg Fuscoe and the pair who showed up here. A black guy, Sanders, and another one called Krantz. From our side, there was Dame Helen, Saul and myself. They came to apologise, which was generous. For their behaviour. They said that in their zeal to repossess what they had seen as their stolen property, they had allowed themselves to get carried away. They now wanted to propose a different approach – a more collaborative way of working. Whichever party found their way to the encryption key first would promise to share it with the other, because of the Special Relationship. By way of a peace offering, they had some interesting drone footage to share, proving conclusively that Fisher was murdered by an assassin dressed in black.'

'That's one puzzle solved. I never believed Fisher shot Doherty. This assassin. Do you think it was the Russians or the Chinese? It has to be one of the two.'

'I'd wager the Russians. I mentioned it in passing the other day to the Russian ambassador, but he blew me off.'

'In what way?'

'Told me not to make wild-ass guesses unless we could substantiate such a claim.'

'Tell me about the Russians.'

'There was a hell of a shouting match about Polunin's murder. The police, MI5, and various Russian forensics people have been all over his flat with a fine-toothed comb. As you suggested, there were no prints that gave any clues to the murderer's identity. The alarm system had been tampered with.'

Both men look at each other in silence, Sullivan raising his eyebrows before drinking some tea.

'Anyway, the SVR operation in London must now be down to the absolute barest minimum. We had to expel four of them for the incident in Soho the other night. That only leaves your friend Ivankov to worry about. He's gone to ground. We haven't seen him for a few days.'

'Maybe he's back in Moscow getting fresh orders.'

'Let's hope he doesn't come back. Which leaves the Chinese. We hauled in their ambassador two days ago along with a man called Cheng, their head of London Station. Sir Philip Musson was there. My godfathers, did they get a roasting. The agent who was arrested for Li-Jing's murder is having the book thrown at him for murder. I hope for his sake they keep him in a British prison and don't deport him. He'll be a dead man if he's sent back to China. The other person who dragged you to that gravel pit has already gone home, as have the two you sent on that wild goose chase to Highgate. Plus the bogus medics who tried to kidnap Holly. Oh, before I forget.'

He digs in his pocket and withdraws a set of keys and hands them across.

'These are yours. I thought you might need them back.'

Lewis smiles and puts them gratefully back in his pocket.

'Thanks. What you're suggesting is that everything appears to have quietened down, for the time being. I'm not sure I believe it.'

'I wouldn't be so cynical.'

'Have the Chinese expressed any interest in the encryption key?'

'It wasn't specifically mentioned but it's clear that they want it. It was hinted at, obliquely of course. Very Chinese. Their cyber-analysts had traced Doherty's missing one hundred million dollars. It went, via a circuitous route, to an account in his name at a London art gallery. The money was used to buy a Mark Rothko original. A private sale from a collection owned by Qatari clients. No one has any idea where the painting is now. It was strongly hinted at that if we recovered whatever Doherty had taken and were prepared to share the bounty with them, then all sorts of beneficial UK-China economic trade deals might be forthcoming.'

'So, a good time for you to be visiting the No-Tell Motel.'

'I agree. Talking of which, I should be on my way. I'll ping you a Tweet in the next day or so, once I've spoken to Holly and Saul.'

Lewis sees his friend out to the car and waves to him as he drives off.

With Sullivan telling certain people about the Ben Lewis resurrection story, Lewis no longer feels confident about who will know what any more. Which brought its own risks and threats. If nothing else, of breaking the peaceful calm of the last few days. Especially if Lewis's recent past was allowed to catch up with him.

The no man's land between Ben Lewis, on the one hand, and Tom Ruff, on the other suddenly feels under threat. As Sullivan departs, the border crossing back into his old life closes once more. However, this time the gates no longer feel as securely shut as they did previously. Lewis needs the boundary to remain impenetrable until it becomes safe and appropriate for Ben Lewis to resurface for good. What had been a deserted and tranquil haven now feels as if menace might once again be lurking at its edges.

Chapter 65

Having apologised and grovelled in front of her British counterparts, Kathleen Thomas is no sooner safely airborne in her Langley-bound private jet than Greg Fuscoe is calling an impromptu meeting with Sanders and Krantz in his office. They are about to get new orders.

During Thomas's visit to London, Langley's official line had been all sweetness and promised co-operation in the spirit of the Special Relationship. Privately, Fuscoe wants Sanders and Krantz on a different agenda. *Sotto voce*, the message from the White House is unequivocal. Do whatever it takes to get the encryption key and screw the Special Relationship.

'What do you guys think?' Fuscoe asks, once he has outlined the new game plan.

'The zillion-dollar question is whether Lewis took the encryption key with him to his grave,' Krantz says.

'Assuming that Lewis is dead,' Sanders adds sharply.

'What do you mean by that?' Fuscoe asks. 'Of course he's dead. The man's just been cremated, for God's sake. You heard Sullivan yesterday. He was so fucking depressed, I thought he was about to burst into tears.'

'What do we know?' Sanders persists. 'Sullivan's a spook. He might be a world-class actor. All I'm saying is that it's just a little too convenient that Lewis is no longer with us.'

'You've got to stop being so cynical, Oscar. We need to move on. If

245

Lewis miraculously resurrects himself, then for sure, let's rethink the plan. For now, what other options do we have?'

'The Chinese nearly kidnapped the girl,' Krantz continues. 'That says they needed the leverage and are no nearer the encryption key than we are. Ditto for the Russians. They kidnapped the detective's children to put the screws on Lewis to reveal all. Besides, from what we hear, they've been largely wiped out for the moment. Except for that fucking giant, Ivankov.'

'Realistically, is the girl likely to know anything?' Sanders asks. 'I doubt it.'

'Very unlikely,' Fuscoe adds.

'I still maintain we're being played,' Sanders persists. 'Shut out all too conveniently by the Brits. Whether Lewis is alive or not is irrelevant. I suspect Sullivan knows more than he's prepared to let on. Why don't you keep him under surveillance? Ivankov as well. If any new leads are going to develop, it's likely to come from one of these two.'

'What about Lewis's detective friend? It was his kids who the Russians took.'

'Sure, if we have enough resources. By the way, do we know why the kids were released so quickly?'

'I never got around to asking Sullivan yesterday. Maybe I should have?'

'Tough for Polunin that he had to take a bullet for his troubles. How convenient. London's becoming a dangerous place these days,' Krantz says.

'I vote we focus on Sullivan and Ivankov for the time being,' Sanders chips in. 'Let's not spread ourselves too thin. They seem to be the main players.'

'You happy with that, Mickey?' Fuscoe asks Krantz.

'Works for me. What resources can you spare, Greg?'

Chapter 66

The night after Sullivan's visit, Lewis decides to place the Glock under his mattress. He sleeps less deeply as a result, the old vigilance back. He wakes at daybreak and makes himself a coffee, worrying how Holly will be coping, wondering how she will react to the news that he's still alive. He places the Glock back behind the sofa cushion whilst he fixes himself a light breakfast. The morning is then spent back outside chopping yet more logs, working up a sweat in the chilly air and then stacking the logs neatly beside the fireplace. He takes a long shower and looks at himself in the bathroom mirror.

Is he Ben Lewis today or Tom Ruff? Does it matter? It feels odd but okay to have a new persona.

Lunchtime approaches and the lure of the Lamb and Flag feels like an irresistible magnet. He didn't go the previous day. The place is empty, apart from one table where two business types are eating in a corner. Sarah is once more behind the bar, smiling broadly when she sees him. She comes forward to give him a warm, welcoming embrace, her eyes sparkling with genuine pleasure. Tom Ruff is happy to reciprocate, opting once more to sit at the bar. By default, he's now almost a regular. He orders fish and chips off the lunch menu and selects a pint of local beer. She, in turn, flirts with him more than ever, happy to find himself relaxing in her company. When it's time to clear his plate, she leans across the counter and whispers into his ear.

'If you're not busy, you could always come by at three and pick me up?' she says softly. 'It'd be fun to spend a little time together, don't you think?' She fingers the collar of his jacket. 'I have to be back by five-thirty, though – I'm working the evening shift.' She breathes warmly into his ear. 'That would still give us over two hours to fill.' She wrinkles her nose at him as she pulls away, smiling, her head on one side.

Tom Ruff is tempted. Ben Lewis might be spoken for, but it is not hard for his alter ego to imagine the wild passion that would, without question, flow during an afternoon with Sarah. To his regret, after due consideration, Tom Ruff finds himself slowly shaking his head.

'I shouldn't. It's so tempting, but I'm spoken for, I'm sorry,' he finds himself saying, mindful about what he is turning down. 'It's a tough call, and very tempting, but I think not.' He pauses. 'Not right now at any rate.' He smiles sheepishly.

'Who might this lucky woman be who lures you like a siren away from my clutches?'

Lewis laughs at her theatrics.

'Her name is Holly. You might meet her someday.'

'I'd like that. It won't stop me lusting after you, though.'

'I should hope not. Nor me you in reverse. You're a beautiful, sexy woman, Sarah. A warm ray of sensual sunshine. I'm sorely tempted but, for the moment, the answer is no thank you. Does that make sense?'

She leans across the bar counter and kisses him.

'Not particularly, but I'm happy to wait. Let's say that for now, the offer remains open, shall we?'

Chapter 67

He doesn't turn on his electronic device until he's back in Middlesbrough. It's a Ben Lewis trait, not a Tom Ruff trait. Ben Lewis would always be worried that someone might trace him to the farmhouse if he turns on the device at home. Tom Ruff might have been getting more relaxed about these things. Until, that is, Jake Sullivan had turned up, having been telling 'just one or two people' from Lewis's old life about his reincarnation.

He pulls into a cul-de-sac and connects to the network. Five bars of signal strength appear, along with one Tweet. It is from @MadDog3x. The Tweet was posted at 2.56 pm. *York station 10.32 am tomorrow. Bring the mistletoe!*

Lewis is about to have a visitor. Given Sullivan's cryptic Tweet, it can only be Holly!! He posts his reply. From @HairyHound4 posted at 3.45 pm. *Fab. Assuming the package knows to travel black.* Lewis doesn't need Holly's mobile phone left on by mistake.

Returning to the farmhouse, he has his work cut out. He wants the house to be spic and span for Holly's arrival, so he spends the evening giving the place a thorough going-over, even discovering a vacuum cleaner in a downstairs cupboard. On the way home from Middlesbrough, he had stopped by a store and bought food and some flowers, the latter already in a vase on the table by the fireplace. He looks at the chocolate-box picture sitting above the mantelpiece. It is a rather uninspiring mountain landscape, probably somewhere in Switzerland or the French Alps. Set in an old gold frame, it is a picture that in Lewis's home would have been consigned to the bin and replaced by something more modern and cheerful. In any event, his domestic duties stop with the vacuuming. Dusting paintings and their tatty old frames are not his forte.

As the day progresses, he worries about being able to protect Holly adequately. Her recent incarceration had been primarily because of him and Lewis is not prepared to let that happen again. The farmhouse needs to remain secret. His own safe haven – totally undiscoverable. The weakest link was Sullivan. However, Sullivan had always known about the place and who was he likely to have told? It had been acquired for Doherty and Fisher to use as a training base. It felt unlikely that the head of either MI5 or MI6 would have got into that level of operational detail. Lewis tries imagining Sullivan's recent three-way meeting where his resurrection had been discussed with Dame Helen and Sir Philip.

'So where is Lewis at the moment?'

'Somewhere safe and off the grid.'

'Are you in contact with him?'

'Only if or when I need to be.'

'Is he in London somewhere? Could we, perhaps, meet?'

'In good time. My advice is that we lie low for the moment. The trail to the encryption key has gone stone cold.'

'Does Lewis have any idea what Doherty did with the encryption key?'

'I don't believe so, no.'

'You don't think he knows how to acquire it?'

'Again, I don't believe so.'

At least, that is what Lewis hopes had been the limit of what Sullivan had felt obliged to divulge. Not a scintilla more.

Who else knows about the farmhouse? Zeltinger, tangentially, but only because he traced Doherty's black BMW to that registered address. If he learns from Sullivan that Lewis is alive, what reason would he have to believe Lewis might be hiding there? Next to none. True, the Americans know about the place, but they are unlikely to return. They only ever believed it to be some kind of dead letter drop. Besides, they think Lewis is dead.

Could someone have followed Sullivan on his recent day-trip? It's possible but not likely. It wouldn't have been hard to trace a flight from Northolt to Durham Tees Valley airport, but to what avail? The only clue beyond the flight would be the recorded mileage on the rental car. Someone would have to draw a circle with half that distance as the radius around the airport to see where he might have driven to. Would that lead them to the farmhouse? Hardly. Certainly not quickly. That circle would have a radius of at least thirty-five miles, which meant that the circumference was at least two hundred and twenty miles. Without more information about which direction he had driven in, it would be almost impossible to guess. Assuming Sullivan had followed his own procedures and turned off all electronic devices, it was unlikely that anyone would yet know about the farmhouse.

That assessment is what allows Lewis eventually to sleep that night. The Glock, however, remains close at hand, once more under his mattress. Next morning, the sun is shining, and there is not a cloud in the sky. It is an auspicious omen. The early morning air feels fresh on his face as he drives down the single-track lane and onto the main road towards York. He arrives in good time and parks the bike. With his keys back in his possession, he has even removed the paperclip and reconnected the ignition cable connector.

The 8.30 am train from King's Cross is running two minutes late. Lewis has no idea where to stand on the platform. Unusually nervous, he finds himself pacing. He is excited. This is the end of a rollercoaster few days. He doesn't quite believe that Holly is shortly to arrive. Earlier, he checked his Twitter account. There were no new Tweets. Therefore, everything should still be going to plan. By the time on the station clock, there is just one minute to go. He heads towards the end of the platform. That way, she is likely to see him as the train enters the station. He stops near where he gauges the back of the train is likely to be and looks down the tracks into the distance. A train is approaching. He can feel his heart beating loudly already. Get a grip, soldier, he tells himself.

The train sweeps alongside the platform gracefully, slowing gradually until finally it crawls to a stop. Lewis moves back from the platform edge to have a good view of the whole train. He starts to walk down the platform towards the middle when he hears a voice behind him. Turning, he sees her, looking magnificent, happy, beautiful – and safe! With her characteristic, slightly lopsided smile and golden hair, she drops her small overnight bag and runs towards him, hair trailing in her wake. Lewis catches her and holds her close, spinning her around. Her feet eventually touch the ground and they kiss. A lovers' kiss, a passionate embrace. Tom Ruff no more, Ben Lewis is back once again. More to the point, he's got his girl.

The guard's whistle blows and the train begins pulling out of the station. Lewis and Holly are still embracing. They don't notice the small handful of passengers on the train turning their heads to stare at the happy couple. They don't see one man in particular. A man who had looked at first, then turned away. A man with a wry smile on his face, sitting on his own, two rows behind where Holly had her reserved seat. A large individual who, even by Lewis's own description, was a massive brute of a fellow, well over two hundred pounds in weight. Someone happy to have found Lewis. For the moment, alive. However, as Pyotr Ivankov is only too aware, the day is still young.

Chapter 68

During the journey back to the farmhouse, Lewis feels the warm, protective hug of Holly's arms around his waist. When they eventually arrive, he parks the bike behind the outbuildings as usual. He lifts Holly's small bag from the pannier and, locked arm in arm, they walk to the front door. They have so much to say but, for the moment, are content to bathe in each other's silence.

The door closed and locked, Lewis drops Holly's bag on the floor. Gently, he takes her head in his hands, kissing her softly. Whilst Tom Ruff might have been tearing off her clothes and dragging her up the stairs, Ben Lewis takes Holly by the arm and leads her cautiously to the sofa. Slowly and tentatively, gently and tenderly they come together. Every moment is for savouring. They kiss, they hug, they caress. In time, they find a reason to laugh, the laughter quickly turning to tears of joy. Their lovemaking begins on the sofa. The rawness is intoxicating, their hesitancy an aphrodisiac. Only later do they make their way to the bedroom. Only later still do they come up for air.

Lying in each other's arms, they slowly begin to talk. They have so much ground to cover, the conversation has no logical flow. They speak in sound-bites; snippets of what has happened; snippets about how they felt, their worries, their fears. Slowly these snippets get strung together. They lose track of time, and it is early afternoon when they emerge downstairs, Holly wrapped in a blanket, Lewis finding his discarded clothing and getting dressed. She takes a small bag out of her overnight case and heads to the bathroom. She is gone for ten minutes. When she emerges, Lewis has made coffee. Strong and black. The way he remembers she likes it.

'You were gone a while,' he says.

'I had to send a text to the hospital. To tell them I won't be in tomorrow.' She looks at Lewis's face and frowns. 'What's wrong, Ben?'

'Is your phone off now?' he asks.

'Not yet.'

'Turn it off immediately.' His tone is unexpectedly harsh, the magic in the room broken.

'Of course. Sorry, I had to let them know.' She fumbles with her phone and then holds it up to show that it is no longer connected. 'See?'

'Promise,' he says sternly, his expression severe, his brow furrowed. 'Never to turn it on again while we're here. It's a homing beacon. They'll be able to find us. Did you get a signal?'

'Yes. Four bars out of five.'

'Shit!'

'Who's going to want to find us, Ben?'

'Anybody! Everybody! The same people who've been chasing me all week. The people yanking Doherty's chain. The ones who took Saul's kids. The rule here is no phones, no internet, nothing. Do you understand? It's really, really important.'

She apologises and the tension in the room eventually diffuses, but not before Lewis slides his hand down the back of the sofa cushion to check that the Glock is still in position.

Chapter 69

Krantz and Sanders only just make the train. In their haste to follow Ivankov, almost too late they discover that he, in turn, is tailing Lewis's girlfriend. Krantz manages to take the last available seat in the rear carriage, three rows away from the Russian. Sanders is forced to take a seat in the next carriage. When the train pulls into York station and Lewis is on the platform, very much alive and waiting to greet Holly, Sanders, in particular, feels vindicated. He had suspected something like this all along, Lewis faking his death. Now he has living proof. About to jump off the train, he receives an urgent text from Krantz. Ivankov is staying on the train. There has to be a good reason. Sanders sends a rapid text back.

Follow the Russian. I'll take care of Lewis.

With Lewis distracted by Holly's arrival, Sanders leaves the train. He makes his way towards the exit just as the train is leaving the platform. Though continually checking over his shoulder, Sanders fails to notice the former Spetsnaz soldier who also left the train further up the platform. Passing the station toilets close to the platform exit, Sanders stops and turns. He appears to check something on his phone but in reality, has eyes only for Lewis. He pretends to type a message, leaning against the stone brickwork adjacent to the men's toilets. His positioning provides a clear view along the platform to where Lewis and Holly are still in an embrace. Sensing someone advancing towards him, too late Sanders turns to look. A man in urgent need of the bathroom. The oblique angle and speedy nature of the approach cause the man to bump clumsily into Sanders. All too easily, the four-inch, spring-assisted steel blade penetrates deep into the American's stomach. Before Sanders comprehends what has just happened, the Russian is dragging the wounded agent inside the toilet block. In doing so, he jerks the blade upwards before hastily dumping the body, wiping the knife clean, closing the blade and then heading outside. The whole procedure has taken less than ten seconds.

Ivankov, still on the train heading north, receives a text from his new operative back at York station. It brings another smile to the Russian's face. He contemplates the message. He has twenty minutes until he needs to get off the train at the next stop. More than enough time. He heaves his bulky frame to his feet and walks purposefully to the rear, checking each of the passengers carefully. After the stop at York station, the carriage is now half empty. Seeing nobody he recognises, he turns and walks back, past his seat. Three rows beyond where he had been sitting, the Russian comes to a halt. He recognises the American, a man desperately pretending that Ivankov doesn't exist. Ivankov heaves his bulky frame into the empty seat directly opposite.

'Krantz,' is all he says. The American looks up apprehensively. This was not going according to the rule book.

'Are you following me, Krantz?'

The American says nothing, staring blankly at the Russian. Without warning, Ivankov grabs Krantz's mobile phone from the table in front of the two men.

'Hey, put that down!' Krantz shouts, struggling to snatch his phone back but failing. Ivankov's large fingers have already enveloped the device.

'You won't be needing this anymore,' Ivankov says, crushing the device in both hands until the screen cracks and then shatters.

'Oh dear, your friend won't be able to call.' Ivankov smiles at his little joke. 'He is, how do you say, unavailable!' With that he laughs, then quick as lightning grabs Krantz by the jacket collar and thrusts a hand deep into an inside pocket, pulling out Krantz's handgun.

'This you also won't be needing either,' he says, pocketing the gun. Krantz tries clambering out of his seat, but Ivankov extends a massive arm to restrain him.

'Sit!' he says, his eyes never leaving him.

They remain like this for several minutes, staring at each other in silence. An announcement over the Tannoy states that the train will shortly be arriving at Darlington station. The people sitting directly behind Krantz stand and make their way to the exit. Which is fortunate since, when Ivankov surreptitiously draws a handgun and fires two silenced rounds under the table directly at Krantz, there is no risk of collateral damage. Ivankov rises from his seat as the train pulls into the station. Opposite him, Krantz's slumped body looks, to all intents and purposes, as if the man is simply sleeping deeply.

Chapter 70

Holly and Lewis talk all afternoon, wandering around the garden and then into the woodlands at the back. Arm in arm, it is a meandering, purposeless stroll. At one stage, she stops and turns to face him, both arms draped around his shoulders.

'Are we really in danger?' Her blue eyes look into his, searching for the truth. For a while Lewis says nothing. He then kisses her and they start walking again.

'Maybe,' is all he says in time. Then a little later, he stops and turns to face her once again. 'Plan for the worst, hope for the best. I'm here to protect you, Holly. You don't need to worry.'

'That thing with my phone earlier. I'm sorry, Ben. It was foolish, a stupid mistake. Will it have caused any trouble?'

'I doubt it,' he says to comfort her. 'I hope not.'

'I worry more about what might happen to you.'

He smiles and shakes his head.

'Put it out of your mind. Let's change the subject. What do you want for dinner? I bought loads of food yesterday.'

'Flowers as well.' She kisses him. 'I noticed.'

Lewis checks his watch. The time is just after four in the morning. Holly is deeply asleep beside him. He sits up, instantly alert. Something has disturbed his sleep, and he knows he needs to investigate. Retrieving the Glock from underneath the mattress, he slips out of bed and into the bathroom. Getting dressed in the dark so as not to disturb Holly, he tucks the silenced weapon down the back of his trouser waistband before heading back into the bedroom to look out the window. He stands still and listens. For a while, he hears only the wind. Then he hears a voice. Muted, distant, but definitely a voice. Lewis had left the bedroom window open for this very reason. He goes back to Holly's side of the bed and kneels on the floor beside her.

'Wake up,' he says urgently but quietly, shaking her roughly as he speaks.

'What time is it?' she asks groggily. 'You're dressed. What's happening?'

'Shh! Listen to me. There are voices outside. I'm going to check. I want you to get dressed quickly and quietly. No lights whatsoever. Keep away from the windows. Go downstairs, into the back where the utility room is. You'll be safe there. I'm going to give you a gun.'

'I don't want a gun!'

'Just take the gun.' He places the Glock beside her on the bed. 'It's ready to fire. There's no safety catch. All you need to do is aim and pull the trigger. Only use it in extreme emergencies.'

'What about you?'

'I can take care of myself.'

'I'm terrified, Ben.'

'Good. The adrenalin will help. Take care, Holly. I'll be back soon.'

'I love you, Ben.'

Chapter 71

Lewis leaves the house by the side door at the rear of the kitchen, soundlessly pulling it closed behind him. Without the Glock, his weapon of choice is the length of fence pole he'd found and cut to size a few days earlier. Old technology at its reliable best. The pre-dawn night is heavily overcast. Tonight, there is little moonlight to see by. He sets off in a crouching run around the back of the house towards the nearest outbuildings. When he reaches the wall, he flattens his body against the brickwork in order to listen.

For five minutes, he remains stationary, listening. The wind is gusting strongly off the North Sea, making it difficult to differentiate sounds. Nothing that he hears feels out of the ordinary. Then, just as he's preparing to go and check his bike, a thin pencil of light flashes on and off across the far side of the courtyard. Close to where the rear of the outbuildings leads into the forest trail. It confirms what Lewis had feared. He and Holly have company.

Night vision goggles would have been perfect. Without them, Lewis has to make do with his own eyes. He does have the home advantage of knowing the terrain. He loops around behind the outbuilding and into the woodlands at the rear, planning to creep up on any visitors from behind. Within thirty metres of where the light source had been, he stops to peer around the large trunk of a tree. It is an action that probably saves his life. Moving slowly towards him is an armed assailant: a soldier, special forces or equivalent. Lewis recognises the gait, particularly the way the man moves with purpose, vigilance and stealth. From a distance of ten metres, Lewis sees face paint and an assault rifle. This is not good news. Lewis tries to melt his body into the trunk of the tree. Moments before reaching Lewis's position, the soldier stops abruptly and turns.

Lewis hears a few words muttered into a neck microphone. Russian words. Ivankov's crew! Ivankov would doubtless be somewhere nearby. The big Russian had scores to settle. This other man, however, is no longer moving, standing two, perhaps three metres away from Lewis at most. Had he heard Lewis? Then Lewis understands: the man is busy answering a call of nature. Too much coffee drunk in the early hours. A man who's been trying to stay awake – Lewis had been there many times. With the sounds of the man's pissing covering his approach, Lewis swings the length of fence pole, aiming directly at the back of the neck. The Russian sinks to the earth without a sound. One down. Lewis rolls the man over and searches his pockets. In addition to the rifle, there is a Glock 17 handgun in an armpit holster. Lewis checks the magazine. Fully loaded. He puts the gun in his inside left jacket pocket.

Armed once more, Lewis discards the length of fence pole and heads back the way he'd come, towards the clearing in front of the first outbuilding. Which is when he makes his first and only mistake. As he emerges from the forest onto the concrete hard standing, he forgets to check his rear. He incorrectly assumes that the only person he has left to contend with is the one he can now see directly in front of him – a massive brute of a fellow, well over two hundred pounds in weight. Unfortunately for Lewis, another of Ivankov's colleagues had been hiding in the forest, covering Ivankov's rear. The man is now jabbing the cold muzzle of an AK-12 rifle into Lewis's neck. Before taking two steps backwards. To keep Lewis from swinging around, grabbing the gun and disarming the man.

'What pleasure to find Ben Lewis alive!' Ivankov speaks slowly, his words laboured as he lumbers towards the former Marine. 'You killed Polunin, *da*?' Spittle flies as Lewis remains rooted to the spot, saying nothing. 'You bastard!' Ivankov coughs up phlegm and spits it onto Lewis's face. 'It was you, I know it was. Like you killed Oleg Panich. Now, it's your turn to die. It will be my pleasure.' He says something quickly in Russian to the other man and Lewis receives a sharp kick to the kidneys from behind. It's a move that sends Lewis sagging onto his hands and knees.

'Don't be a baby,' Ivankov says and stamps on Lewis's left hand, fingers instantly breaking under the weight of the Russian's heavy boot. 'Sorry for being so clumsy!' He looks at the other Russian and they laugh. 'Get to your feet!'

Lewis makes an effort to stand, his injured left hand now hanging uselessly by his side. Ivankov approaches Lewis on the left whilst the other Russian approaches on the right. Just as Ivankov tries to deliver a massive uppercut to Lewis's chin, the Russian with the assault rifle simultaneously swings the butt end down hard on the vulnerable part of Lewis's right knee. Lewis had seen Ivankov's incoming fist and swerves his body to avoid being hit. However, the sledgehammer blow from the rifle butt collapses his right leg and he falls to the ground in acute pain.

'Get up!' orders Ivankov once again. He starts kicking Lewis to get him to respond. Lewis, no longer in a strong position, can only use his left knee and right hand to get to his feet. He struggles, unable to put weight on his injured leg, which is why, when the Russian with the assault rifle decides to snap a powerful kick into Lewis's groin, Lewis falls to the concrete once more. Seriously wounded, there is still fight in the former Marine yet. Whilst the two Russians share a joke at Lewis's expense, Lewis's right hand darts quickly into his jacket pocket to reach for the Glock. He manages to fire two shots in quick succession at the Russian with the assault rifle. Both soft-nosed bullets hit the man in the shoulder moments before Ivankov kicks the Glock out of Lewis's hand. The big Russian is now apoplectic with rage. He rains powerful kicks all over Lewis's body. Everywhere is a target: ribs, stomach, the kidneys, Lewis's head and his legs. All receive multiple assaults from Ivankov's heavy boots. Lewis curls himself into a ball to try and protect his head and vital organs. He is fighting a losing battle. Unable to get to his feet to fight back, his body must absorb blow after blow like a punchbag. Ivankov, sensing that Lewis is close to blacking out, stops for a moment to draw breath. He nudges Lewis's broken ribs with his foot, deliberately using pain to prevent Lewis from losing consciousness.

'Maybe Ben Lewis is not so invincible now?'

Lewis tries to laugh but finds he is coughing up blood.

'Perhaps you would like bullet in knee?' Ivankov pulls a Glock pistol from under his armpit and points the gun at Lewis's left knee. 'Just like you did to Alexei, eh?' He fires a shot, deliberately missing. He laughs at the frightened look on Lewis's face.

'Not so funny for you now, eh? Next time, I don't miss.'

'Ivankov?' Lewis mutters. The Russian, happy to see Lewis's suffering, comes nearer to hear what the British man has to say.

'Yes?'

Lewis takes time to draw strength to speak. A weak smile appears on his face. Ivankov seems puzzled.

'Well? What is it?'

'One . . . thing.' He pauses, struggling to conserve his breath. 'Why . . . don't . . . you . . . fuck . . . off . . . and . . . die . . .' he mumbles, his eyes finally closing as he loses the battle to stay conscious.

Chapter 72

Holly, scared out of her wits, dresses quickly and is already descending the stairs by the time Ben is pulling the back door closed behind him and slipping quietly into the night. The Glock feels a dead weight in her hands. She takes a coat from the hook by the entrance to the kitchen, trying – but failing – to stuff the unwieldy weapon with its long silencer into any one of the pockets. With no option but to continue holding the gun, she grabs her mobile phone from its charging point and makes her way to the back door. Opening it just a fraction, she listens for any strange or unfamiliar sounds. All she can hear is the wind.

This is all her fault. If she hadn't been so stupid as to switch on her wretched phone earlier, no one would have found them. For that reason alone, she is determined to go and help Ben.

It takes a few moments for her eyes to adjust to the darkness. She edges cautiously around the side of the house, soon able to make out a stone barn some distance away across the open courtyard. About to cross to the stone barn, she suddenly freezes, rooted to the spot. Up ahead, she has seen someone. A huge man, moving out of the shadows, now standing with his back to her, about thirty metres away. When she sees Ben emerging from the trees, her heart sinks. Behind Ben is another man, this one with a rifle, pointing directly at him.

'What pleasure to find Ben Lewis alive!'

The voice is unmistakably Russian. It makes Holly's skin crawl. Ben is outnumbered, at least two to one. Perhaps there are more? What should she be doing? She can't just rush in shooting left, right and centre.

'You killed Polunin, da? You bastard! It was you, I know. Like you killed Oleg Panich. Now, it's your turn to die. It will be my pleasure.'

It is then Holly realises that, without her intervention, this is going to end in disaster. Sure enough, when Ben is kicked from behind and falls to the floor, she finds it difficult to stifle a scream. She sees the bulky man stamp on Ben's hand. She is going to have to use the Glock: the question is, when? If she fires from her current position, she's almost sure to miss. She needs to get nearer without being seen. For the moment she has little choice but to remain where she is. Tears fill her eyes as she watches Ben being systematically beaten. Suddenly, two gunshots ring out in quick succession, her spirits lifting to see one of the Russians fall to the floor. Her euphoria is short-lived, however, as Ben's bulky opponent kicks a gun from his hand. In a blinding rage, the Russian has become a man possessed, raining blow after blow at Ben's increasingly inert form on the ground.

With the odds changed, Holly's mind is laser-focused on how to kill the Russian. Casting aside any fear, she begins walking slowly and purposefully towards the ugly scene unfolding in front of her, Glock in her right hand, aimed directly at Lewis's opponent.

Twenty-five metres to go.

'Perhaps you would like bullet in knee?'

Holly freezes as the Russian points a gun directly at Ben, now curled up on the ground to protect himself. She almost cries out to distract the Russian, just managing to stop herself as she continues advancing.

Twenty metres to go.

'Just like you did to Alexei, eh?'

Nearly losing control as the sound of another shot rings out yet emboldened by the deliberate miss, she uses all her willpower to keep advancing. She's in the zone now, oblivious to all and any distractions, the objective of killing the Russian never clearer.

Fifteen metres and closing.

'Not so funny for you now, eh? Next time, I don't miss.'

Holly keeps advancing.

Ten metres.

She can faintly hear the sound of Ben's voice, although not what he's saying. She watches as the Russian steps closer to Ben, straining to listen to his words. This is Holly's moment. She advances now more brazenly.

Five metres, four, now down to three. It is time!

She raises the gun so that it is pointing directly at the Russian's back. At the last moment, she looks directly into Ben's eyes and sees him looking at her. There is a faint smile on his face.

Which is when Holly pulls the trigger. Once, twice, three times and more. She keeps firing as the Russian falls to the ground, losing count of the number of bullets until eventually, the gun clicks empty.

Chapter 73

Ten days later, two weeks before Christmas.

Zach and Nate Zeltinger have never been on a private jet before. For that matter, neither have Saul or Hattie. The exuberance and excitement shown by the twins at being allowed on an adventure quite so exciting are worth more than any Hanukkah present their parents could have given them. Sullivan had even laid on a chauffeur-driven car to ferry the Zeltingers to RAF Northolt. Sullivan was a last-minute addition to the passenger manifest, arriving unannounced at the VIP terminal shortly before the flight to Durham Tees Valley was ready to board.

'How is he really?' Saul asks Sullivan sometime after take-off. Hattie has taken the twins to see the pilot in the cockpit.

'Fair. It was touch and go for a while. He suffered multiple breaks and fractures. Overall, some twenty-five fractured or broken bones. The ones in his hand were a nightmare. What they were most worried about, apparently, was his knee but they are quietly confident he should make a full recovery.'

'The whole incident caused quite a diplomatic stir, by all accounts.'

'Yes, the Russian ambassador was sent packing. Given a right bollocking. He'd had a warning from the foreign secretary only a few days earlier.'

'I expect there will be repercussions.'

'Already have been. Ten of our people have just been expelled from

Moscow.'

'How's Holly?'

'She's strong. Full of surprises, actually. If she hadn't had the guts to pull the trigger and kill Ivankov, Lewis would be dead, no question. How she handled the whole clean-up was impressive.'

'In what way?'

'Well, cool as a cucumber, she rang me and then rang the hospital in Middlesbrough where she knew there was a major trauma centre. It was she who organised the air ambulance and then tended Ben's injuries until the medics turned up and ferried him away. After all she'd been through, I think that's impressive.'

Both of Zeltinger's boys are running down the aisle to talk to their father.

'Daddy, Daddy, we've already passed Peterborough and we are soon going to pass over York. The captain says if we're good and you say yes then we can stay in the cockpit for landing. Pleeease Daddy, can we?'

'Go on Daddy, he promised we could do it if you say so. Pleeease may we?'

'But boys, since when have you ever been good? I thought both of you were always terribly, terribly bad?'

'Stop being silly, Daddy. This is serious. Pleeease may we?'

'Okay, just this once! But you have to do what the captain tells you. And don't touch anything!'

The boys race away exuberantly.

'When's this whole business going to end, Jake?'

'It's puzzling, isn't it? The moment that Ben plays dead, everyone gets back in their box and pretends nothing has happened. Life goes back to normal. Then, the instant there's a whiff that he might be alive, people go a bit crazy once more.'

'Ben mentioned that Doherty and Fisher might have been working for some parallel organisation, outside of either MI5 or MI6. Do you believe that?'

'There might be an element of truth in it. It certainly proves one thing. The lack of accountability and oversight in such an arrangement dramatically increases the body count, no question.'

Chapter 74

Lewis is sitting up in bed when his visitors arrive. Apart from puffiness around the cheeks and eyes and some discolouration, his face looks remarkably unblemished. Generally, they all agreed afterwards, he was in good spirits.

He beams broadly when he sees Zach and Nate.

'It's the Terrible Twins,' he jokes. All the boys seem interested in is firing pretend guns in Lewis's direction. Lewis returns the gesture in kind, much to their amusement. His left hand is set in plaster, with just the very tips of his fingers showing. 'If you don't behave, boys, I have a gun inside this plaster cast,' he says to them mischievously. They suddenly stop and stare at the cast in amazement.

'Is that really true, Mister Lewis?'

'Of course. Do you want to see my bionic knee?' He looks at Hattie and she nods quizzically. Lewis throws back the bed covers and reveals the contraption attached to his right leg. The knee is secured in an open splint, an electric motor constantly winding and unwinding two parallel metal threads that keep the knee bending and unbending.

'When I am out of here, I am going to be able to run so much faster than you two with my new knee.'

'Why is there that motor thingy?' one of them asks.

'Because I'm too lazy to bend the knee myself. It's a new way to get exercise.'

'Can we get one, Mummy?'

'No, we can't,' Hattie says. 'Now, haven't you boys got something to say to Mister Lewis?'

'Thank you, Mister Lewis,' they begin in unison, 'for doing whatever you did to rescue us from those horrid people.' Then each of them in turn steps forward to shake Ben's hand. 'Can we go and play now, Mummy?'

'I'll take them for a moment,' Saul says to his wife. 'You stay here and chat with Ben, darling.'

'I'll come with you too, Saul,' Sullivan says, getting to his feet and following in the children's wake.

'You look good, Ben,' Hattie says once they've disappeared. 'Am I allowed a kiss?'

'Sure. But no hugs. I've got a few too many bruised and broken ribs.'

Hattie kisses Ben tenderly on the cheek and then grips his right hand in hers.

'I've no idea what you really did to save the boys, Ben,' she says, fighting back the tears. 'All I know is that I can never say thank you enough. I can't tell you how grateful Saul and I are. When you were supposedly killed and we had to go to your wretched funeral, it was nearly more than I could take!' They laugh, a moment of levity that breaks the ice. 'Seriously, Ben. I love you for the courage you showed and for what you did for our family. Thank you.' She raises his hand to her lips and kisses it softly.

'You'll get us all weeping if you keep talking like that.'

Which is the moment that Holly appears.

'I hope I'm not interrupting the pair of you having a moment,' she says. Holly and Hattie give each other a warm hug.

'Not at all, I was just thanking Ben for saving Zach and Nate from those odious Russians.'

'Well, whether he likes it or not, this particular man is out of action for the next few months. Recovering, resting, and then getting back to full fitness.'

'What about you, Holly?'

'I've decided to take leave of absence from the hospital for a while. I am going to look after Ben.'

'Ben Lewis,' Hattie says, smiling, 'you're a lucky man. Don't let this lady out of your sight! That's an order.'

'What's an order?' Saul says, returning with Sullivan, the twins still running around the corridor outside. 'Hello, Holly. It's so good to see you again.'

They all embrace, and Hattie takes it as her cue to go and look after the twins. Holly goes with her, leaving the three men alone together.

'Did you bring a chess set?' Lewis asks Saul.

'Do you know, I didn't. Damn! How very remiss of me.'

'Please remember next time. I'd enjoy a game with a human being rather than constantly losing to a computer game. Last time you stood me up, remember? If you hadn't, none of this might ever have happened.'

'You're lucky to be alive, Ben,' Sullivan says. 'I'm so glad you made it.'

'Not nearly as glad as I am. Holly saved the day, not me. She gets all the credit.'

'She's too good for you, Ben,' Zeltinger adds.

'You sound like you've been speaking to her neighbour in Canterbury. She told me the same thing.'

'Well then, listen and take note. Seriously, it's so good to have you back from the dead.' Zeltinger pulls up a chair next to Sullivan and sits down.

'Am I back from the dead? Am I Ben Lewis once again or should I stick with my new persona in the afterlife, Tom Ruff?'

'It says here, Jake,' Zeltinger says, lifting the medical record file clipped to the base of Lewis's bed, 'that the patient in this bed is called Ben Lewis. It sounds like you're back from the dead, Ben.'

'I guess that settles it. Tell me, Jake. Have you been on your holidays yet? I thought you were heading down to the Devon coast.'

'Yes, I did end up going down there.'

'Find anything interesting?'

'I found a prepaid motel room that was completely empty.'

'Empty?'

'Unused. Waiting for guests to arrive. Nothing in the room whatsoever. No envelope, no parcel, no key, nothing.'

'Did you take any photos, Jake?'

'I have a few on my phone. Let me find them.' He plays around with his phone for a moment and then hands it across. 'Take a look. Tell me if you see anything.'

Lewis thumbs his way through Sullivan's photos. Nothing stands out apart from the last one. It is a photo of the back of the bedroom door.

'Why did you take a photo of the back of the door?'

'There was some graffiti scratched into the varnish. I thought it might be relevant. It's only four letters. I've searched online for possible acronyms but nothing fits the bill.'

'What are the four letters?' Zeltinger asks.

'FOBH,' Sullivan says. 'It's not particularly clear in the photo. Mean anything to you, Ben?'

'Sorry.' He hands the phone back. 'What next?'

'You tell me. I was rather hoping you might have the answer. As it is, we've reached a dead end. No more hunting for the encryption key. No more clues as to what happened to the missing money.'

'Are you sure there was nothing else in the motel room?'

'I looked, Ben. I searched high and low. I even checked with the cleaning staff. The room hasn't been touched for three weeks.'

'Is that the end of the matter? All this chasing around, death and destruction, and now a dead end?'

'Unless you have a better idea.'

'What do Dame Helen and Sir Philip say?'

'They seemed relieved that we've finally come to the end of the affair. This way, no one wins. However, the biggest losers are the North Koreans, who suddenly seem in a very precarious position financially. Dame Helen and Sir Philip want to know whether you might be interested in some new and exciting work opportunities. When you are fully recovered, that is.'

'Tell them I'll think about it. I need to spend time getting my health back first.'

'Understood.'

They spend a few moments exchanging idle gossip before Sullivan, ever the fidget, looks at his watch and gets to his feet.

'Saul, I think we're in danger of outstaying our welcome. Ben, we'll come and visit soon, I promise. It's been great seeing you again.'

'You too, Jake.' They shake hands and Sullivan wanders off to find Hattie and tell her they are about to leave.

'I just wanted to say thanks as well, Ben,' Saul says when they are alone together. 'I don't pretend to know all that happened. I probably don't want to know either. You saved all of our lives, not just the twins. I owe you.'

He holds his friend's hand in a warm clasp for several seconds.

'You'd have done the same, Saul. Just don't forget about me while I recuperate. I'm going to get bored, and I need a chess partner!'

A short while later the visitors, having said their goodbyes, wait for the lift to take them to the ground floor. One of the twins keeps pressing the call button.

'Why don't the rest of you carry on down to the car and wait for me there,' Sullivan suddenly announces. 'I've just remembered something I forgot to say to Ben. I won't be long.'

Holly is beside Ben's bed when Sullivan returns. She moves aside when she sees Sullivan.

'I guess you'd like to say something to Ben in private. I need to powder my nose anyway.'

Jake comes around to Ben's bedside.

'One more thing, Ben,' he says once they are alone. 'Officially, I am content for Doherty's No-Tell Motel clue to be a dead end. Officially. However, unofficially, if FOBH means something that you're not yet prepared to divulge, all I ask is that you bring me into the loop discreetly and immediately if, or when, you know anything further. This business has not yet been put to bed. There are too many loose ends. In my mind, it's simply dormant. Dormant things have the nasty habit of waking up unexpectedly. Sometimes they can even surprise us. Do we understand each other?'

'Sure. Just to put your mind at rest. As I explained once before, Jake, aside from Holly, there are only two people I trust in this whole matter. Saul is one, and you're the other. If anything does develop for any reason, you'll be the first to know. I promise.' He holds his hand out to Jake so that they can shake on it.

'Thanks,' Sullivan says, gripping Lewis's hand carefully. 'We haven't yet got to the bottom of everything. We will. It just might take a little time.'

'I agree. However, we're getting close. Now it is dormant, the good news is that no one else will realise how close we're getting until probably too late.'

'I hope to God you're right.'

Chapter 75

A week later

Holly has gone back to the farmhouse to prepare for Lewis's homecoming. The doctors are hopeful he will be discharged in the next day or so. Lewis is dozing when he senses he has a visitor. He opens his eyes to be greeted with a warm, welcoming smile, glistening long, dark brown hair and sparkling blue eyes.

'Sarah! What are you doing here? How did you know . . .?'

Sarah reaches across the bed and places her finger on Lewis's lips.

'Shh! Pleased to see me?'

'Delighted! Do I get a kiss?'

'Am I allowed to touch the patient?'

'Only on the lips. No hugging. Yet, that is.'

Sarah manoeuvres to a position where she can get close to Lewis. She gives him a long, lingering kiss on the lips.

'That was nice! How did you find me?'

'Holly came to the Lamb and Flag and introduced herself. I'm jealous, Tom. Or is it Ben I should be calling you?'

'Jealous – why?'

'She's so perfect, damn it.'

'I know. I'm lucky. I was also lucky meeting you, Sarah.'

'How are you? I've heard about some of your antics from Holly. My God, you're a dark horse, Ben Lewis.'

'I'm better, thanks. Certainly better than I was. I might even be going home tomorrow, which would be great. How are you doing?'

'Me? Life is good. I may have a new man.'

'Well done you! You don't hang around. Where did you meet?'

'Same way you and I did. He was in the pub for dinner the other night. We hit it off. He's divorced. Split up a couple of years ago and recently moved to Whitby to start a new life.'

'Sounds a familiar story.'

'Tell me about it! We seem well-suited.'

'I'm pleased. Fireworks in the bedchamber?'

'Now, now. Actually, not bad. I think you and I would have been better, in fact I'm sure of it, but, hey! No complaints at the moment.'

'I hope it works out for you both.'

'If not, I intend to come and hunt you down!' She flicks away a strand of hair nervously. 'Holly has been telling me all about the real you. Are you Ben now or should I still call you Tom?'

'Call me whatever you like.'

'Despite my being insanely jealous of Holly, I just hope you and I can remain connected. I'd like that.'

'So would I, Sarah. Though it might be tough keeping this sexual attraction thing between us under control, don't you think?'

'All any of us can ever do is try our best.'

A silence falls between them. Sarah uses the moment to take hold of Ben's right hand in hers.

'Is it true that you killed someone the other day?'

'Don't ask, Sarah. I do whatever I do because I believe that I'm doing the right thing. Think of me as Tom Ruff. I'd prefer it that way. Change of subject. I have a favour to ask. Since you've already met Holly, would you be willing to take a day off work sometime soon? I need Holly to do something for me in London. I would be so much happier if she had someone to accompany her.'

'Am I about to become a spy? Will it be dangerous?'

'No, and I sincerely hope not. Holly's had a rough time herself, of late, if she hasn't already told you. I simply don't want her wandering around London on her own, that's all. It's nothing dangerous. I just need something collected that I can't currently do myself.'

'Then, of course I'll do it. I'd love to help. It means a lot to me, you asking.'

Chapter 76

FOBH. Conversations between fellow-Marines are one constant swear-athon. Every other word is a profanity – an Effing-and-Blinding masterclass. FOBH was a stupid private expression that Lewis and Doherty had invented and then used over and over. Their own private *lingua franca*. They said it to each other all the time, especially during the final Commando tests. The hardest, most gruelling assessment of their readiness to wear the Green Beret. The tests that some failed outright and even more simply didn't have the stamina to complete.

First, the nine-mile speed march, when legs were always aching, screaming, crying out to slow down.

'Can't we ease up for fuck's sake? My legs are fucking knackered, Doherty.'

'FOBH, you wimp, Lewis.'

Next, the six-mile endurance course, with the body pushed to its very limits. So much so, it became virtually impossible to concentrate on any task they were meant to be doing.

'If I have to do another fucking endurance test, I'll fucking kill someone. Aren't you ready to fucking quit yet, Lewis?'

'FOBH, you lazy arsehole, Doherty.'

Then to the Tarzan Assault course, every sinew burning and screaming, every muscle worked to its limits and beyond.

'I hate this stupid fucking Commando shit. Aren't you fucking ready to fucking throw in the towel yet, Doherty?'

'FOBH, you lazy bastard, Lewis.'

Finally, the killer: a timed, thirty-mile march. Everyone so exhausted, all they wanted to do was to lie down and give up.

'Why don't you fucking want to quit, for fuck's sake, Lewis? My knees are fucking killing me, you useless fucking bastard.'

'FOBH, you useless piece of shit, Doherty.'

FOBH. Always FOBH.

Fuck Off Back Home.

A stupid expression that somehow always worked its magic. Spurring them on to bigger and better things. Just when they had otherwise been about to give up.

The fact that Doherty has scrawled it on the back of the door was a good sign. A very good sign. It meant that they were getting close to the end-game. It was also a coded instruction to Lewis.

'Don't fucking give up, soldier!'

Doherty might have been on the side of the angels, after all, spurring Lewis to do the right thing from beyond the grave. Encouraging him to get to the finish line. In the way that only one Marine can tell another.

Fuck off back home, Keiran! Thank you. May you rest in peace.

Chapter 77

A few days before Christmas

London's Oxford Street is busy with Christmas shoppers. Holly and Sarah waste no time getting into the festive spirit. A pair of shoes each – a Christmas gift to themselves – and various small presents. They emerge from Selfridges, two hours after their assault on Oxford Street had begun, laden with an assortment of carrier bags. They stop along the way for a welcome coffee, two friends enjoying a Christmas outing together.

'I hope Ben's all right,' Holly says, looking at her watch. 'I did tell him not to do anything stupid.'

'Men are a law unto themselves. I'm sure Ben's being good. I still think of him as Tom. He was sexy as hell as Tom. As Ben, he's unquestionably off-limits and most definitely yours. I'm only jealous, Holly.'

'What about your latest man, Sarah? Isn't he sexy too?'

'Yes, but in a different way. Ben's, well, Ben. Envy, envy!'

'You're not allowed to fancy him, Sarah. He's mine. Hands off!'

'I know. I'm not a boyfriend-snatcher, I promise. I'm just rather touched that he asked me to help you today.'

'It's because he trusts you. Come on. Are you ready to play your part on the big stage?'

'Is it far away?'

'About fifteen minutes' walk.'

Saul Zeltinger had promised his friend that he would keep a careful watch over Holly and Sarah that day. Not that anyone was expecting trouble. Lewis simply didn't want to take any risks. Zeltinger and Meilin are thus sitting in an unmarked Vauxhall Corsa, parked some thirty metres from the property's entrance, just off St James's Square. Meilin is behind the wheel whilst Zeltinger sits patiently in the passenger seat with a notebook in hand.

'I think this is them coming now,' Zeltinger says, watching a pair of Christmas shoppers strolling along the opposite pavement, about to approach the main entrance. 'Yes, it's Holly. The other must be Sarah. Is anyone following them or showing any interest?'

'Not that I can see at the moment, sir.'

'I don't see anyone either. I suggest we stay in the car. They shouldn't be long.'

Sure enough, a few minutes later, the pair emerge and start walking towards them, on the opposite side of the street.

'Perhaps we should be kind and offer them a lift?'

'Why not? They appear to be carrying a lot of shopping.'

'I agree.'

Meilin starts the engine and, performing a quick U-turn, pulls the car to the curb some ten metres in front of where Holly and Sarah are walking. Zeltinger winds down his window, waiting for them to pass him by.

'Good day to you, ladies. Do either of you need a lift to King's Cross station by any chance?'

'Saul! Finding you here is a bit of a surprise,' Holly says once they are both inside the car. 'Did Ben ask you to follow us?'

'He might have done. Did you find what Ben was looking for?'

The two women look at each other and shrug.

'We might have done.'

'Very good. I'll phone and tell Ben you're on your way back, then.'

Approaching King's Cross Station, Zeltinger is finishing speaking with Lewis on the phone when Holly asks him a question.

'Are you coming to see us anytime soon, Saul? Ben would like that.'

'Sometime over the Christmas period, for sure.'

'Good. It would be lovely to see you. Ben misses playing chess enormously.'

'As do I, Holly. I'll be up as soon as I can, I promise.'

Chapter 78

By the time Holly and Sarah return to the farmhouse, it is beginning to get dark. Lewis is lying on the sofa, as he was instructed to by Holly.

'Have you been a good patient?' Holly asks, planting a lingering kiss on Lewis. Her professional nursing eye glances beside the sofa to survey the evidence of what might have been consumed in her absence. 'What are these, Ben?' she says, holding up a packet of biscuits. 'Where did you find them?'

'In the kitchen cupboard. You told me that I could get out of bed if I went carefully. So, I went carefully.'

'What about the fruit I bought? Too many biscuits in your condition are going to make you fat.'

Lewis makes a face behind Holly's back, and Sarah laughs, blowing a sneaky kiss in Lewis's direction.

'Come on, what did you find?' Ben asks. 'I'm itching to know.'

FOBH. Part of the joke that Doherty and Lewis had shared all those years ago was finding and agreeing between them a place that might suitably be labelled 'Home'. They quickly determined that the home in FOBH was less about where they lived, more where one aspired to belong. Former SAS and SBS members had their 'home' in the Special Forces Club in London's Knightsbridge. There was nothing so grand for former Marines, an anomaly that the two young Marines felt needed to be rectified.

As a consequence, the Naval and Military Club in St. James's Square became their aspirational 'home'. They had thus both become members. Also known as the In & Out Club, it's a club for former officers and gentlemen of the British Armed Forces. If FOBH meant anything, it meant that Doherty had left a clue for him in his mailbox there, which is why he'd sent Holly and Sarah to go and see. It was a location that no one except Lewis would think to check.

'We found Saul Zeltinger and a female policewoman loitering outside the club when we came out. You didn't have anything to do with that, I suppose?'

'I have no idea what you are talking about.'

Holly comes over to the sofa and perches on the edge.

'Thanks for doing that, Ben. It was a nice touch. It made us feel safe. He even gave us a lift to the station.'

'Saul? He wasn't driving, was he? He never drives.'

'No, the policewoman drove. By the way, he promised to come up and play chess with you soon.' She opens one of the many shopping bags that she and Sarah have brought back with them, lifting out a handwritten envelope, postmarked London, which she duly hands to Lewis. It is addressed to 'Ben Lewis'.

He looks at the handwriting and smiles.

'This looks like Doherty's scrawl. Let's see what it has to say.'

He slips a finger under the back flap and tears open the envelope. Inside is a small white card with eleven words written in Doherty's scrawl:

Check out the landscape in Yorkshire to see the bigger picture

'What does that mean, Ben?'

Lewis shakes his head.

'I don't know. Keiran loved using Americanisms when we were playing soldiers. One of his favourites was *Check this out*'. He used it a lot. You know: '*Hey, what's happening, bud? Check this out!*' or '*Check out this food, Lewis!*' Schoolboy humour. Banter. Usually, with a few more swear words thrown into the mix. So, Keiran: what in hell's name does this message mean?' He shakes the card in his hand, closing his eyes as he tries to think. Holly and Sarah don't say a thing, waiting to see if Ben gets any inspiration.

A long time passes with nothing spoken. Then, without warning, Lewis opens his eyes wide and stares at the fireplace, smiling.

'I've got it. Holly, pass me the phone. We've got to get Saul and Jake up here, *pronto*. I know exactly what this means. You're a sly old fox, Keiran! A sly old fox!'

Chapter 79

They arrive shortly before eleven the next morning. It is raining heavily, the sort of incessant, constant rain that Sarah had warned was typical of the North Yorkshire Moors.

Zeltinger runs from the car door to the front porch in his raincoat, a small leather case held over his head to keep off the worst of the rain. Sullivan reaches into the back of the car for a collapsible umbrella which then fails to open. In the end, he abandons it, making a run for the house with his briefcase also over his head, just as Zeltinger had done. Only this time he gets drenched in the process. Holly is there, on the porch, waiting to greet them. To their surprise, Lewis is also on his feet, one crutch in his right hand and with his left leg taking all of his weight.

'It's great to see you.' Lewis shuffles across to shake hands. This turns out to be a clumsy procedure requiring Ben to move the crutch under one armpit whilst wobbling precariously on one leg.

'Careful now,' Sullivan says, helping Lewis back to the sofa.

'You're soaking wet, Jake. Forgot your umbrella?'

'Bloody thing wouldn't open.'

'I bought a chess set with me,' Zeltinger says. 'Just in case we have time.'

'We'll make time!'

'You're looking so much better than when we last saw you,' Sullivan continues. 'It has to be Holly's care and attention.'

'It is. She's been unbelievable, haven't you, Holly?'

'Spare me my blushes, the lot of you. Now, I have a fresh pot of coffee on the go. Also, some cake. It's only shop-bought, but it is fruitcake. Any takers, anybody?'

'Cake? We never have cake!' Lewis says. 'Yes please!'

'It's not for you, Ben. You have to watch your waistline. It's for our guests.'

'You see what I have to put up with?' They spend a few moments catching up with the gossip and gently satisfying themselves that Lewis is firmly on the road to recovery.

'I saw the surgeon yesterday. The man who worked on my hand,' he says, lifting the cast in the air. 'With luck, this thing will be off before New Year. Then, after some physio, all being well it should be back to near normal in a couple of months.'

'How about the knee?'

'The knee is going to be okay. Fingers crossed. A lot of muscle tissue and nerves were damaged, but I should be weight-bearing soon. So they say. Then it's just the slow process of building strength and flexibility back up.'

'Come on, Ben. We're all itching to know why you dragged Saul and me out here. What have you found?'

Which is when Ben explains about FOBH and the little outing that Holly and Sarah had made to London two days earlier. He leaves out Zeltinger's part in that for the moment, catching a glance at his friend as he is talking, finding himself on the receiving end of a knowing wink and a soft smile.

'Why didn't you tell me about FOBH the other day at the hospital, Ben? I could have had someone collect whatever it is from the In & Out Club. Or I could even have done it myself? I thought we were meant to be trusting each other?' Sullivan's tone is miffed, which Lewis had been expecting.

'We are, Jake, and we do. As discussed before, we need this kept well away from all official channels until we know what we are dealing with. Anyway, sure enough, Doherty has sent one, I hope final, clue.'

He shows them the card. The two men look at it, read it, look at each other, and shrug.

'What does it mean, Ben?' Sullivan asks, still slightly put out.

'Have a guess. Saul, you're the detective. Why do you think I brought you all the way out here?'

'I don't yet know, Ben. Holly, have you any idea?'

'Goodness, no. Ben's been waiting until you both arrived. He hasn't told me a thing.'

Zeltinger stands motionless, palms together, contemplating Doherty's message. His chin now rests on his fingertips, a form of prayerful thinking pose that Lewis has seen him assume before. In this manner, he starts wandering around the room, pacing back and forth a few times before stopping suddenly. He then returns to his chair, a gleam in his eye.

'It's the picture over the fireplace, isn't it, Ben?'

'Yes, I think it is – the chocolate-box landscape. Doherty and Fisher used this place a lot. It was their training base. What more perfect place for them to hide whatever they needed to hide than here, in plain sight. I think the Rothko and who knows what else may be hiding behind that picture. 'Check out the landscape in Yorkshire to see the bigger picture.' It's like a cryptic crossword clue.'

'Well, what are we waiting for?' Sullivan says, leaping to his feet, all evidence of his earlier sulkiness now vanished. 'Come on, Saul. Give me a hand and let's take a look!'

The picture is surprisingly heavy. Definitely a job for two pairs of hands. They lift it off the wall carefully and place it gingerly on the table. Lewis is on his feet. Assisted by Holly, he hobbles to the table to see for himself.

Taped with duct tape to the plywood at the back of the painting is a USB stick. There is also a small white envelope with Ben's name written on it in ink.

Chapter 80

Ben

I hope it is you reading this? Otherwise, a lot of lives will have been lost for no reason. Those who continue to subvert the system will have won the day.

On the face of it, you and I've had a chequered past. It wasn't always like that, and I'm sorry, mate, for our falling out. It was mostly my fault and I apologise. Deep down, I knew I could always count on you to do what was right. I am trusting you on this now. Don't let me down!

When Helen Morgan and Philip Musson invited Nigel and me to join their trusted band of outlaws, I have to confess that it seemed a no-brainer. We actually both had a blast reinventing ourselves. Literally dying and being reborn with a new identity was amazing. Very liberating. We had freedom, we had money, and we had little accountability. What was not to like?

The mission to destroy Gunter Markov started as a simple operation but quickly became a nightmare. It began with a private conversation between the PM and the newly elected president of the United States. The PM, keen to impress, pledged her support in crushing the North Korean regime economically in return for the president's promise to secure the UK a rapid and favourable trade deal, post-Brexit. Not having a fucking clue how she might deliver this, the PM spoke with Morgan and Musson who thought this might be a job for Fisher and me. The initial brief was simple. Destroy Markov and his operation. At a stroke, this would eliminate a major source of North Korean foreign currency and severely damage the Koreans financially. The Iranian nuclear money was an unexpected bonus. None of us had seen that coming.

The complication was finding out along the way that the CIA had secretly been running Markov as an agent for years. He had this penchant for sex with underage girls. In return for keeping his perversions sated, Markov agreed to help the CIA by sharing information and working on the occasional project for Langley.

The original idea of what became known in the CIA as 'the Markov Portfolio' was possibly a brilliant American project that only latterly began to spin out of control. Langley commissioned it as the ultimate fake news project. Markov and his team were meant to announce to the intelligence community that they had hacked their way into discovering the goods on many of the world's top politicians. They hadn't, but no one except the ultimate owner of the portfolio (the Americans) would ever know this. Imagine the shit storm if full details of secret bribes and backhanders paid to senior politicians the world over were made public? Including full and intimate details of offshore bank accounts and shadow companies used along the way? The Americans believed the Chinese and Russians, in particular, would go nuts when they learned about the existence of this stuff. Leadership elections in both countries threatened to be overshadowed by the disclosures. Washington wanted something to give them an edge in their discussions with China and Russia; Markov's fake portfolio looked like it might just deliver. The fake portfolio was thus never intended to be about the information it purported to contain. Instead, it was meant to be about the power that <u>implied</u> ownership automatically conferred – the ability to negotiate better deals and outcomes from a fictitious position of strength.

The project might have been perfect if Markov had played along instead of being such an awkward, arrogant son of a bitch. What irritated Markov was the fact that it was not a genuine hack but a bullshit project. He didn't like that because he thought it was likely to damage his credibility – essential things to hacker motivation. So, very privately, he began working on creating his own blockbuster portfolio. Something, he believed, was many, many times more potent and valuable. The hack to end all hacks.

We only found out by accident. One of Markov's team, a man who found himself with, how shall I put this delicately, a serious and life-threatening conflict of loyalties, felt the need to spill the beans. Markov's real portfolio was a complete list of foreign agents on Russia's payroll: their names, their code names and how much they had been paid – and where. Here's the good part: both overt and covert operatives. Not that long ago, such information might have been dreamt about but been impossible to obtain. Today, everything's computerised. Buried deep in some electronic record somewhere, no longer just handwritten on a piece of card stored in some hidden Kremlin safe. Totally secure behind all those electronic firewalls and top-secret access codes, right?

Well, maybe. Unless you are unlucky enough to have one of Markov's team pay you a visit.

Fisher and I suddenly needed to change our game plan. Markov's real portfolio felt like an unbelievable prize. A portfolio of spies! Definitely worth getting hold of before we eliminated Markov and destroyed his business.

He may have been an arsehole, but Markov wasn't stupid. He encoded the portfolio using one-time encryption, making it impossible to decode without his unique encryption key. He then went and posted an encrypted copy of the damned thing on the internet. All anyone needed was the key. The intelligence community, fuelled by false American rumours, believed that what was posted was an encrypted copy of the fake portfolio. Only Fisher and I knew what it really was. We felt it vital to acquire the encryption key before completing our mission to kill Markov.

We had a lucky break. We ambushed Markov's technical guru when he was flying back into Rostock airport and relieved him of the only copy of the key. Shortly before he died, Markov confessed that he'd been keeping the existence of the real portfolio a secret deliberately. Avoiding a big reveal so that he could max out the money he might earn from it all. That and the kudos in the hackosphere. Perhaps we should have taken a leaf out of his book and kept quiet about it? Sadly, we didn't. We initially told Musson everything. Why not? He and Morgan were our notional bosses. He accused us of going off-piste, risking destabilising the intelligence community. He was keen to put a lid on everything. He demanded we hand over the encryption key as well as the Iranian money. Which was when we suddenly got cold feet. In a moment's foolishness, you see, I had also spoken to the Americans, telling them that I now owned the encryption key. They went ballistic. The shit was completely out of the bag, and there was no way to get it back in. When we learned that kill on sight orders had been issued, we realised we had crossed a line. We were suddenly dead men walking. Story of my recent life, I guess.

Which is why, my friend, I involved you in all of this. I'm sorry, mate, for any grief it may have caused. Please apologise to Holly. I never wanted to hurt her, and that's the truth. Eli Rosin's interview suite in the Barbican is a more luxurious version than most. If you read this and you haven't yet found Holly, go and see Eli at the Israeli embassy and he will take you to where she is. I genuinely hope she's okay. You will have gone around the houses to get to where I hope you now are. I had to leave you clues that I was confident only you could solve. As a thank you, I leave you in sole charge of the Rothko, for you to decide what to do with it – hiding behind the landscape. I was pleased with that riddle. I don't personally like his paintings, but they are a great investment, by all accounts.

Finally, I leave you the decision about what to do with the enclosed encryption key. Lives have been lost because of this damned thing. Choose wisely, Ben. If you are reading this, Fisher and I will not have been so lucky.

One final thing, mate. FOBH. Once again, JFDI. This time, do it for me, do you understand?

Good luck with your life.

Keiran

Chapter 81

Afterwards, there is only silence. A needle could be heard to drop, such is the effect that the letter has on all four. Even Holly has read it, Lewis concluding that she had become so invested in the whole business that she has a right to know what Doherty had been up to.

The USB stick sits there, staring at them – the one-time encryption key. If Doherty's letter is to be believed, this will open Pandora's Box. Information powerful enough to get people killed. A list of all agents and foreign spies secretly in the pay of Moscow. Imagine who might be prepared to kill to get their hands on that information? Imagine who might also be prepared to kill to ensure that such information never saw the light of day?

'I'll get lunch ready,' suggests Holly, getting up from the table. 'I've no interest in knowing any more. I suspect you three might. I don't need my life expectancy reduced any more than it has been already.'

'Should we check to see if the Rothko is there?' Saul asks.

'It will be,' Lewis says. 'I suggest we leave it where it is for the moment. It's well concealed. It's probably a job better suited to an art curator than the three of us, anyway.'

'Ben's right,' says Sullivan. 'Meanwhile, we have weightier considerations. I suspect that I ought to be the custodian of the USB stick, don't you?'

'I'm like Holly,' Ben says. 'I have no interest in knowing what it might reveal. It's more your neck of the woods, Jake.'

'I agree. Do what you have to, Jake,' Zeltinger adds. 'Did you bring your laptop with you?'

'I've got it here,' Sullivan says, holding up his briefcase.

'Then take your time. We're in no hurry. Whilst you're busy decoding, perhaps you and I could have that game of chess, Ben?'

Sometime later, Sullivan has still not uttered a sound. His face has taken on an ashen hue, the colour drained from his skin. Earlier, after plugging the USB stick into his notebook computer, he had copied and pasted the enormous one-time encryption file into a special field linked to an MI5 secure database. He had then watched in amazement as the garbled nonsense on his screen had slowly been decoded and replaced by plain text. Ever since, he had been staring at the screen and scrolling through the information in silence.

Lewis and Zeltinger are already on their third game, their faces a study in concentration. The match is level at one game apiece. Holly is afraid to announce lunch, fearful it might break the spell of silence that has pervaded. Slowly, Sullivan lifts his head from the screen, saves the file to some secret server and then closes the lid of his notebook computer.

'Conclusions, Jake?'

'Grave,' is the one-word answer Lewis receives. 'Will you excuse me? I need to make a phone call.'

Outside the rain has eased. Sullivan opens the front door and makes a quick dash to the car to make his call out of earshot of the rest of them.

'Sounds ominous,' Ben says to Zeltinger as he makes a well-considered move.

'It was always going to end badly,' Zeltinger says. His eyes are suddenly gleaming as he spots an opportunity. He moves a bishop diagonally across the board, next to Lewis's rook. 'Check,' he announces triumphantly.

'Oh, bugger, I missed that completely,' Lewis says, moving a pawn in front of his king to take him out of check. Which is Zeltinger's cue to pounce on Lewis's rook. 'Damn! I think you might win this one, Saul. I wasn't concentrating hard enough.'

'With good reason. There's been a fair amount to distract us this morning.'

'Do either of you want to eat? Jake can catch up when he's finished his call. It's gone one o'clock already.'

'Good idea. I'm starving. I'll cede you this game, Saul. Nice play.' They shake hands, and Zeltinger clears away the chess pieces.

Sullivan reappears some thirty minutes later.

'You look like you could do with a drink?'

'I would love a drink, but I mustn't. Saul, we need to be going in about thirty minutes. I've got a slot with the PM and the cabinet secretary at six this evening.'

'Nothing important then,' Holly says and everyone laughs. 'Come on, there's plenty of food. Help yourself to what you want.'

'Is there anything we can do to help?' Lewis asks once Jake has cleared his plate of food. 'You've hardly said a thing. We don't want to pry, but if you want to talk about it, we're all invested in this business.'

'Thanks, Ben. Yes, I know you are. I think I need to sort one or two things out first. Hence my meeting later today. We've moved into different territory suddenly.' He nods to the envelope that is still resting where he had left it on the far end of the table.

'What do you want to do about the painting?' Ben asks.

'That we can discuss. I was mentioning it to the cabinet secretary just now. Technically speaking, we're confused as to who the legal owner might be. Doherty stole the money from people we all wish didn't have it. He then used the money to buy a painting in good faith before indicating that he was handing over custody of the painting to you. Let's skate over the vagaries of death duties for one moment. It seems to us that you might have some kind of partial claim on it.'

'Me?'

'We have a suggestion. When the dust has settled, we hand the painting back to a professional curator and get it reframed and then sold. Whatever proceeds it makes, any amount up to one hundred million dollars, we think we might gift to the Chinese as part of Britain's efforts to negotiate a new trade deal. If the painting makes more than one hundred million, then we propose that the UK government keeps half of the excess and you keep the rest.'

'Wow! Is that likely? For it to sell for more than what was paid for it?'

'Who can say? However, the cabinet secretary is going to make some enquiries. We can discuss this again down the road. For the time being, I suggest we leave the Rothko in its present disguise, here. If you don't mind, Saul, can you give me a hand to hang it back on the wall? Then, I'm afraid we need to be going.'

Chapter 82

Two days before Christmas

The time is seven-thirty at night. The location, Onslow Square, near London's South Kensington. It seems an appropriate choice of location for a person in such a position. A specialist from the Service had visited earlier in the evening to tamper with the alarm system. Someone extremely skilled. Someone who had done this before. Her tradecraft now allows the latest intruder to enter the place undetected while the alarm system outwardly gives the appearance that it is still set.

The intruder waits in the drawing-room, sitting patiently in the dark. Deep in the intruder's inside left pocket is a Glock 19 handgun. Suppressed, of course. Hollow-point ammunition. Fifteen rounds in the magazine, as ever. More than enough for the job in hand.

Ten minutes ago, he had seen a Tweet that had caught his eye. It was one of his old Twitter friends, @CrazyHarry46. The Tweet was posted at 7.22 pm. It said simply: *Taxi in 15.*

At thirty-four minutes past seven, the intruder hears a key in the front door latch, the sound of deadbolts being unlocked. Then, a second key in a different lock and finally, the door is opened. The alarm starts to beep. The intruder hears the sound of a keypad being used to disable the security system, followed by the front door closing. There's the sound of a hat, coat and scarf being removed and hung on hooks the intruder had spotted in the vestibule. A briefcase is opened, then closed. The person then enters the drawing-room. The light is turned on, the curtains drawn, before the man turns sharply around, pointing a Sig Sauer P320 directly at the intruder sitting in the chair opposite.

'That's no way to greet a colleague, Sir Philip.'

'That's no way to enter my house, Sullivan. Especially when you've not been invited.'

'How did you know?'

'There's a special warning light that comes on beside the front door when someone is in the house. Completely separate from the alarm system. I knew someone was here.'

'You could have turned around, gone away and simply called the police.'

'But then I would have missed all the fun. Why don't you start by telling me why you're here?'

'No, why don't we start, Sir Philip, by you putting that gun down?'

Sir Philip Musson moves into the room and takes a seat in the chair diagonally opposite. The Sig Sauer is still pointed unwaveringly at Sullivan.

'Maybe I don't want to.'

'Have it your way, Sir Philip. I presume that is the same Sig Sauer that you always carry with you in your briefcase? I think you'll find that tonight, the magazine is empty.'

Sir Philip squeezes the trigger, and an empty clicking sound is audible.

'Too bad,' says Sullivan, removing the silenced Glock from his inner jacket pocket. 'Whereas this one –' he pauses as a single round tears a large hole in the left-hand armrest of Sir Philip's chair '– seems to be working just fine.'

'Very clever,' the man sneers, putting the gun down in his lap. 'I suppose you disabled the panic buttons as well?'

Sullivan gives a bleak, disinterested smile.

'It's just you and me, about to have a cosy fireside chat.'

'What about?' Sir Philip begins to rally. 'Why the theatrics?'

'I think we both know the answer to that. This is the end of the line. The journey you began with Doherty and Fisher. We're about to hit the buffers.'

'Did Lewis find that encryption key?'

'He did. We then managed to decode Markov's encrypted post. Not the fake American-inspired bullshit version. The real one. Russia's list of foreign spies who worked for them. Who they are, what they're called, how they are paid, even. Names such as Thomson, for example.'

'Interesting. Why wasn't I told?'

'You are being told now.'

'I see. May I pour myself a drink?'

'No.'

Silence engulfs them both. The only noise is a grandfather clock ticking somewhere in the recesses of the house: that and the muted sounds of the occasional passing vehicle outside.

'Why are you here?' he asks eventually.

'I think you know the answer to that. The PM and the cabinet secretary thought I should be the one to come and visit.'

'I see. Do they know everything?'

'They do.'

'Am I to suppose that you'd like an explanation?'

'Not particularly.'

'Motives are never easy to explain or understand,' Sir Philip says, seeming to ignore Sullivan's answer. 'Did you know that in certain tightly knit circles, I'm something of a celebrity? The most senior-level spy the Russians have ever been able to place anywhere. More senior than Burgess, Maclean or Philby. More senior than Aldrich Ames too. How good is that? Until now, no one has had any idea. I am rather proud of that. No one even suspected. To think. All brought to an end because the bureaucratic geeks who rule the world felt the need to computerise everything. They call that progress! How bizarre.'

'Doubtless, you thought it was for the greater good or something?'

'Not particularly. I did it because no system is flawless. Sometimes the arrogance that comes from supposed success needs rebalancing. No government is ever good without an effective opposition. I simply saw myself as giving the other side a helping hand. Not all the time, only occasionally. Always on my terms. I never gave them anything that they specifically asked for. Only what I thought would be helpful. That used to infuriate them. I remember once having a blazing row with someone who is now, shall we say, in arguably <u>the</u> highest office in Russia. *Give us the bloody information we want, Thomson, you bastard.* That was my cryptonym. Thomson. I never knew whether it was meant to be with a 'P' or not. Anyway, I refused. You may choose not to believe it, but it was all part of a game to me. I was levelling the playing field. Seeing what I could get away with, without being found out. I was a good spy, by the standards we judge spies in MI6. Imagine, a spy getting all the way to the top of MI6? The only thing better would be having the PM as a spy as well. God help us!'

'Why are traitors always so righteous?' Sullivan delivers the words heavy with disdain.

'You call me a traitor . . .?'

Sullivan stops him mid-sentence by firing another round. This one tears into Sir Philip's calf muscle, causing him to fall, writhing, to the floor.

'You bastard! You self-important, arrogant little shit!' he spits. 'You have . . . no idea . . . who . . . you're . . . dealing . . . with.'

'Maybe. I suppose you thought you were above it all? More recently, you even had your own private army, Doherty and Fisher, at your beck and call. Dame Helen left you alone to run the show, didn't she? Leaving you free to order the pair of them to kill whomever you wanted. Markov first, then who would have been next? There was no accountability. The only thing was, the assignment to kill Markov completely backfired. You had no idea what he'd been working on. Doherty and Fisher unexpectedly got much too close to exposing you. So, you had to have them killed. You asked your Russian friends to take care of them. The rooftop assassin with the succinylcholine poisoned dart. The question was, could you limit the damage that had already been done? Then there was all that stupid bullshit at the opera with me. You really wanted to ensure that Lewis was silenced. You were determined to make sure that the list of spies never saw the light of day. You failed. It has. You sadly are its first victim.'

Which is when Sullivan steps forwards, deliberately pointing the handgun at the pathetic, cowering man on the floor in front of him.

'Sweet dreams, traitor!'

He then fires a single round at point-blank range, the gun barrel aimed directly between Sir Philip Musson's eyes.

Chapter 83

They make love on Christmas Day morning. It is the first time since Lewis had been injured. It's their special present to each other. Tentatively and carefully: gently and lovingly. It is such a precious moment that they feel duty-bound to celebrate with champagne. Which, in turn, leads to a repeat performance lasting beyond lunchtime. Their planned roast turkey lunch becomes an overcooked mid-afternoon feast. The potatoes are overly crisp, the gravy lumpy, and the Brussels sprouts soggy. Both would say later that it was one of the most memorable meals they'd ever had.

Sometime in the late afternoon, Lewis receives a text. It is from Jake Sullivan.

Don't miss today's six o'clock news. Btw, I am told a Saudi investor is willing to pay $105m. Don't spend your share too quickly! Happy Christmas Jake

'Does that mean what I think it means?' Holly asks in amazement.

'I think it might.'

'I'm speechless.'

'If it ever happens, half is yours.'

'Or all of it is ours. Oh, Ben, I am just pleased we're both alive.'

In the early evening, they watch the Christmas Day news on Holly's tablet computer over a glass of red wine. The third news item reports that the Director-General of MI6, Sir Philip Musson, has been shot dead at his home in South Kensington. The Metropolitan Police commissioner is calling it a callous crime. Tributes are already pouring in from all parts of Westminster, many calling him one of the brightest and most able civil servants of his generation. Police say that Sir Philip disturbed petty thieves in his house and was killed by a gunshot wound to the head as they made their escape. They are calling for witnesses to come forward.

'I feel the hand of Jake Sullivan at play,' Lewis says at the end.

'Jake?' says Holly. 'People like him don't go around bumping off senior civil servants. Sir Philip was the head of MI6. It must have been a foreign spy that killed him.'

'Perhaps,' Lewis says vaguely. 'Though he wouldn't have texted if it hadn't been in some way connected to this Markov business.'

'For the time being, Ben Lewis, you are better off out of that world.'

They chink glasses.

'To be honest, Holly, I'm not sure it's all over yet.'

Holly looks up at Lewis, an expression of shock on her face.

'What do you mean? Jake is now in possession of Markov's list of spies. What else is there to worry about?'

Lewis strokes Holly's hair as he considers his reply.

'You remember Doherty's letter. You read it, the same as me. Did anything strike you as odd?'

'Odd? Ben, ever since Doherty reappeared in our lives, the whole of my life has been feeling odd. What in particular about the letter is worrying you?'

'Think about what he said at the very end. *'One final thing, mate. FOBH. Once again, JFDI. This time, do it for me, do you understand?'* The wording looked and sounded odd when I first read it.'

'Forgive me, Ben. JFDI?'

'Soldier shorthand. *Just fucking do it.* The sentence looked clumsy the moment I read it. On the face of it, he was repeating himself unnecessarily. Most readers wouldn't have given it a second glance. They'd have put it down as unnecessary repetition, written in haste by someone with a lot on his mind. I don't think it was. I think he was sending me another message. Something once again that only I was going to understand. Regardless of who else I showed that letter to.'

'You've lost me, Ben. Explain.'

'Think about what he's saying. *FOBH. Once again, JFDI. This time, do it for me, do you understand?'* I think there's something else that Doherty's left at the In & Out Club. Something he left in his name and not mine. Something he didn't want anyone else to see.'

'Such as?'

'Who knows? One thing's for sure. If Doherty worked so hard to cover his tracks, whatever else he might have discovered has the potential to be even more deadly than Markov's list of Russian agents. If that's the case, this whole business may yet be far from over.'

The End

THE LATEST THRILLER BY THE SAME AUTHOR

Visit: www.davidnrobinson.com

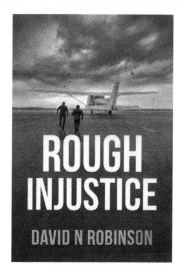

FOR A MAN LIKE RICKY BAXTER, FORGIVENESS DOESN'T COME EASILY

Ostensibly just this disabled guy running a simple charity in a London backwater, anyone underestimating Ricky soon discovers their mistake. He's a man driven to right some of the wrongs of the world – a man who simply doesn't care who gets hurt along the way.

Or so he likes to believe.

When an abused pole dancer comes to him for help, he has little idea of the murky depths of modern-day slavery that he's about to get dragged into. Too late he finds himself up against violent gangs smuggling migrants across Europe, people who'd go to any extremes to exploit their human cargo for profit. People who make Ricky question himself. Has he really got what it takes to stop these people? Or will he find himself losing the moral high ground, drawn into acting more like the gang leaders themselves and, in the process, sinking to their level?

Acknowledgements

I am a lucky person. Some people say you make your own luck, but I don't always feel that's the whole story. Firstly, I am unbelievably lucky to have an amazingly supportive wife and family. I couldn't write without their helpful ideas – and occasional 'suggested' course corrections! Their editorial comments are always insightful. Thank you, Team Robinson!

I am also lucky to have a growing population of friends who, with hardly any prompting, volunteer to help me improve the quality of my first-draft manuscript. I would like to say a huge thank you to them all – you know who you are! Plus, to the many more friends, wider family and loyal fans who seem to love my writing and continue supporting me with their reviews, comments and suggestions.

Author's Note

As a self-published author, I have, in the past, tried all sorts of different methods to get my books in front of readers yet to discover me. I've tried Facebook and Twitter, I've tried free books to build mailing lists and spent money on book sites like Bookbub and Goodreads. I've even used paid advertising on both Amazon and Facebook as well. All these have helped, but the returns on investment are meagre.

The funny thing is that whilst many successful self-published authors tell new authors like me that I must build a mailing list of my most loyal fans, I've learnt over time that most readers rarely want to be bombarded, week after week, by yet more emails from an author they have only read a few times? I don't think so.

So, these days I rely on people like you who read my books to do three things:

i)   if you could leave an honest review on the Amazon page you bought or downloaded this book from, that would be the **very** best help you could give;

ii)   two, if you enjoyed the book, perhaps you might tell a few friends and family members about it? and

iii)   finally, maybe I might even be able to tempt you to try a few more of the books that I have written?

Thank you for taking the time to read The Markov Encryption. I sincerely hope you enjoyed it.

In case you're wondering, I do offer a free book on my website, **www.davidnrobinson.com** – but you no longer need to subscribe to a mailing list to download it!

David N Robinson

For many years before COVID 19, I was a business leader: always out and about meeting people, travelling the world regularly. Endless plane and train journeys provided ample time for reflection. In between work, I would read books and plan for a different life.

These days, I am happy to be grounded, living my new life as an independent author. Working from home and living the dream. Writing thrillers, the sort of books I always hankered after on yet another long-haul flight. Fast-paced, contemporary page-turners – with plenty of twists and action along the way. Books about topical subjects that I love researching.

Most of the time, when I'm not researching a new book, my wife and I live in England, close to the fabulous city of Cambridge. The walks are fantastic, the bike rides not too challenging and the streets full of interesting and inspiring people.

Visit **www.davidnrobinson.com** to learn more about my writing.

Printed in Great Britain
by Amazon

11989410R00183